ALSO BY E.

To my family

1

Michael was not really Colin O'Brien's father, or so Michael's wife Líadan had claimed during a Christmas celebration. Though no one but Michael's mother paid attention to the allegation. Líadan had always been thought of as eccentric, and everyone gathered around the small table had long ago become accustomed to her nonsense.

"Colin has eyes like a stormy ocean," the granny commented to her son. "Only one person in our family has eyes that color, and it's not you or your missus."

"Ah, Mother, be quiet," Michael said. "You've had too much whiskey in your coffee."

"Still," the granny continued. "You can't help but wonder..."

The young Colin himself never questioned his parentage. All he knew was that his hair was the same coal-black as his father's, and they even had the same smile. His mother was blonde with green eyes, and had been born in New York City to Irish and Welsh parents, returning to Ireland with her father as a young teenager after her mother's death. None of her children looked much like her, not just Colin; they mostly looked a lot like their father.

It was Colin's father's final decision to move to New York, but it was his mother who had initiated the idea. Líadan could hardly get out of bed on some days, but she had talked endlessly about the city of her girlhood. The city, where in her words, every person, no matter where they lived, had a marvelous view; where work could be found practically at the drop of a hat; and where education was provided for free for the entirety of one's life. Where, if one worked hard enough, a home could be bought in the country, a house with a barn and a large acreage with enough room for horses. Where they had doctors who could help his mother get better.

It had sounded pretty good to Colin's father. After all, the family was living with their granny and Colin's father worked as a clean-up man at the local abbatoir, mopping up blood and the sorts of nasty things that fell to the floor from dead animals when they were stripped for their meat.

Colin was six when the idea came into his mother's head, and he was eight by the time she had actually convinced Colin's father to make the journey. At eight years old, Colin might not have known much, but he wasn't sure he wanted to live in this place called the United States.

"Don't they have cowboys there?" he asked his father. "And the Indians, who live in animals?"

His father chuckled softly and took a break from reading the newspaper. He looked over at Colin and watched him through his eyeglasses. "A long time ago, they lived in shelters covered with the skins of hunted animals."

"Will we live in an animal skin in New York?"

At this his father chuckled greatly. "No. I expect we'll be living in what we call a flat here, and what the Americans call an apartment."

"Apartment," Colin said several times, as though it was very important for him to remember the word. "When will we be going there?"

"Your mammy and I will be leaving in a month or so to get everything settled first. Then your sister, your brother, and you will meet us there."

Colin's older brother, Danny, entered the room. "Meet who?" he asked.

Michael looked up from his reading again. "I was telling Colin your mam and I will be leaving for New York first. Then you'll be meeting us there."

"You'll probably leave us here," Danny said, and left the room.

Colin could hear his sister, Maureen, who was a little younger than Danny, singing softly in the other room. Maureen was the smart one in the family, and would have been attending a posh school in Belfast next year on a scholarship if the family hadn't been moving to New York.

Colin's father sighed and Colin smiled at him.

"Will we really be meeting you and Mammy there, or are you going to leave us here with granny?" Colin asked.

His father frowned. "Of course you'll be coming."

"Will you play your accordion for us?"

"Now?"

Colin nodded.

"Not tonight. It's getting late." He gestured for Colin to leave. "Go to bed."

Two months later, Colin's parents had sent word for their children to meet them in New York.

Colin sang as he boarded the large passenger ferry with Danny, who looked weighed down by their belongings.

"Be quiet," Danny whispered as Colin sang loudly. "You should really carry your own luggage. You aren't little anymore."

"But Maureen doesn't carry her own things, and she's older than me," Colin said.

"I'm helping her out because she's a girl."

Colin sang high above Danny's voice.

"Why did Mam and Da go to America first?" Colin asked when he'd stopped singing.

"They had to find a place for us all to live before we came there," Danny said.

Colin's eyes widened. "A big house?"

Danny smirked. "I wouldn't count on it."

Maureen was inside the cabin buying them a snack. Danny reached into his coat pocket, took out a coin and leaned against the thick railing that kept them from falling into the churning, foamy sea. He tossed the coin into the fast-moving water as the heavy boat plowed through the crest of a wave.

"You wasted money," Colin shouted at his brother.

A few other passengers turned to look, but then quickly went back to their own troubles.

Danny shrugged. "It was only a coin."

"Granny says one coin is worth more than the moment of joy you get from throwing it."

"I don't care what she believes."

"Why not?"

"Granny's an old woman. She's got old ideas."

Colin looked up at his brother, who was a lot older than him, both physically and in his way of thinking. "Will Granny die soon?"

"I don't know." Danny seemed uninterested in the thought.

"Da will be sad."

"He might be glad. Granny isn't very nice."

Colin looked at his brother, appalled. "But she's his mam."

"Doesn't mean she's nice."

"What about when our mam dies?"

"I don't really think about that yet," Danny said.

"Why not?"

"Because Mam's younger, and I don't like to think that far ahead."

"What will America be like?" Colin asked.

"It will be different than home."

"What does that mean?"

"It might be better. It might be worse. I don't know. Stop asking me questions."

Colin fell silent as his brother turned away from him. He didn't want to displease Danny.

Colin began to focus his attention on the other passengers. There was a shorter boy, but who he assumed was close to his age, standing not too far to his right. The boy had combed brown hair and an approachable look in his large, light eyes. He was dressed in a dark suit and tie, as if he might have been coming from church or from a wedding. He appeared to be by himself.

After Danny started flirting with a girl, Colin walked toward the other boy.

"Hello," he said with a wave. "What are you doing?"

The boy sized him up. "Minding my own business. Unlike you." The boy had an American accent, which Colin had never heard before, and maybe only once or twice on the radio at his granny's house.

"I'm going home after a vacation. My parents are in the cabin," the boy said after a while.

"You're a Yank?" Colin said excitedly. He thought he might make an American friend before he even reached America.

The boy, who had since turned his back to Colin, whipped around to face him. "What did you call me?"

"Are you a Yank, because of your accent?" Colin wasn't trying to be rude. He simply didn't know any better. "I'm on my way to America. I'll be living there."

The boy glared at him, and Colin wished he'd never said hello. His body quivered. He recoiled and ran away from the other boy.

A few minutes later, when Colin went to use the toilet, he came out of the room and found the boy waiting for him on the back deck of the ferry. Colin didn't see Danny or Maureen, and there was no one else at that part of the ferry, which was a cold and windy place to stand or sit.

The boy waited in his path so that Colin couldn't walk by without colliding into him. Colin tried to walk past him, but the boy shook his head and wouldn't move. So Colin tried politeness.

"Excuse me." He attempted to walk forward again.

Although Colin stood over the boy he froze, because now he could tell the boy was older than him and he had a menacing look in his eyes. The boy shoved Colin backwards into a wall. Colin had never been in a fight, and he felt a sensation he had never felt before. He felt genuine fear for his life.

The boy took off his suit jacket and threw it on the ground by Colin's foot. He wasn't wearing cufflinks and easily rolled up his shirtsleeves. Then he punched Colin in the chest.

Colin fell to the dirty ground, which felt hard and painful to his thin body.

The boy picked up his jacket and ran off, shouting over his shoulder.

"I just gave you your first American greeting."

It was Colin's first taste of what might be waiting for him overseas. And even at a young age it scared him. Was this what America would be like?

"Where have you been?" Danny asked Colin when he found him sitting on a bench and looking out at the stormy seas.

The swells made the large ferry rock back and forth, and some passengers were retching into the sea.

"Are you ill?" Danny asked.

"No."

"Then why are you bending over and holding your stomach?"

Colin pointed at the standing passengers who were ill. "I'm not throwing up like them, am I? I have a stomachache, that's all."

As much as Colin feared the older boy who'd punched him, he feared even more what Danny might do to the boy if Colin told him what had happened. Danny might have acted as though his younger brother annoyed him, but Colin knew he wouldn't permit anyone to hurt him and get away with it. He also didn't want Danny to find out he'd been beaten by a boy whose build was slighter than his.

"You're ill from the sea," Danny insisted.

Colin rose to his feet. "No, I'm not." He winced at the pain he still felt in his chest. The cool air tasted like salt.

Danny looked puzzled. "What's wrong with you?"

"Nothing."

Maureen appeared with fish and chips wrapped in paper and held Colin's hand. She smoothed back his hair. "Are you all right, Colin?"

"The sea's making him ill," Danny told her.

"No, it's not. I'm just hungry."

Maureen kissed his cheek and showed him the food. "Here, this'll make you feel better."

∾

"Mam says New York is the place of dreams," Colin told his brother and sister as they watched their ferry dock in England.

Danny smiled at his brother. "Maybe it is."

"Do you think that we'll be living in a big house?" Colin asked. "Mam had a house when she lived there."

"I'm afraid not." Maureen's green eyes softened.

Danny shrugged, as though he didn't want to dissuade too many of Colin's dreams.

"In America, they call minerals 'soda pop'," Colin said. Maureen smiled at him.

They took a crowded bus to a large docking station. Colin had never been to England, while his brother had gone there a few times with their father. He stared out the bus window, not speaking much, quietly taking in all he could see. With the third-class tickets their parents had mailed from the US, they boarded *The Lady Anna*, an immense ocean liner that would take them the remainder of the way to New York City.

The Lady Anna varied in its passengers. Some were tourists returning to the States from vacations in Europe, others were English couples and families traveling to visit New York – and a few, like Colin and his siblings, were immigrants.

Colin stayed close to his brother and sister as they boarded the giant white ship. He feared that the boy who'd hit him might appear again.

Colin's eyes went huge when he saw the numerous people boarding alongside them and in front of them.

"Are they all going to New York like us?" he asked his siblings. Danny shrugged.

"But where would they go if they didn't go to New York?"

"We don't know," Maureen said. "They probably aren't all going to New York."

"Good, because I don't want them all living with us." Maureen and Danny laughed.

"Our Uncle Rick lives in New York, you know," Maureen told Colin.

"Da's younger brother?" She nodded.

"Will we be living with him?"

"We don't know." Danny grabbed Colin's and Maureen's hands to board the ship.

"Will we sleep on the ship?" Colin asked.

"Yes. We'll be staying in a cabin," Maureen said.

Colin's father met them at the dock in New York less than a week later. Their mother, his father explained, was at their new home, tidying up and getting the place settled and ready for their arrival.

Despite what Maureen had said, Colin envisioned his new home would be a palace, or at the very least a beautiful large house painted white on the outside and with red shutters. He had seen pictures of such homes in American magazines that his mother had sent away for in Kilrea. His father had assured him that their lives would be better in New York, and, to Colin, a large house would mean a better life.

His father was eager for news from home when he met them at the port. Colin kept craning his neck to get a better view of the Statue of Liberty in the harbor that his granny had spoken to him about.

"How's Granny?" Colin's father asked Maureen after they had loaded the last of their luggage into a taxi.

"She's well."

Colin gaped around the place where their ship had landed. It wasn't a pretty area. It appeared desolate, and had a heavy feeling about it, as though it was a person who was lonely.

Colin's father grabbed his hand and put him in the taxi in

the seat next to Danny. Maureen sat alongside Colin, and their father rode up front with the driver. The taxi smelled of cigarette smoke. Colin looked out the smudged windows. He had thought they would be leaving this ugly place to travel to their new home, but when the taxi headed deeper into the awful, dirty place, he knew this wouldn't be the case. The sky, what he could see of it, seemed unusually bleak. Broken glass, cigarette stubs, and pieces of old newspaper littered the fractured sidewalks, the congested streets overshadowed by dark warehouses.

"This is our home?" Danny asked when the taxi pulled in front of an old brick building.

"Yes. It's a start," their father said with a sigh.

The outside of the building was in need of a thorough washing, the brick discolored from urban soot. The building's steps were broken in many places. Colin's face couldn't hide his disappointment. He helped his father and brother unload their luggage from the taxi.

His father patted his shoulder. "Cheer up, lad. It's only for a little while. We'll find a better place soon."

Colin's disappointment only grew when they entered the building and he discovered that even if it was ugly it was not even their own house. There were other people who lived there, too. One of the apartment doors was wide open and Colin could see an old woman and man playing cards on a table inside the cramped room. The woman gave him a toothless smile and he recoiled. The long, dim hallway held a feeling of entrapment, like a big dog in a little cage. The smell of cigarette smoke and brewing coffee, as well as another, stronger, less pleasant odor, were present. His granny's stone cottage in Kilrea was small, but it had a fireplace and was warm and inviting. Colin followed Maureen and Danny behind their father up the stairs.

"Hello," Colin's father called out once they'd entered an apartment.

Footsteps hurried out from somewhere inside the small rooms. Colin's mother stood in front of the four of them. She kissed Colin on the forehead. She hugged Maureen and Danny. Her face was flushed, and she had dark circles under her eyes, but it wasn't unusual for her to appear that way. To Colin she still looked as pretty as she always did.

"How was your journey?" she asked Colin and Maureen. Danny and their father moved the luggage from the hallway, which had a damp smell, into their apartment. Michael had insisted he didn't want to leave their belongings out in the hall, and Colin wondered if his father feared someone might steal them.

"It took too long, and I'm hungry," Colin answered his mother's question.

Líadan smiled at him. "I'll make some sandwiches for all of you."

"Can we buy them instead?" Colin asked. "I want an American sandwich."

Líadan laughed a little. "There's a shop around the corner. You can go outside and buy some if your brother comes with you."

Colin looked at Danny. "I'll go with you."

"Get something for me and Da and Mam too," Maureen said.

Colin noticed his mother and father hadn't unpacked some of the wooden crates and trunks they had left home with months ago. His father's elaborate red accordion case inlaid with brass looked untouched.

His mother took money out of her red apron and handed it (Colin saw it was a genuine American dollar) to Danny. Then she turned to Colin. "Lads, have fun. Button your coats. And Danny," she said, looking at him again, "keep this money in the bottom of your shoe. This is New York and one can never be safe."

What his mother had said frightened Colin.

"Why did we come here if it isn't safe?" he asked Danny on the way out of the building.

"We came here so Mam could get better, and because it was her dream."

"Is it Da's dream as well?"

"Who knows? He's trying to find work, but he does whatever she wants."

2

In New York, a boy named Johnny Garcia was Colin's only friend. "I'll take pity on you," Johnny had told Colin a few minutes after they met for the first time outside Colin's building. Johnny had introduced himself to Colin and had said he also lived in the apartment building. Colin had seen Johnny around the neighborhood but they had never spoken. He seemed friendly enough, so Colin started talking to him.

"Why would you take pity on me?" Colin asked.

"You're a big guy but you're soft. Without my help, it's obvious you're going to get yourself killed around here someday," Johnny said matter-of-factly. "These guys who live here, they won't just mess with you, they'll kill you if you ain't careful."

Colin looked at Johnny, shocked. "I was already beaten."

"When? In this neighborhood?"

Colin shook his head. "On the journey over here."

"Did you retaliate?"

"No. He was older than me."

"That's not good."

"Why? It was long ago anyhow."

"Doesn't matter." Johnny put his arm around him. "Suppose you were to run into this guy again someday and he remembers you, what are you going to do then?"

"I'm not sure."

"See? That's why you always have to retaliate. Because if you don't then they think they can keep kicking your ass."

Colin had never heard anything so harsh being uttered by someone his age before, but he hadn't made any friends since arriving in New York a year ago and he wanted Johnny to become his friend.

"He will?"

"Yeah."

"You're darker than the people we have back home," Colin observed.

Johnny glared at him. "What's that supposed to mean?"

"You look like coffee with milk, is all I meant. I'm sorry. I wasn't trying to be mean. My mam loves to drink coffee with milk."

"Your mam? What the hell is that?"

"My mother. That's what we call mothers where I'm from."

"Ireland?"

Colin nodded.

"Okay, Irish, so you say I look like coffee with milk? Then I think you look just like the milk."

Colin laughed, and Johnny did as well. "I think I'm going to like you, Irish."

Johnny was a change from everything Colin had ever known before. He'd been born and raised in New York and had never once been out of the city. Johnny was an only child who lived with his mother, Annette, upstairs from Colin. Johnny's father was serving time in prison for killing another man in Brooklyn, and Johnny hadn't seen him in years. Johnny was a few months older than Colin, but they were in the same year at school.

Johnny was half-Cuban in a mostly Italian, Jewish, and Irish neighborhood. Colin would help Johnny when the older boys, sometimes even the adults, played cruel pranks on him, such as spraying him in the face with beer from a can, and calling him names like 'chocolate bar'. They even said his mother should be the only one allowed to live in the building because she was Irish and Johnny should be forced to live somewhere else. But Colin supported Johnny, and he admired how Johnny remained strong and never let anyone bring him down.

One day, Johnny called for Colin outside their building as Colin left for school with Maureen.

"You're going to school today?"

Colin nodded. "Aren't you?"

"Not today. My mother already left for work and won't notice if I don't go. Do you want to *not* go with me?"

"I'm not sure."

"Why would you want to go to school anyway? It's full of girls." Johnny glanced at the pretty Maureen and smirked.

"Be quiet, Johnny Garcia. Colin's going to school, and you should be going with us," she said.

"I don't have to if I don't want to."

"Oh, what do you know anyway? You're just a little boy!"

"You're not a very tough guy if you let your sister speak for you," Johnny said to Colin. "O'Brien, didn't I tell you that you won't make it around here unless you're tough?"

Colin looked over at Johnny, who was bolder than him, and wanted to ask exactly what he meant. Colin knew his father wasn't a tough man. He had been told by others over the years that his father was a large, serious man but soft – not a man devoted to the cross, but not one of the tough blokes either. But his father seemed to have done all right for himself. Did you really have to be so tough to survive? And what exactly did tough mean? How tough did you have to be? Colin guessed he'd have to be tough – whatever that meant – in the Bowery to survive. After all, Johnny seemed to know everything, from what was under girls' dresses, to why Colin's boozy uncle Rick had headaches in the morning.

Maureen grabbed Colin's hand and pulled him along to school. "All right, I'll go with you," Johnny called out and followed them. Colin could tell Johnny fancied Maureen.

Life in New York wasn't what Colin had expected for his family or for himself. Life in New York wasn't easy for them, almost as hard as it had been back home, perhaps even harder in some ways. The Great Depression intensified some of the city's lifelong residents' dislike of immigrants, and Colin's father had trouble finding consistent work despite great effort. Back at Granny's, the children had gathered around him as he played the accordion in the evenings, but he hadn't removed the instrument from its case once since coming to New York. Colin's mother, who'd sometimes worked as a hairdresser in Kilrea, seemed to have no interest in finding work in New York. There wasn't enough money for her to see a doctor, or enough for the family to move back to Kilrea. There was barely enough money for them to survive. And when they received word in the post that their granny had died, they lost their connection to home.

Colin's family was living in their own apartment, but they rented by the week, and the family had to share a bathroom with the three other families on the floor. The building was noisy all the time with adults yelling, and laughing and crying children, and the sounds of people making love through the walls.

In the autumn and the wintertime, the landlord sometimes purposely forgot to heat the building to save money; and in the late spring and summer, the tenement had a constant stench. It was the stink of its occupants' sweat, and garbage tossed into the hallway and down the stairwell. Even if you opened a window, there was the rank scent of the warm city, of trash left on the busy sidewalks and streets, and the noise of cars speeding past the building and sometimes hitting a neighborhood child or a pet cat.

Uncle Rick had come to the United States five years before Colin's family, and Colin knew Rick was part of the reason for his father agreeing to move their family to New York in the first place. Rick was married to a kind Polish woman named Georgette. He owned and operated *O'Brien's* pub just outside the Bowery. *O'Brien's* was frequented by Irish dockworkers, petty thieves, and assorted locals who told tales so complicated and untrue that they took hours to narrate them and seconds to change them.

When he saw Rick now, Colin thought how much he looked like his uncle. They had the same eyes and the same laugh, and customers in the pub would comment how they could be father and son. Colin's father and Rick had always laughed at this.

Rick was Colin's only uncle in America. He had uncles in Ireland, but even if they all came over here, Colin felt that Rick would still be his favorite. Rick cracked jokes that always made Colin laugh. Colin wanted to grow up to be a publican like Rick, or maybe a policeman.

Colin's father didn't drink at the pub, but even at a young age Colin knew Rick was always at his pub and that if Colin's father wanted to see him then he had to go there to do so. Rick took much pleasure in the drink. He drank while tending the bar. When Rick drank, he would sing in an off-key voice, and Colin found it amusing. Colin learned what drunk was early on, and how some people became angry when they picked up the bottle, and some became friendlier, while others got ill and some of them passed out. Women who drank would sometimes throw themselves at men, and some men did the same to the women. Mostly people yelled more when they drank.

"Colin," Uncle Rick said loudly when Colin went inside the pub with his father.

It was early in the afternoon, and Rick's face was already ruddy with the drink. He was a large man, tall and broad-shouldered, like Colin's father. His dark O'Brien hair was tinged with silver. "You've grown since I last saw you." He grinned.

"Since yesterday you mean?" Colin said sarcastically.

Rick chuckled. He looked at Colin's father. "It really does seem like he's getting bigger every day. Maybe he'll be a boxer someday. Soon he'll be as tall as us."

"Don't I know it," Michael said.

Colin ran behind the bar and gave Rick a hug. Rick pretended to groan as he raised him high up into the air, and Colin smiled at his uncle. Rick smelled smoky like his pub.

"Interest you in a drink, Mike?" Rick put Colin down as he spoke to Michael.

"You know I never touch the stuff."

"Do you want a cup of milk, Colin?"

Colin pouted at his uncle and shook his head.

Uncle Rick chuckled. "Would you like a ginger ale, Colin? Michael, do you want one too, then? Or maybe Colin wants a beer himself?" He winked at Colin. "You're getting on to be ten years old, aren't you, lad?" He glanced at Colin's father. "I reckon our da gave us our first taste of the drink when we were around your age, Colin. Isn't that right, Michael?"

Colin's father touched his shoulder with his large hand and looked at his brother. "Colin's not having that kind of a drink." He used a firm tone.

Rick's posture tensed. "All right, then, Michael. I'll get you two those ginger ales."

In turn, Colin looked up at his father for his approval, and his father smiled. Colin nodded yes at his uncle.

"Come on then, sit down." Uncle Rick gestured to the bar. Colin waited for his father to sit and then he sat.

"You still smoke, don't you?" Rick asked Michael with a sparkle in his bright blue eyes.

Colin's father nodded.

"Me, too," Uncle Rick said. "Do you know what's interesting? I bought this wonderful box of cigarettes the other day from Daniel. He's selling them for the Dubliner who lives below you."

Michael stared at Rick and didn't say anything. Colin couldn't tell what was going on between his father and uncle. He didn't know if Rick was trying to pick a fight with his father.

"Did you know Danny's been working for that fella?" Rick dried a mug with a clean rag and the motion caused it to squeak.

Colin's brother Danny was now fifteen years old, strong and tall for his age. He had left school and planned to enlist in the Air Force.

"I'm aware of it, yes," Colin's father said to Uncle Rick.

"What do you think of the Dubliner, Mike? Do you think he's crooked like they say in the neighborhood? Some say the cigarettes he sells are stolen." He set the ginger ales on the bar.

Colin's father handed him one of the drinks.

"I'm not sure exactly what that man does. But you know, Rick, it's not the job I'd wished Danny had taken, but at least he's doing something with his life – and he needs to do something to keep him out of big trouble. Of course it isn't my first choice for him. But he's not been going to school, and he needs to do something for money. I told him that if he won't finish school then he needs to earn money."

"Make him go back to school, then."

"If only it were that easy. The school doesn't want him back because they say he fights with the other lads too much."

"Does he always win?"

Colin's father nodded. "The girls like him though."

Rick laughed. "I bet. Handsome devil he is."

Colin's father managed to laugh only a little. "I don't know, though, Rick. Sometimes I feel like New York is the devil and he's pulling my family into his clutches."

"It's different here from home, that's for sure. I have an idea. Why doesn't Danny come work here with me? I'd pay him fairly."

Colin's glass of ginger ale started to topple and his father reached out to balance it.

"Thanks, but I don't want Danny around the drink all day."

"Really, Mike, you'd rather have him working for a possible crook instead of his uncle?"

"No, that isn't it at all. I just don't want him surrounded by drinking all day," Colin's father stated again, this time more firmly. His pale face turned red.

Colin felt that the relationship his father had with Uncle Rick was typical of Irish brothers, one where there was plenty of fighting and rivalry, and, of course, love.

"You've become a saint in your old age," Uncle Rick remarked to Colin's father.

Michael laughed slightly but Colin could tell the remark had irked his father.

Colin took another drink of his ginger ale. He eyed his father and uncle. The postures of both men were now tense and Colin moved in to diffuse the situation. He didn't want it escalating into a full-scale fight. He knew Irish brothers well because he was one himself.

"Uncle Rick, you said you could take me to play baseball in the park like the American boys do, and I want to do it tomorrow." Even then, Colin was good at easing conflict.

Uncle Rick looked across the bar at him and smiled. "Sure we can, Colin. A promise is a promise. We'll do it tomorrow."

Colin grinned. His mother had mentioned Rick had boxed competitively all over the world in his younger days, until he'd damaged his 'knockout' arm in a pub brawl when he was twenty-three. He had come to New York to start over, like Colin's family had.

"How's Georgette?" Colin's father asked Uncle Rick.

"She's doing very well."

"Is the baby coming along all right?"

"Yeah. She's about six months along, so the time's almost here. I hope it's a boy myself, Mike. If it's a girl then I'll be having to keep an eye on her all the time when she gets older. God bloody well knows I've sometimes been a bastard to women myself in my younger days, and I wouldn't want no fella treating my daughter the way I treated some girls as a lad. You've gotten lucky with Maureen. She's a pretty girl but you've had no trouble with her."

"And don't I know how lucky I am. Maureen's smart and she's strong."

"Perhaps she'll become a nun."

Colin's father chuckled. "I doubt that."

"How's Líadan getting on these days?"

Rick asked about Colin's mother often. Sometimes he'd give Colin's father a bottle of beer to take home to her.

"Sometimes she seems fine, but then sometimes, well, you know."

"Must be hard to keep up with her moods," Uncle Rick observed. Colin's father nodded but didn't say anything.

Rick glanced over at the ticking clock on the wall. "It's a few minutes after four. The after-work crowd should be coming in soon."

A heavy man in longshoreman's garb walked in and took a

seat at one of the booths in the back of the pub. He hollered, "Rick, bring me a pint!"

"Be right with you."

"Colin and I should be getting home. See you laters, Rick," Colin's father said.

Colin hopped off his barstool and followed his father out of the pub as Uncle Rick waved goodbye to them.

Outside the pub the autumn air was strangely warm, and it felt a little like the early summer as Colin walked with his father down the block and crossed a side street. Colin's father reached for his hand but he declined.

"I'm too big for that." Colin then tugged at his father's sleeve. "Da? How come you don't like to drink like Uncle Rick does?"

His father looked down at him and his brow furrowed. Colin wondered if he'd asked the wrong question. "Because the drink makes me a mean man."

The sun had still been visible when they'd left Uncle Rick's pub, but as they walked on it disappeared behind the vast skyline. All that was left in Colin's presence were gray shopfronts and row after row of suffocating tenements with the occasional shout coming from an opened window. As Colin walked on with his father, it only grew darker. Soon the moon shone bright in the sky above him, somewhere he wouldn't be able to see from the dirty streets down below of the Lower East Side. How could his mother and father ever have thought this place would be better than home?

By the time Colin arrived at the tenement with his father, Maureen had already set dinner on the table.

"You were at Uncle Rick's, weren't you?" she asked as they took off their coats.

Maureen wore their mother's red apron, which fit her well. She seemed annoyed, as if the food was cold because they were late, even though they weren't. She had just set the dinner out earlier than usual.

"Yes, we were visiting your uncle for a bit," Colin's father said. "Are we late for dinner? I didn't think we were."

Maureen shook her head as she stood in front of the stove. There was no separate kitchen in the apartment. The only spaces that were separated by walls were the two small bedrooms. The stove, the icebox, and the sink were part of the main room that you stepped into when entering the apartment. They had to boil water if they wanted to fill the bathtub in the main room and everyone else had to leave for privacy.

"Thank you for dinner, Maureen," Colin's father said. "Has Danny come home yet?"

Maureen shook her head as she went over to the small dining table. She was already taller than their mother, and she was clever and self-taught.

"I suppose he's still working," she said. "What time did Danny leave for work?"

"I'm not sure. It's not unusual for him to be late." Maureen sat down at the table and waited for them to take a seat.

"Where's your *máthair*?"

"In bed."

Their father sighed and then sat down. Colin sat next to his sister. Maureen put her hands in position to pray, and Colin and his father followed her lead.

"Dear Lord," she began, "bless this food and the members of our household. We pray for their safe departures and their swift returns—"

Someone knocked at the door.

"It's open," Maureen hollered as she started to eat her potatoes.

Colin watched as their father scolded Maureen for her boisterous behavior.

She shrugged. The door opened and Colin began to eat. Most likely it was a neighbor wanting to borrow a frying pan or a paring knife.

But Mr. Duffy who lived downstairs burst into the apartment shouting, "Come quick, Danny's been shot!"

He had to shout again before the startling news sank into the mind of anyone at the table. "Danny's been shot!"

Maureen gasped and started to cry. Colin's father dropped his fork and ran over to Mr. Duffy. Mr. Duffy was almost crazed with madness himself. His white hair went this direction and that, and his spectacles were falling off his face.

"Where is he? What happened?" Colin's father asked.

Mr. Duffy fixed his spectacles and whispered into Michael's ear. "I see," Michael said. Then he spoke to Colin and Maureen, "Stay here." He began to walk out with Mr. Duffy and Colin started whimpering.

"Da, don't leave without me." Maureen rose from the table and ran over to where he was.

He took her by the shoulders gently. "I have to. I can't take Colin with me so you need to stay with him."

"No..." Maureen touched their father's shirtsleeve but he shook her off.

Colin's father didn't grab his coat as he left the apartment.

Maureen's entire body seemed to shake. She left the door open and lingered in the doorway for a few minutes after their father had left, almost as if she was waiting for him to return. She didn't shut the door, and went back to the table and sat down next to Colin.

"You should finish your dinner," she said.

"Where's Danny?" Colin began to eat his food again. "Someone hurt him with a gun?" He wiped some food from his face.

Maureen slowly nodded as she dried her eyes. "Yes, Danny's been hurt."

"Who did it?"

"I don't know, Colin."

"Will he be all right?"

"Da's going to find out for us."

"How come Mam didn't go with him?"

"Da left in a hurry."

"Why did you stay? I'm big enough."

"I stayed so you wouldn't be alone."

"But I'm not alone. Mam's here."

"Yes, but she's sleeping," Maureen said gently.

Colin's mother spent a lot of time shut away in the bedroom when her sadness and fear overcame her.

"Doesn't Mam care what happens to Danny?" Colin asked. "She does, but she's anxious."

"Anxious about Danny?"

"If she knew then I'm sure she'd be worried about him, yes, but she's anxious all the time."

"Will she feel better soon?"

"There's no cure for what she has."

"I don't like it when she's this way."

"I don't either." Maureen squeezed his shoulder and then got up and stepped into the bedroom their mother wasn't using.

Colin sat at the table alone. His face felt hot but he wasn't crying. His mother entered the room in her bedclothes. She yawned as she walked and barely managed to keep her eyes open.

"Why is the door open?" she asked and then closed it.

Colin thought she must have been a very deep sleeper to not have heard the commotion.

"Hello, handsome," she spoke sleepily to him. She walked to

him, put her arms around his neck and hugged him. "*Stór*," she cooed in Gaelic.

Colin looked back at her.

"It means *darling*. That's what your father used to say to me when I was younger and prettier." His mother laughed slightly and kissed the top of his head. "You're my favorite child. Don't tell the others." She winked. "I know you'll make me proud someday."

"Something bad happened to Danny," Colin said. "What's going on?"

"He was hurt. Ask Maureen."

"Oh, Lord." His mother looked around the kitchen. "I would ask Maureen, but where is that girl?"

Colin pointed at one of the bedrooms. "She went into there."

His mother sniffed and held back tears. "I don't know if I can handle this right now. Why don't you go and cheer your sister up? I need to stay here and smoke one of your father's cigarettes for a bit to relax me and then I'll talk to her." She'd been smoking his father's Lucky Strikes more and more since coming to America.

His mother's eyes and hands searched the table for the pack of cigarettes, but they weren't there. She eventually found them near the stove.

She patted his back. "What are you waiting for, sweetheart? Go on."

Colin rose from his chair and went over to the bedroom Maureen had entered. His mother sat down in the tattered blue armchair in the corner of the main room and exhaled. She never smoked in bed because she didn't want to start a fire. She took a cigarette out of the pack then got up again to look for a match. Colin already knew her routine by heart.

〜

Colin was in the middle of asking his neighbor Mrs. Finnegan and Uncle Rick when Danny would be coming home when his father arrived. Uncle Rick had shown up a little while ago before Mrs. Finnegan came over from across the hall to see how the family was coping. Bad news traveled fast in the tenement. Colin's mother and Rick were smoking the Lucky Strikes at the table.

Mrs. Finnegan had brought cake and tea with her. Colin devoured the cake with relish.

"Michael," his mother spoke to his father. "Why did this happen to our son? Who would do such a thing?"

"He had a dispute with a customer he sold cigarettes to."

"Has he died?" she inquired softly.

Colin's father shook his head. "But he was shot twice, and his arm is in a bad way. We can't let him work for that man anymore." Colin's mother dragged her cigarette away from her red lips with a pale, thin hand, and blew a curl of smoke out of her mouth. She nodded slightly, and Colin could see tears shining in her eyes.

She was trying to remain composed but failing.

"We're all praying for him," Mrs. Finnegan said. Then she remarked with pleasure as Colin gobbled up a piece of her sweet cake, "He's a growing young man, isn't he?" She patted him on the head.

Colin's mother smiled at him, and he saw how other peoples' compliments about him pleased her.

"Da," Maureen shouted as she ran in from the bedroom where Colin had left her a little while ago. "Is Danny okay?"

Michael calmed her down and gave her a hug. "He's in surgery now. I have to return to hospital," he told everyone in the room. "You and your mother can come with me if Rick can stay here and watch Colin," he said to Maureen. "Colin's too young to come with us. Will you watch him, Rick?" He looked at his brother.

"Sure I can." Uncle Rick began to eat a piece of cake.

Colin sat with his treat and then began to fret about Danny again. Johnny's mother had stopped by an hour ago to say that Johnny would be in to see Colin as soon as he came home from visiting his cousin, so Colin had that to look forward to.

Colin's father looked at Maureen and then at his wife. "Let's go, girls." He nodded at Uncle Rick. "I'll ring Mrs. Duffy upstairs if I need to reach you, Rick. They have a telephone."

"We'll be saying our prayers," Mrs. Finnegan said.

"I'm not sure even prayers will be enough," Colin's father mumbled.

"Can we go play baseball?" Colin asked Uncle Rick after his mother, father, and his sister had left.

"Now?" Rick said.

Colin nodded. "I don't want to wait."

"Surely, child, it's too dark outside to play baseball," Mrs. Finnegan interrupted.

"It isn't," Colin insisted.

Mrs. Finnegan frowned at him.

"I'm afraid we can't do it right now," Uncle Rick said gently. "You see, we have to stay in the building to wait for any news of your brother. Your brother's been hurt, you know."

"Will he get better?"

"I expect that he will." Uncle Rick smiled.

Mrs. Finnegan gave Colin's uncle a look of disapproval.

"Let's have some more of this cake Mrs. Finnegan was so kind to bring us," Rick said to Colin.

Mrs. Finnegan beamed with pride as Uncle Rick cut them a few more pieces from the cake using the small pop-up knife he had in his shirt pocket.

"Danny would have wanted me to play baseball," Colin said. Mrs. Finnegan smiled at him. "Yes, but not now, sweetheart."

She smelled like baby powder, and Colin thought about asking her why she smelled that way since she seemed too old to have babies at home.

"I'll tell you about my father, your grandfather," Uncle Rick suddenly said to him. "Say, do you know if your da keeps any beer around the house?"

Colin shook his head.

Rick sighed. "I thought as much."

"My John has some," Mrs. Finnegan said. "I'll go fetch it."

"That's very kind of you, ma'am." When she left, Rick spoke to Colin, "I feel like having myself a drink. It keeps the nerves off."

Colin smiled along with his uncle although he hadn't entirely grasped what Rick meant.

Uncle Rick began to tell a story. He started out slowly but he became livelier and beaming with exaggerated detail after Mrs. Finnegan brought the beer.

"When I was a child..." Uncle Rick had already finished his second bottle. "...your grandfather would take me to his pub with him, like your da takes you to my pub. I'd sit and watch my da work. He'd give me a ginger beer. Sometimes your da would come along with us."

"I never knew my grandfather," Colin said.

"He died before you were born. He was a great man, full of laughter, and love for this world. Everyone he met loved him. He played the accordion like your da. He was quite talented. Your da is a skilled player as well though you wouldn't know it these days." Uncle Rick looked at Mrs. Finnegan after he'd started drinking his third bottle. "Do you happen to have any more beer at home?"

29

Mrs. Finnegan nodded. "But you've already had three. Do you really think you should have another?"

Uncle Rick gave her a sheepish smile. "If you wouldn't mind, I'd really love another."

Mrs. Finnegan was too polite to not carry out Rick's wish. "Thank you," Uncle Rick called out as she left. He smiled at Colin when she was gone, and Colin smiled back. "Now, what were we talking about?"

"Your da."

"Yes, him. You look very much like him. Did you know that?" Colin shook his head.

"Well, you do. You're both big, handsome devils." A twinkle shone in Uncle Rick's eyes and he gave Colin a wink.

Colin laughed.

Mrs. Finnegan returned with two more bottles and Rick thanked her generously as she set them on the table.

"I have to go now. Let me know if there's any news of Danny. And, Colin," she said, wagging her finger at him, "don't stay up too late."

"Goodbye, ma'am, and thank you again," Uncle Rick said as she closed the door behind her. "What a lovely woman." Rick opened a bottle using the table's edge and toasted Colin.

Colin giggled at the toast his uncle had given him.

"Come here," Rick said to him after a moment. "Come now and sit on my lap. I bet you're tired. You can sleep."

Colin shook his head. "I'm too big."

"No, you aren't." Uncle Rick gestured for him to sit. "Come on." He grinned when Colin hesitated. "You're not afraid of me, are you?"

Colin slowly shook his head and then smiled at his uncle. He had never sat on anyone's lap before except for his parents' laps a few years ago. But Uncle Rick was a relative so Colin figured it would be acceptable. He got up and went over to Rick.

Uncle Rick lifted him up. "You're getting big and heavy." Rick leaned his cold, unshaven face against Colin's "Have I ever told you what a good lad you are, a good nephew?" His breath smelled bitter like beer.

Colin sat up and tried to get off his uncle's lap, but large Rick, so much stronger than him, had his arm around Colin's waist, holding him tightly.

"You are a good lad."

Colin wasn't a slight boy, but each time he tried to break free, Uncle Rick used his even greater strength to hold him back. Rick was slurring, and he had a difficult time keeping his eyes open. He put his hand on the front of Colin's pants, and Colin jumped. His body squirmed as he, again, tried to wrestle free.

"Did I ever tell you you're my favorite nephew?" Rick smiled awkwardly. He slipped his hand into the front of Colin's pants, inside his underwear. "But you have to be quiet now. Calm down." He put his other hand across Colin's mouth to muffle his shouts.

Rick's cold, rough hand felt awful against Colin's warm skin. He wriggled and tried to escape again, but he failed under his uncle's persistent force.

"All right." Rick pulled his hand out.

He ceased covering Colin's mouth and tucked Colin's shirt back in. Then he lifted him off his lap and set him on the floor. Uncle Rick tried to fix Colin's ruffled hair but Colin ducked out of his reach.

"Go and get ready for bed now." Rick gave Colin a terse push toward the bedroom. He didn't look him in the eye. "Don't tell anyone about this," he warned. "I'll come in the middle of the night and hurt you if you do."

Colin glanced back at Rick as he ran to the room he shared with his older brother and sister. Uncle Rick was now slouched over in the chair at the table. His head moved up and down once in a while as he snored. Colin hurried into the bedroom and shut the door. He didn't understand what had just happened. Colin didn't want to grow up to become a publican anymore. He used all his strength to push Maureen's bed against the inside of the door to keep the monster out. Colin feared Rick would hear the noise and try to come into the room. His eyes were damp, but he never cried out loud.

3

Years passed. Danny had lived. The Dubliner he'd worked for had paid the hospital bill, but Danny had lost his right arm and the hand he'd depended on to join the Air Force. World War II was raging, and Colin's family had to use ration books, but there would be no going to war for Danny now. Líadan had given birth to another son a few months after Danny's injury. It wasn't intentional, of course. The family had named the little boy Patrick, and he had his mother's looks.

Uncle Rick was present in Colin's life less often, and when he was there, Colin tried his best to avoid him. If Colin's father would go to the pub and ask him if he would like to come along, Colin always said he was busy.

Johnny's mother wanted to move out of the Bowery to the countryside, but she only made it as far as Twenty Second Street. In the process, Johnny got himself a girlfriend; a pretty, brown-eyed girl named Donna. Colin got into the habit of skipping school with them. He hung out with Johnny and Donna at a drugstore near Johnny's new apartment building and ate hamburgers and drank cola while people watching and telling obnoxious jokes. Sometimes they bought beer from older boys, which they'd end up paying double for. But the lightheaded joy it gave them on endless weekend afternoons made the money spent worthwhile.

Colin received his first kiss that same year, from a shapely friend of Donna's named Peggy. He lost his virginity a month after to that same girl. He wondered if this meant he had a girlfriend. He wanted Peggy to be that.

"It's getting hot." Johnny raised the edge of his shirt toward his face and wiped the sweat from his brow.

"These guys are going to get us beer?" Colin asked.

"Yeah. And this time I think we're actually getting it for nothing."

"You're sure?"

"Yeah. Especially now that I'll remind them you're Irish, they'll be even more generous. Micks stick together. Right?" Johnny grinned.

Colin laughed. Their friendship was strong enough for them to insult one another in jest. "Can I ask you something?" he said after a moment.

"Go ahead."

"Do you think it means that since I've been with Peggy, I'm her fellow?"

Johnny chuckled. "Who knows? Peggy's been with a lot of guys and they all ain't her 'fellow'. Do you like her that much? To get serious?"

"Serious? What, like you and Donna?"

"Like Donna and me."

"If you mean it like that then I'm not sure."

Johnny smiled. "Sometimes Donna drives me crazy—she acts like we're married—but I really like her."

"I know you do."

Colin knew how much Johnny was stuck on Donna. Johnny always had his arm around her waist and would whisper into her ear. "Have you ever seen the Dunleavys's sister Alison?" Johnny asked.

Colin shook his head.

"She sure is something." Johnny whistled. "Great figure. Beautiful eyes. Sweet, too."

"Then why don't you go for her too, then, Johnny?"

"I don't think Donna would like that very much."

"Probably not."

Johnny laughed. "This guy, Freddie, is one of the people we're meeting, one of the Dunleavys. He's lucky. His old man let him leave school last year to come work with him. Now he's making like fifty bucks a week. My mother tells me I have to stay for as long as the school will have me." He imitated his mother's voice, which made Colin laugh. "Yours, too?"

"I don't know what my mother thinks. She hardly leaves the apartment."

"What's wrong with her, is she sick?"

"She's sick but she's not getting better, if you know what I mean. She's worried something bad will happen to her if she goes outside, and she sleeps a lot when she's feeling sad. That's how Maureen explained it to me." Colin didn't believe Johnny understood his mother's condition. He hardly understood it himself. "My father will make me finish school. He won't have it any other way."

They walked to the Dunleavys's building. There was only one Dunleavy loitering in front of the steps today. The Dunleavy family owned the place, and the building was better kept than most others in the area since the family made substantial money. The Dunleavys's place wasn't considered a 'tenement'. It was a white four-story building with two street-facing windows on each floor. Those windows glistened like wintertime ice in the sun. It impressed Colin that the windows were kept so clean. In his family's home, the outsides of the windows were forever grimy because of a lack of interest or a lack of an effort in cleaning them, or they were fogged with thick steam from cooking inside. "O'Brien. Garcia," Freddie Dunleavy said to them as they approached.

"How's it going today?" Johnny asked.

"I'm doing all right. You?" Freddie looked directly at Colin. Colin nodded at him.

Colin sized Freddie up. Freddie was smaller than him, but he was seventeen and already raking in significant cash. He worked for his father's beer distribution company full time. The Dunleavy family supplied all of the Irish pubs on the East Side of Manhattan. Freddie had on a pressed dark suit with a red silk tie, and his hair was slicked back.

"You're going to buy beer from us today," Freddie stated. "O'Brien here is from the old country." Johnny pointed at Colin.

"That so? I never knew that."

"Yeah," Colin spoke up.

"Where's your accent?" Freddie asked.

"I lost it when I came here."

Freddie stared at him as though he was trying to assess whether Colin was telling the truth. Then he smiled at him. "I'll give you a discount, then."

"Uh, Freddie?" Johnny said.

"Yeah?"

When Johnny didn't talk, Freddie said, "Yeah?" again.

"When I spoke to your brother he said you'd be giving it to us for free today."

"Which brother?"

"Frank."

"Frank? That explains it. Frank's been a little slow lately. He isn't right about that. We don't give it away for free. Never."

"I don't know if we're interested, then."

Colin couldn't believe the way Johnny was speaking to the

powerful older boy. He knew Johnny had guts, but he didn't think he was rash enough to challenge the Dunleavys.

"I was told I'd be getting it for free." Then Johnny looked over at Colin. "Come on, let's get out of here and go to those other guys." There weren't any 'other guys'. Colin knew Johnny was bluffing and hoping to change Freddie's mind so he played along with Johnny's plan.

"Where the fuck do you think you're both going?" Freddie shouted as they started to leave. He pulled out a knife.

Johnny didn't eye the knife. Colin knew that if his friend had looked at the knife, then Freddie would have sensed his fear. And Johnny couldn't let Freddie think he feared him.

"We're going to someone else," Johnny said to Freddie.

"You're going too, giant Irish?" Freddie stared at Colin. "Or are you going to let him speak for you?"

"I'm going with Johnny." Colin held Freddie's stare.

"Not smart." Freddie switched the blade up and shook his head at both of them. "I think one of you should stay here and pay for this beer we got for you." He gestured to the box of brown bottles on the building steps. "And I think it should be you, Irish."

"Are any of your brothers fighting in the war?" Colin asked Freddie to diffuse the situation.

"Why are you asking me that?" Then Freddie nodded. "Yours?" Colin shook his head.

"Why not?" Freddie asked.

"My older brother lost his arm."

"So he's a cripple?"

Colin nodded.

"That's too bad for him. Or maybe it isn't. At least he won't get killed in the war, right?"

Colin shrugged.

Freddie clutched the knife at his side in his pale, thick hand

and looked at Colin. The look caused a long-simmering rage in Colin to boil over. It was the same kind of look his Uncle Rick had given him the night he was drunk. It wasn't that Colin sensed Freddie Dunleavy wanted to touch him, rather it was that Freddie gave him a look like he was going to hurt him and there wasn't anything Colin could do about it. Colin didn't like the feeling. Freddie was older than them, but Colin was larger. Soon he was grasping Freddie's knife. Freddie was on the ground a second later, and then Colin violently kicked Freddie's back.

Colin didn't speak or yell as he continued to kick Freddie. His face and body felt very hot. Sweat wet his back. Kicking the shit out of Freddie was revenge for his childhood, albeit revenge taken out on the wrong person. Payback for a childhood that Colin figured had been stolen from him. And Freddie, at that moment, was the unfortunate incarnation of the robber.

"Stop it," Johnny shouted at Colin. "You're going to kill him!"

But Colin kept kicking. His mind told him to stop but his body didn't want to. It was his first taste of physical release, and it felt wonderful.

"Holy Mother. Colin, stop. You're going to kill him." Yet Johnny didn't move from where he stood watching.

In the end, Johnny began to move and pulled Colin off of Freddie. When Colin snapped out of his rage, he clutched Freddie's knife as he stood above him. Freddie moaned and rolled around on the ground. His forehead was bleeding. He looked helpless, but Colin continued to hold the knife. It was as if it gave him added security.

Johnny tugged at Colin's sleeve. "We need to get out of here." He spoke to Colin as they ran. "You didn't stab him, did you? I couldn't tell. There was so much going on."

Colin shook his head. He wiped the handle of Freddie's knife with his shirt and then flung it into a street gutter.

Colin ran with Johnny as far as they could without stopping

to catch their breath. They stopped at the corner of Thirtieth Street and Third Avenue, unable to run any further. Respectable businessmen stared at them like they didn't belong near the large office buildings. Colin looked over his shoulder and saw they were near a police station.

Colin pointed out the station to Johnny. "Do you think I should turn myself in?"

Johnny didn't smile. "You know, Colin, I really thought you were going to kill him back there."

"But I didn't."

Johnny grinned. "You're tough and you're a good fighter. Maybe you'll be a boxer someday."

Colin smiled at his friend's compliment. "Do you think Freddie's brothers will come after me?"

"Yeah. You're screwed." They both laughed.

"Too bad we forgot to take the beer with us," Johnny said.

Colin saw a dead body being taken away to the morgue one night when he was coming home from the movies with Maureen and Johnny. The body was lying in the middle of the street and was covered with a bloodstained sheet.

At the movies Colin had warm, buttery popcorn and a cola. Colin was starting to believe Johnny was sweet on Maureen despite having Donna. Johnny had insisted he sit next to Maureen at the theater and he'd bought her candy. Colin wasn't sure if he approved of Johnny showing interest in his sister, but he didn't blame him. Maureen was growing into her face and looking pretty. She already had herself a boyfriend, a young dockworker. Colin was sure she wasn't interested in Johnny, who was younger than her.

The dead man under the bloodstained sheet had been shot

by the husband of the woman he'd seduced, at least that's what all the adults said the next day over breakfast or at the pub. A sudden, violent death in the Bowery wasn't considered shocking because it happened so often. The sad occurrence would be discussed, but only casually.

Johnny stepped closer to Maureen. "Goodnight, beautiful." He kissed her hand.

Maureen laughed.

Johnny said goodbye to Colin and then left to return to his home farther uptown. Johnny turned his head every chance that he could, to glance at the body under the bloody sheet.

"I don't want you to be looking at that," Colin and Maureen's father said to them when they had entered their apartment.

Michael was sitting on a chair at the table. There was an empty glass next to his hands, which were folded and resting on the tabletop.

Colin glanced at his father as if he didn't know what he meant. "I saw it out the window," his father replied.

"We've seen it so many times here in New York, it doesn't mean anything anymore," Maureen said.

"It should."

"Where's Danny?" Colin asked.

"You're both fifteen minutes late." Colin's father ignored his question. "And Colin, you haven't been going to school. The Duffys got a telephone call for me this morning about it."

Colin looked at his sister for what to say.

"We were just with Johnny," Maureen said to their father. "We were at the movies. We weren't doing anything bad."

"You shouldn't be running around with Johnny Garcia. Either of you." Colin's father didn't turn his head to face them, rather he spoke staring ahead.

"What's wrong with Johnny?" Maureen asked.

"He's always getting into trouble, and his father's in prison."

Michael rose from where he sat and went close to where Maureen stood near the doorway with Colin. "Don't ever talk to me like that again, girl." He bent his big self over and leaned in close to her face. "I'm going to use the strap on you if you do," he threatened.

Colin smelled alcohol on his father's breath. "Don't hurt her!"

Michael looked away for a moment, as if he was ashamed at his behavior. He shook his head and muttered something Colin didn't understand.

"Maureen, darling, I'm sorry." He turned and embraced Colin's sister in his arms and kissed her gently on the forehead. "You know I'd never hurt you." He patted her back as his voice slurred.

"I know, Da." Maureen sounded afraid.

"He's been drinking," Maureen said to Colin and Danny that night. "He never drinks."

"He's never drank his whole life," Colin added.

"Ha," Danny commented from the floor where he was resting flat on his back on a threadbare quilt. Colin and Danny were too big to share a bed, and their parents hadn't gotten them a new one. Danny stared up at the white ceiling covered with a little black mold. He was smoking one of their father's cigarettes. "He's a goddamn drunk and a hypocrite."

Doctors had told Colin's brother he would have to learn to write all over again using his left hand. But Colin noticed Danny only got frustrated trying to write with his left hand, and his frustration continued to grow. Then one day he seemed to give up. He took a part-time job as a clerk at a drugstore, and went out at night alone. Colin didn't know what his brother did at night.

"What's a hypocrite?" Colin, and Patrick, who was now five years old, asked at the same time.

Patrick had grown to become a quiet little boy who had difficulty learning to read.

Colin assumed a 'hypocrite' must have been something very important, something only an older person would know, and Danny was the eldest.

"A hypocrite preaches against something and then goes ahead and does it anyway," Danny said. "Da's always saying drinking's bad for us and that he'd never do it himself, and neither should we, but he is doing it so he's a hypocrite."

"Maybe he's not doing it," Colin suggested.

"He's doing it. I saw him bring home that bottle of mick whiskey myself. Mam's been drinking it with him."

"Don't use that word." Colin abruptly rose and shouted at his brother.

"What are you going to do about it? What, are you going to ruin my only arm and leave me with nothing?" Danny said with sarcasm. "Anyway, I'm Irish so it's okay for me to say that word. Calm the feck down."

Upon hearing the word 'feck', young Patrick burst into giggles. "He said the bad word!"

Danny smiled at Patrick then looked up at the ceiling again. "I give him a month until he blows."

Colin watched him light another cigarette with his Ronson lighter.

"What's 'blow'?" Patrick asked.

"In this case, I meant until he hits the bottom."

"Why's he going to hit the bottom?" Colin said, suddenly worried.

"He's going to drink and drink . . ." Danny put out the cigarette to go to sleep. "And then they're going to get him."

"What are you talking about?" Colin asked him. "Danny?" But it was too late. Danny was already asleep.

4

Colin's father owed a lot of money to a Bowery loan shark named David Burke who had been a rumrunner during Prohibition. Burke had taken to confronting Colin's father at the building sites where he sometimes worked. Danny had been the first in the family to find out what had driven their father to the drink.

But Colin still believed his father would be all right, that he'd somehow come out of it okay.

"Why do you think you're going to die?" Colin asked his father one day when his father had mentioned the possibility.

"You never know what can happen. Things like that, people dying unexpectedly or getting killed, you read about it in the newspaper every day. Just yesterday I read about this man who suddenly dropped dead in the middle of the park. It happens all the time."

"Da, I don't think you need to worry about that. Besides, I heard that man was shot, he didn't just drop dead."

"You just never know."

A week later, Colin's father managed to scrounge up fifty dollars, but when he met with David Burke to give the money to him, Burke refused to accept anything less than the full amount he was owed. Colin's father had run out of time.

When Colin and Danny found out how much their father really owed Mr. Burke, thousands of dollars, they thought they could pick pockets to get the money needed to save their father's life. But they didn't manage to get enough.

Colin's father didn't come home for dinner one night. His body was found later in the evening. He was identified by Danny and Colin at the city morgue early the next morning on behalf of their frantic mother. But David Burke hadn't killed him. Colin's father had shot himself in the mouth in the back of an alley with a gun he'd bought. Colin had planned to ask his father when he got older if he was really his father. Now he couldn't.

Danny and Colin sat on their steps when they came home from the morgue. Danny was sitting quietly, staring up at the clear sky through the tall city buildings. His hands were folded in his lap. He seemed strangely calm. Colin's body felt hot and ached from anger.

"I can't believe he did it," Colin said about their father. Danny murmured in agreement.

The air was thick with a humidity that day that never seemed to end – the oppressive, tiring humidity that always clung to the city in the summertime. The tenement, out of respect for the deceased Michael O'Brien, was nearly silent, except for the occasional howl of Colin's mother or the wailing of Maureen and Patrick.

Residents had lit tall white candles in decaying copper holders and set them near the entranceway. The landlord took them away a few hours later, claiming they were a fire hazard.

Colin and his brother brushed off the tender pats offered by neighbors on their way up the steps to their apartment. Danny never looked up while Colin stared back at the sympathetic faces. Colin would never let them know he was afraid what would happen now that his father was gone, and that inside, he ached with all his heart. He stepped into his apartment with a numbing ease. This time, his brother followed him.

Their father had come home for lunch that past afternoon but had never returned home for dinner in the evening.

"Goddamn mick," Colin had muttered under his breath as he left the morgue with Danny. He hadn't meant it of course. He was just angry at his father for not telling his family about how serious his troubles were, and, eventually, leaving them.

Colin and Danny had gone into a church on First Avenue after they left the city morgue, and Colin had cried in the pew at what he had said. Danny had given him a hug, which was rare.

"It's just Mam and us now," he told Colin. "It'll never be the same."

Then Danny got very angry and swore revenge, but they both knew that it was impossible. Mr. Burke had won.

In Ireland, Colin's granny had instructed the children how to use the old shotgun her husband had hunted pheasants with, something Colin's father hadn't liked; and Colin knew he could buy a gun in the street and shoot David Burke. But what good would that do? Because there would always be a family member wanting to avenge Mr. Burke's death, and there would always be another man waiting to take Burke's place. Violence never ended in the Bowery.

The funeral took place at a small church frequented by the Irish. Their neighbor Mrs. Duffy had suggested the place. The tenement occupants had collected enough money to give Colin's father a simple ceremony.

Colin hadn't wanted to go to the funeral. He wanted to sit in the bedroom he shared with his siblings and concentrate on nothing. He went to the funeral only for his mother. She had stopped crying when he stepped out of the bedroom wearing his black Sunday suit. His mother waved his father's box of Lucky Strikes in the air. "Colin," she said in between her loud weeping. "You look just like your father. You have to go to the funeral. Please. You're the image of him."

The service was crowded, which was a testament to how well-liked Michael was in the community. The family had contemplated saying that Michael's death was a murder and not a suicide, but they had decided against it in the end. Too many people already knew too much, and many had connections to the police and therefore to the truth.

People speculated as to why Colin's father had *really* taken his own life. Was his pretty, pompous wife cheating on him? Was it because his eldest son was missing an arm? Some in the neighborhood even snickered that Colin's father was a coward and 'not a man' because he'd killed himself. Colin had hit a man he didn't know well for saying those exact words. He was only fourteen years old and the man had decided not to call the police, but people in the neighborhood began speculating it was because of Colin and his temper that his father had done what he had.

"And now one of the family will speak," the priest said from the pulpit. "Michael O'Brien's eldest son, Daniel."

The priest nodded at Danny in the front row. He was an old priest, a decaying man with droopy skin and dark circles under his fading blue eyes. He was depressing for Colin to watch. Every time Colin glanced up he thought he might laugh, but he reasoned it'd be more than shameful to laugh at his father's funeral. His father's casket was closed because of the damage he'd done to himself.

Danny rose from where he sat with Colin and the family. He clutched a wrinkled piece of paper in his left hand. Colin had sat with Danny late last night as Danny dictated and Colin scribbled his words on the paper.

Colin's mother wouldn't cease her crying at the funeral, and when Danny made his way up to the front of the church and stood behind the lectern, she started to bawl even more.

"Our father was a good man," Danny shouted above their mother's cries. "He came here from Ireland and worked hard in America to support us, his family."

He looked at Colin from where he stood. Danny began to read louder as his confidence seemed to increase.

"Da loved us."

And it seemed as if Danny might shed a tear or two at that moment, but he didn't, he just kept reading, appearing as proud as ever.

"He had four children. Me, my brothers, Colin and Patrick, and a daughter, my lovely sister Maureen. His favorite thing to do was to spend time with his children and his wife, our mother. And he enjoyed visiting with his brother, Rick. He went to Rick's pub almost every day, but he never drank. Da was sober until the day he died."

Colin thought how Danny made the lie sound real. "He was decent and led such a good life..."

Colin knew Danny had more written down, but Danny's voice cracked as though he might cry and he stopped speaking. So he ended with that, and that was enough, apparently, because the funeralgoers rose to their feet and clapped, some even called out words of praise or admiration.

"Now let us lead the O'Brien family in a prayer," the old priest began after Danny returned to his seat and the commotion had settled down.

All in the audience bowed their heads, and, if they were Catholic, which most of them were, they knelt on the rests.

"In the name of the Father, Son, and Holy Ghost."

The words echoed through the small church, heavy with the

scents of myrrh and frankincense. Fingers crossed patiently over chests.

There wasn't a funeral procession afterwards. People just dispersed and returned to Manhattan to the family's small apartment for an impromptu wake while two glum workers buried Colin's father in the ground at the potter's field on Hart Island. The immediate family had been invited to watch the burial from afar. Colin's mother declined to go and took Patrick home with her instead, but Colin, Danny, and Maureen went. When it was over, Colin returned home with Maureen and Danny and found the apartment overflowing with guests, including Johnny.

Initially, most of the adults had a drink of whiskey, and the older children each had a shandy. Then one drink turned into a couple of drinks for the adults, and soon most of them were pretty drunk. Songs were sung. Someone broke out into "Auld Lang Syne" and then another fellow mentioned it wasn't the appropriate season and a fight almost broke out. A man was dead. The atmosphere at the gathering, however, was not.

Uncle Rick came by the reception already drunk. Colin hoped he might drink an entire bottle himself and lose his head so he could finally have it out with Rick once and for all, to confront him about the awful thing his uncle had done when Colin was a little boy. Colin watched Uncle Rick give Líadan a few white flowers, but other than that his uncle seemed to avoid the family at the reception, as if Michael's death might rub off on him somehow if he got too close to them.

5

Colin quit school a few weeks after his father's funeral. He reasoned an education wouldn't do him much good now, not that it ever would have. A boy from the Bowery wasn't going to use many books in his life, unless they had to do with the horse races. He was a man of the household now, and all he needed to do was to find ways to earn money.

Despite his large stature, he had difficulty finding work where most men did – like down at the piers unloading gigantic cargo ships – because of his young age. So Colin filched rich men's wallets and unsuspecting deliverymen's bicycles, until he found a job selling stolen cartons of cigarettes for a downstairs neighbor, the man from Dublin. Danny had once worked for the guy. It was the same man who had almost gotten Danny killed.

Colin got five percent of every box he sold. It wasn't much, but it was steady, and he found he had a knack for it. He hawked the stolen cigarettes all over the city, downtown, midtown, and the uptown area. Sometimes he rode the subway to the outer boroughs or hitched a ride into New Jersey or Pennsylvania.

Sometimes the people who bought the cigarettes got a 'bad box', cigarettes that were no good and didn't light, and more than once Colin ended up in an argument with a dissatisfied customer that escalated into a fistfight. Colin had a brass knuckle and won the struggles most of the time, but other times he found his eye blackened, his face cut, his jaw swollen, or a finger broken. Maureen mended his injuries at home. A few times he ended up in New York's juvenile court system for delinquency or truancy. And by the time Colin was fifteen he had criminal convictions and had served almost a year's worth of various minor sentences at juvenile detention centers.

"Colin," Maureen lectured him as he helped her wash the laundry in the sink. "Don't become like the men who hurt Da." She had already tried and failed to persuade him to finish school. A year later Colin was still alive, a year of selling stolen cigarettes and waving at the uniformed WAC girls. He was sixteen and lived in a dim world of smoke and fights. He knew all the prostitutes by name on 42nd Street from selling cigarettes to them in front of the pawn shops. His boss informed Colin there was a high probability of him taking over the business once he retired. Colin looked forward to that prospect.

He was in love with an older woman named Lucille Byrne he'd met at the pub. She was unfairly beautiful considering how poorly she took care of herself. Her brother owned and was the bartender at *Byrne's* in the Bowery, a favorite retreat of Colin's, and where Lucille sometimes worked as a server. Colin had developed a taste for the drink and Lucille had become his drinking partner. It was unofficial, but late in the afternoon, just as her shift ended and before he made his evening cigarette rounds, they'd drink together. Like all the men in Colin's family when they were young, he looked older than his age. But he'd recently told Lucille his true age, and although she promised she wouldn't tell her brother, she started treating him like a boy instead of a man, which wounded him. "What are you drinking today, Lucille?" Colin said to her on one of those afternoons.

"Get us some beers."

"Two beers, Joe," Colin called out to Lucille's brother at the other end of the bar.

Colin sat with Lucille at the side of the bar closest to the front door. The door was propped open with a large rock to allow air inside the warm building. Colin liked sitting near the door because the outside air, no matter how much it smelled of the East River's stench, made him feel more alive.

"How have you been?" Lucille asked him.

"Not bad. You?"

"I'm thinking about leaving the Bowery, Colin. You know, packing my bags and..."

"Sure. Whatever you say," Colin said with a patient smile as he lit a cigarette.

Every other day Lucille said she was going to leave the Bowery and go someplace where the weather was always warm and beautiful, yet almost every afternoon after she was still drinking with Colin at her brother's pub. Lucille was a lifelong Bowery girl, and she depended on her brother. Colin didn't know much about her past, but he inferred her mother was a drinker.

"You'll marry me someday, when you're older?" Lucille half asked, half commanded.

There was a longing in her voice that touched Colin's soul. He glanced at her warm eyes and her pale skin and smiled. "Sure, I'll marry you someday. I'll marry you when I'm the mayor of New York and you're the leading actress in a Broadway play. When that happens, we'll tie the knot."

"You're a crumb sometimes, Colin, do you know that?" Lucille shook her head. Then she laughed out loud.

Colin laughed along with her. "I was only joking before. Of course I'll marry you. When I'm older."

Joe slid the beers across the counter and Lucille smiled as

Colin took the caps off the bottles using the edge of the bar. With a few gulps, his was gone. Lucille finished hers afterward.

"Bring me a shot of scotch," Colin said to Joe. Joe gestured to the different types of scotches. "That one. Thanks."

"You better slow down, handsome," Lucille said.

Colin grinned at her. "Lucille? Can I ask you something?" She nodded.

"How come we've never been together? I like you, and you seem to like me, unless I'm wrong."

"I do like you." Lucille blushed, and he hadn't thought that was possible.

"Do you not find me attractive?" he asked after a moment.

Lucille laughed a little. "No. You're attractive. And don't you know it."

He continued to stare into her eyes.

"Quit it, Colin. You're making me nervous. You're too young for me to really be interested in you."

He still watched her.

She rolled her eyes. "What do you want, some kind of prize?"

"A prize would be nice," he said with a smile.

"Ha."

But there was a look on her face that told him she might be considering it.

"You mean it?" Colin's voice deepened at the prospect of sex.

"Let's just drink now, okay?"

Colin nodded. He faced the bar and drank his scotch. Lucille ordered a ginger ale.

"So I don't get a stomachache," she said.

Lucille lived at a fleapit called the First Avenue hotel. Colin had suggested she better move out soon before she found herself strangled by a lunatic in the stairwell. Lucille had retorted that Colin was young and didn't know what he was talking about. Still, Colin would often walk Lucille home to make sure she was safe.

Colin walked Lucille back to her place like he usually did. One thing led to another, and the two found themselves in a drunken embrace in the stairwell and she kissed him a little. She was drunker than him, and he didn't think it would be right to sleep with her so he went with her into her room, took off her shoes and helped her into bed with her clothes still on.

She looked pretty and calm sleeping in her bed. But he knelt down at her side and took her pulse to make sure she was okay. After all, she'd had quite a bit to drink. Colin had taken the pulse of many people in his life because he had run into a lot of people who might have been dead. But Lucille's pulse was strong, and her wrist warm and soft. Assured, he left.

He stepped outside around six o'clock. His head hurt, and he reasoned he'd skip work altogether tonight. He had done it only once before, but the Dubliner wouldn't mind as long as he made up for the lost time during the next few days.

He walked toward *Mann's* garage, where Johnny, now seventeen, worked three days a week. On his free days Johnny stole items such as car tires for the owner of the garage. Johnny was living what Colin thought was the high life, spending money on Donna at nightclubs.

"You look tired, Colin," Johnny said when he saw him. Colin smiled at his friend's honesty.

"I haven't seen you in what feels like forever," Johnny said. "It's been days. Where'd you disappear to?"

"I've been working a lot."

"How's things with your boss, with what's his name?"

"We just call him the Dubliner. He's all right."

"Is Danny okay with you working for him?"

Colin shrugged. "We don't talk about it. But I think he understands I need to make money. Got a cigarette?"

"Why are you asking *me* for a cigarette? You're the one who sells them."

"I know, but I left them at home."

Johnny seemed unconvinced but he handed Colin a cigarette from the pocket of his denim work shirt.

"Got a match?"

Johnny shook his head.

Colin gave him back the cigarette. Johnny accepted it and then dropped it to the ground.

"What did you do that for?" Colin said.

"It touched your mouth."

Colin shook his head.

Johnny shrugged and gave him an innocent look. "That's some solid work you've got with that Dublin guy."

"It's all right." Colin couldn't offer to put in a good word for his friend because he knew the Dubliner only hired Irish. He didn't want to upset Johnny and was relieved when he changed the subject.

"Do you feel like getting something to eat? I'm starving. Didn't have breakfast or lunch. So, what do you say?"

"Sure. Let's go."

"*Byrne's?*"

"Nah, I just came from there."

Johnny chuckled. "Was Lucille there with you? Is that what really happened to those lost days, you've been spending them with her?"

Colin shrugged then laughed. He didn't want to admit Lucille had only kissed him.

"How about we grab us some Cuban food? You always said you wanted to try it."

"Let's do it."

"I know of this place uptown—"

"You sound excited about this place, Johnny, and I think

that's great," Colin said to let his friend down easy. "But my head is killing me, and there's no way I'm going that far just to eat."

"You drank too much with Lucille." Then Johnny smiled. "I promise you this is the best Cuban food in New York."

"Nope. Sorry, Johnny."

Johnny sighed. "All right. Have it your way. Though you're so damn lazy sometimes." He grinned.

Colin laughed.

"There's a vendor across the street." Johnny pointed to the other side of the street where apparently there was a food cart, though Colin couldn't see anyone from where they stood.

"I don't see anything."

"Come on, I'll show you. How's your sister doing?" Johnny talked as they walked.

They waited for the traffic to stop so they could cross the street. "Maureen's doing all right. She's not married yet, if that's what you're asking." Johnny blushed.

"You always had a thing for her, didn't you? I mean, when we were younger?"

"Yeah, I did."

"She asks about you once in a while. She asks how you're doing."

Johnny smiled. "She does?"

Colin nodded.

"It's nice to know someone's asking."

"How are you and Donna?"

"We're all right, but sometimes I think she's bored with me."

"I'm sorry to hear that." Colin patted his friend's back. "Where's this cart? You said it was across the street. Right?" He looked around for it.

"I guess the guy moved. He must've just moved a little farther up."

Colin hesitated. "Maybe we should just go to *Byrne's.*"

Johnny either hadn't heard or he pretended not to have heard, because he didn't reply. He kept walking and Colin followed.

They reached a delicatessen and compromised on going in there. Colin and Johnny were outside the Bowery and in an unfamiliar neighborhood at night. People wouldn't know them there, and Colin was convinced the guy working behind the counter gave them a menacing look when they stepped inside. He wondered if there was going to be a confrontation. Would the owner call some of his friends and inform them two strangers had entered his shop and one of them was 'dark'? It had happened to Colin and Johnny before.

But nothing happened this time. Colin and Johnny finished their sandwiches and left.

"What's it like living on your own?" Colin asked Johnny as they walked back to the garage.

"It's pretty good. You ought to consider it."

"I don't think I could ever leave my home. Maureen's such a good cook." Colin grinned.

"I ought to marry that girl. Of course, I don't know if she'd have me."

"She likes you. But I don't think I'd want to let you into my family."

Johnny chuckled. "Come on, we're practically brothers."

"I consider you my brother," Colin said with sincerity.

Johnny patted Colin's shoulder. "And I consider you my brother as well."

"Colin, what have you been up to today?" Maureen inquired in a friendly way as he entered the flat.

"Working. How are you?"

"Fine. Did you see Johnny today?"

"I did. How'd you know?"

"He's your best friend."

"Right, he is."

"Have you eaten yet?" Maureen asked.

"Yeah, but I'm still hungry."

"Good because I made dinner. It looks like it's just going to be you and me tonight. Danny took Patrick out for hamburgers."

"He did? When?"

"A little while ago. Want to eat now? The food's hot." Colin nodded.

Maureen had already set out the food so they sat down right away and began to eat the potatoes and shared a small steak.

"How's Mam doing?" Colin asked between chewing bites of meat.

"She's in her bedroom," Maureen said indifferently.

Colin nodded in understanding. "Has she been outside at all today?"

"Surprisingly, she has. She bought cigarettes, Lucky Strikes, like Da used to smoke, and then she sat outside on the steps." Maureen coughed back tears.

Colin tenderly squeezed his sister's hand. He glanced at the corner of the room where his father's accordion case had sat unused and dusty after his death until his mother pawned it. "I better go say hello to Mam and see how she's doing. I haven't seen her all day."

"You can wait until you're done with your dinner, Colin."

"But I really should—"

"Can't we eat in peace?" Maureen sounded exasperated as she cut him off. "I haven't seen you all day either. We all work so hard to support that woman, and she doesn't do anything."

"You explained her condition to me when I was little. I remember you told me her mother had the same problems.

Mam's been tired and anxious her whole life. I remember how she was before we came to New York, and sometimes after, but it's gotten worse since Da—"

"Her mother died in the same way Da did."

The revelation made Colin pause. "I didn't know that. She told you that?"

"No. Da told Danny and me years ago. You were too young to know."

"You don't think she'll..."

"No, I don't think she will. Don't worry, Colin."

"She must have felt terrible after Da..." Maureen nodded and sat there quietly.

"Does that mean we'll end up like her someday?" he asked.

"I'm not sure." After a while she said, "I'm tired. I'm anxious sometimes. But I don't stay inside all day. I work. Maybe I'd like my own bedroom."

"So move out."

"Who would take care of Patrick? Mam?" Maureen laughed bitterly and shook her head.

"I'm sorry, Maureen, but I want to see Mam." Colin rose from the table.

"If you leave this table, don't bother coming back."

"Maureen, please—"

"I mean it." She crumpled her napkin and threw it on the table.

"Maureen."

"Oh, forget I said anything."

Colin went inside his mother's bedroom. Her small, thin body was hidden under blankets and a white pillow framed her delicate face and golden curls. The window curtains were closed, and the room was stuffy.

"Mam? It's me," Colin whispered.

His mother moved slightly. She opened her eyes and looked at him. He started to let some light into the room but she yelled at him to stop. He noticed now more than ever how much she had aged in the past years, and she couldn't be called 'pretty' anymore. Her condition, and then her husband's death, had shattered her. Colin wondered if she privately wished they'd never left Kilrea.

"My handsome boy." She sat up. "You've been out all day. Have you been getting into trouble? You're growing up to be good, aren't you, and not one of those trouble boys?"

"Yes, Mam," he answered in a soothing voice. He disliked lying to her but he didn't want to break her heart more than it already had been. "I've been working. I've been bringing home money for the family."

"You're almost a man, now, Colin, a boy who is becoming a tall, strong man. You'll be a good man like your father was. I'm sure of it." She stroked his face and smiled. Her hands felt very warm.

Colin nodded but inside he doubted he'd ever be considered good anymore.

"Was Da really my father?" he asked.

She frowned. "Of course he was. You look like him. You're big like him."

"Then years ago why did you say he wasn't?"

"You remember that?" She frowned again. "I'd had too much to drink. It was claptrap."

Given her frail state, Colin didn't want to press the matter further. She didn't like discussing his father.

"Is your sister all right?" his mother asked.

"She seems fine. She's in the next room. Why are you asking? Did something happen?"

"I don't know. She's moody all the time. I think she hates me," she grumbled.

"She doesn't hate you. She's upset about what happened to Da, and she doesn't like that you scarcely leave the apartment."

"What is she talking about? I bought cigarettes, didn't I?" His mother scowled and turned away from him. "Darling, I want to rest now."

Colin nodded and left the room. He resumed his conversation with Maureen after he had returned to the dinner table. She didn't ask him how their mother was doing.

"How have you really been?" Colin asked.

Maureen sighed. "Fine, as I said. I guess."

"What do you mean, *you guess*?"

Her eyes darkened, and her lips trembled. "What am I supposed to say?" she shouted as she rose. "Do you want me to lie and say I'm doing wonderful?"

She flung her plate to the ground and it broke apart on the floor. Her fury shocked him. Maureen stepped over a piece of steak and lowered her voice.

"Because you know that none of us are doing well, Colin. We've been cheated. We wouldn't have come here if it wasn't for Mam.

And maybe Da wouldn't have had to borrow money from that man if she'd worked once in a while. Aren't you mad? Just the least bit mad? We gave up everything for that woman in there, who won't even leave her bedroom most of the time." Maureen's voice was hushed but very angry.

"I know. It's not good. Mam's got her problems, but we all have problems. Nobody's perfect."

"Nobody's perfect?" Maureen shook her head in frustration. "You're an *eejit*." She knelt down and began to clean up the mess on the floor.

"Maureen, I'm sorry."

She ignored him and continued to clean.

"You wasted your food," he commented lightly, after a while. She looked up at him and glared.

"Here, let me help you." Colin started to rise from his chair. "*No.*" Maureen reached over and touched his arm to lower him back down.

He accepted her wish and took a few more bites of his food. But he couldn't finish it. "Can I do the dishes this time?" he offered.

"*You* doing the dishes?"

"Why not?"

"Because it's not like you to ask so I don't know why you're asking now."

Maureen rose from the floor and stacked the broken pieces of the dish in the sink and threw away the remains of her dinner. She wet a rag in the sink and used it to clean the floor.

Colin got up and spoke to her. "I'd like to help."

She rose, collected his plate, and put it in the sink. "You don't need to help. Go do something outside. Have some fun. You're young."

"You're young, too."

"I'm older than you," she stated. "And I have to be here when Danny comes home with Patrick."

"Are you sure you don't want me to stay?"

"Go, Colin."

He heard the water running and Maureen scrubbing dishes. Colin put on his coat and quietly left. He said goodbye to her, but she didn't ask him where he was going.

Autumn had settled nicely in the Bowery. The crisp air felt terrific to Colin's lungs as he breathed in. In his life, to have something as definite as breathing often came as a relief to him.

Byrne's was his place and it loomed in front of him like a relic. He could see the outline of Lucille's small, slender body through the thin curtain on the front window. She was smoking a cigarette, had an ashtray in front of her on the bar, and was sipping a drink.

He went inside the warm pub and took a seat next to her. "How are you?"

Lucille had changed into a dark skirt and a red blouse. She turned to look at him. "Did we . . . at my place? I can't remember. We didn't, right?" She sounded worried.

"No, we didn't." Colin watched her pretty eyes.

She exhaled and then drank. Colin ordered a Guinness. "What *did* happen between us?" she asked after a while.

"We kissed and held each other. I helped you into bed before I left. I never touched you after we kissed."

"You're a real gentleman." Lucille stared at him and seemed to be thinking. She sighed. "You're nice to look at. Real sharp too. You're a big guy for your age, but you're too young for me, and, anyway, I'm not looking to get involved with anyone right now." She glanced at the clock above the bar.

"Are you late for something?"

Lucille shook her head. "Just checking the time. Sometimes I forget how long I've been in here. As I was saying, you need a sweetheart, one of those cute redheads. You know, the Irish girls who're always at church on Sundays and every other day of the week; the ones whose parents won't let them date until they're practically married."

"I can't stand the type. I like you better."

"But that's who you're going to end up with, and that's who you need. Honey, I'm too worn for you."

"No, you aren't," he insisted. "You're beautiful." He was eager to please her and smiled at her.

Lucille blushed, and then she frowned and shook her head as though he would never understand, but it didn't bother him. Colin liked the glow in her eyes. Lucille had some hard years behind her, but she was good looking, and her eyes were the most attractive part about her.

Lucille smiled at him. "Come on, handsome. Let's walk to my place."

Colin got up. He couldn't tell why she'd changed her mind. They left the pub and went outside. It wasn't late, but it was a cool evening, and everyone but the nighttime regulars, the drunks, the streetwalkers, and the criminals, had decided to stay inside. Colin and Lucille reached the hotel where she lived.

"Here we are," she said.

Colin asked, with his voice full of uncertainty, "Is it going to be like the last time?"

"What, do you mean are we going to drunk kiss and then you leave?" She smiled at him.

"It doesn't have to be like that. It can be nice this time."

"Oh, honey." Lucille ran her smooth hand across his face and looked up into his eyes. "You sure are handsome," she whispered and pressed her lips to his. Even in high heels she had to reach up to touch his hair. Then she seemed to remember her place, and she pulled away and told him goodnight. "I'll see you tomorrow, honey. We're still friends, right?"

Colin's body turned hot from confusion and hurt, but he didn't want Lucille to see how much she'd wounded him. He mumbled yes, and then said goodbye and strode away.

Colin walked the streets with impatience. He wanted somebody to say something to him that would anger him. He wanted someone to bump into him a little too hard, or to give him a look that was a little too long. He wanted a reason to have a fight. Lucille turning him down made him feel like less of a man, and he hated the feeling.

He contemplated returning to Byrne's or visiting Johnny. Except he knew Johnny wouldn't be home. Johnny would be out on the town with the beautiful Donna. Byrne's seemed like a good second choice, but he figured the pub would only remind him of Lucille. He stopped at a store near his home to get a cola before turning in for the evening.

"Mister, you got the time on you?" he asked an old homeless man sleeping outside.

"Son, if I wore a watch, I wouldn't be out here," the man joked. The old man's laugh was infectious and Colin chuckled along with him. He was grateful for the distraction from Lucille. In his world, it was hard to find joy, so he found it wherever he could. It was cold outside. Life could have been worse for him. His family had come close to becoming homeless after his father died. But they hadn't. Colin and his siblings worked hard to bring money into the household even when their mother couldn't. Colin handed the homeless man some money to get something to eat even though he had little to give.

The old man smiled and reached up to shake Colin's hand. "You're a saint." His eyes shone with gratitude.

"No, I'm not. I'm not even close to that."

6

A handsome Italian man named Carmine Bianchi became his mother's lover. It happened very quickly. One moment Líadan was sitting alone on the steps of the brick tenement, and then she was sitting there with Carmine at her side. She'd met him at the corner shop when buying the Lucky Strikes cigarettes Colin's father used to smoke. Colin frowned when neighbors would openly comment how Carmine and his mother looked so good sitting there together, laughing and smoking, and that they appeared to be in love.

"It's like they were meant to be," Mrs. Donovan commented to Colin as he stood outside the building smoking a cigarette on a sun-filled morning.

He ignored her comment and flicked the cigarette to the ground. Then he headed uptown to deliver a couple of cartons of cigarettes.

Carmine was a little younger than Colin's mother, of above-average height, and was muscular, with a deep, loud voice. He was always clean-shaven and reeked of cologne. His dark hair and eyes gave him the appearance of being good-looking despite his belligerent demeanor. He'd worked as a porter at a respectable hotel for the past seven years. To Colin's mother, Carmine meant a stable future.

"Mam, I don't like him. He's not a good man. I want him out," Colin said to his mother one afternoon when he was taking a break from cigarette runs and Carmine was at work.

"I know you don't like him, but he makes me happy. He brings in money. I've left the house nearly every day since I met him. I feel safer with him around."

"He's not a decent man. I bring in money also. I can protect you. Why does he have to live here with us? If he makes so much money then why can't he live in his own place?"

"He likes being here with me," Colin's mother said pointedly. "We don't want him here. Does he make you feel happy and safe in a way Da never did? I hardly remember you leaving the house when Da was alive."

His mother glared at him and didn't say anything.

"Then I'll make him leave." Colin hit his fist on the table in exasperation.

"Don't do that, Colin, or we'll be living on the streets."

"I make money. Danny sends money. Even Maureen works at the lighting fixture shop when she's not taking care of your home and your youngest for you. We all work except for you. What do you need *his* money for?"

It was as though after their father died Danny didn't want to have anything to do with his family anymore. As though he was happy to forget them. He'd started working fulltime at the drugstore and had moved into his own place. Danny hadn't invited his siblings to move in with him. Colin was sure Danny had what he thought were good reasons. That didn't mean he liked what Danny had done.

Colin's mother had such a thankless look on her face that he wanted to scream at her.

"Maybe I want a better life," she said coolly. "A better life, like the one I moved here to have."

"Moved here so *you* can have? What about us? It wasn't exactly Da's choice to move here, now was it?"

"What's that supposed to mean?" she snapped at him.

"You wanted to come here. Da came here for you. We all came here for you. It didn't matter if coming here made Da miserable and made us miserable. All that mattered was what you wanted. Da's dead. We're miserable. Are you happy now? Right, of course you are. You're in love with Carmine. You're in love with him even though he's cruel to us."

"He isn't that bad."

"Oh, really?"

"Colin—"

He slammed the door on his way out of the apartment.

Summer came. It was one of the hottest summers the city had ever seen. The daily temperature averaged ninety-five degrees. So hot you could smell everyone's sweat around you, the sidewalks stinking with rotting garbage. But the combined stench of the city's summer heat and the refuse made no difference to a permanent resident like Colin. A hot as hell summer was as ordinary as any other season in New York. People shoved past him on the sidewalk and didn't apologize, and neither did he when he did the same to others. It was sweltering and grimy, but he could still get a cup of sweetened coffee or a cold beer from the diner along with the newspaper, and his day would turn out all right. The sounds of people inside the buildings heard through open windows became the music of that summer.

"How was your day in school?" Carmine asked Colin when he came home from selling cigarettes in the dark, humid streets.

There was a bite in Carmine's voice that bothered Colin.

"You know I don't go to school," Colin muttered under his breath. Colin's shoulders tightened. He steeled himself for what might follow, and he readied his comeback. He knew that Carmine was strong, but that he himself was an experienced fighter and around the same size as Carmine. But he didn't think he'd have the courage to pummel Carmine until Carmine put a hand on him; which, so far, he'd never done. If Colin went all out on Carmine before Carmine physically attacked him then Colin feared what his mother would do. She might kick him out of the house and not let him visit Patrick.

Carmine had his long legs stretched out and his feet up on the dining table. Colin stared at Carmine's large boots on the table. Carmine took over the apartment as if it was his place, which Colin figured it kind of was now that his mother had let Carmine move in. Still, it ticked Colin off. Ever since Danny had moved out on his own, Colin had been the man of the household, until Carmine came along and claimed that position. Even if Colin had wanted to move out of the apartment, he was afraid to leave his siblings – and even his mother – alone with Carmine.

"What did you say to me?" Carmine rose.

At first, Colin tried to ignore Carmine and didn't reply. He went over to the cupboard and searched for a snack. "You know what I said," he finally spoke.

Today the radio Carmine had bought Colin's mother was on, and, as usual, Carmine was drinking a bottle of Colin's cola. "Get me another cola," he spat out as he tapped his foot along to the fast jazz beat. "Or are you just as much of an ignorant mick as your old man was?"

Colin walked out of the room, chewing on a piece of bread

with some of the butter Maureen had bought at the grocer's, ignoring him. He'd bought the cola for his family, not for Carmine. He stepped inside the bedroom.

"Get back over here," Carmine shouted.

Everyone in the building had to have heard him. Of course, by then they were probably used to the new tenant and his yelling and fondness for breaking things, including dishes and women's bodies. Like that time last week when Colin was gone for a few days Maureen hadn't tripped on the front steps while entering the building at night as she'd insisted when he returned. Under pressure she'd revealed a nasty confrontation with Carmine that had to do with, as Carmine put it, her 'now able body'. Colin vowed to protect his sister.

Colin closed the bedroom door. He thought about following Carmine's orders and actually going back into the kitchen, and giving him a bullet instead of a cola. Colin knew where he could get a gun.

When dinner came and everyone was seated around the table, Colin's already tense situation with Carmine escalated.

"He's always late," Carmine remarked about Colin, who had been the last person to arrive at the table. "We ought to get him a watch," he said to Colin's mother with a chuckle. "Except he's so dumb, I don't think he could tell the time."

Colin's mother avoided looking at him as Carmine laughed. "I've had enough of this," Colin said.

A few green peas rolled off of his plate onto the table as his thighs hit the edge when he rose. Maureen steadied his wobbling plate gently with her hand. Colin went to the front door.

"Please don't go," Maureen said to him.

"Be quiet," Carmine said. "Let the worthless criminal leave. There'll be more food for us."

As Colin walked out of the apartment, he thought of how much Carmine's laugh sounded like a witch's cackle.

Colin wasn't surprised how warm it was when he stepped outside and went down the few steps leading to the sidewalk. Even the light nighttime rain didn't seem to cool the boiling August temperature. Rainwater dampened his back. He thought about heading to *Byrne's*. But he couldn't go there because of that business with Lucille. He hadn't seen her in weeks, and he hadn't been to Byrne's in that time. He had been leaving the Bowery for a nicer pub over on the West Side. He'd managed to convince them as well that he was old enough to drink. Tonight he ventured there. When Colin was relaxed enough to return home from the pub, he whistled a tune and took his time walking. It had stopped raining, and the sidewalks steamed from the combination of the hot ground and the cool rain. Although the warm weather hadn't bothered him earlier, the bit of drinking he'd done made it irritate him now.

Light-headed, he clumsily jogged up the building's steps and reached the door. Then he realized he'd forgotten his keys when he stormed out earlier.

On a hunch, he pushed the door with his hand and it opened. The landlord, who lived on the first floor, was getting on in years and had difficulty managing the building for the past few months. Hallway lights were often out for weeks, the tiny feet of mice could be heard scampering across the stairs in the early morning and evening hours, and teenagers often loitered on the building steps on weekend nights smoking and drinking beer.

Colin heard a commotion coming from one of the top floors. But this wasn't unusual. The Sullivans, an older, married couple whose children had long since left home, were always arguing. But it was a Monday night, and the Sullivans, Colin had long ago figured out, only squabbled on weekends.

He was looking forward to getting into his bed and, maybe, getting some rest. Colin headed upstairs. As he got closer to the top of the staircase, he realized the noise was coming from his floor, not the one above him. Who could be arguing on his floor? He stepped in front of his family's door and the noise didn't stop.

It was Carmine. But Colin wasn't home, so who was Carmine yelling at this time? For a while Colin didn't make a move. He assessed the situation. He had sobered up walking home, and now his head ached. He tried turning the knob, but the door was locked. He knocked once and then again after no one answered. So he pounded on the door. The noise stopped and the apartment fell silent.

"Who is it?" Carmine shouted from inside.

"It's me."

"Who?"

"Colin."

"What do you want?" Carmine asked.

The sharp ring of Carmine's voice caused Colin to jump a little.

Then he composed himself. "To come inside my home."

"Come back later. Were busy in here. There's no room for you."

Colin's mother screamed from inside the apartment, "Carmine, don't! Please."

She began to cry, and Colin could hear her muttering; a prayer, perhaps. She often prayed when she was nervous or frightened. And Carmine was frightening her, when usually she remained unruffled despite his erratic behavior.

Something wasn't right inside that flat, and Colin sensed it. He removed the switchblade he had bought two days ago with Johnny from his pocket. His shirt was drenched in sweat. He had been in numerous tense situations when selling cigarettes, but he was anxious now because his family's safety might be at stake. He wiped his brow with the back of his hand.

He stopped sweating as he gained courage. Colin nearly smiled at how Carmine must have thought he had given up, and how wrong Carmine was. He charged at the rickety door with all his might, and he broke through it with two thrusts.

Colin gazed around the apartment. He could hear Maureen wailing from what had become their mother's and Carmine's bedroom.

His mother looked over at him from where she sat at the table with his father's old ashtray in front of her and a dying cigarette in her trembling hand, crying softly in between smoking. She put out the cigarette and rose from her chair. She ran toward him, reached out, trying to block him from entering that bedroom.

"Colin, don't go in there!"

She tried to touch his face, but he pulled away. His head throbbed from confusion and anger.

His mother's face was red, and her eyes were swollen from crying. She looked directly into his eyes. She grabbed his arm and he stared back at her. It all seemed to happen in slow motion, like it wasn't real. He thought about Patrick, who slept in the room across from that bedroom. Colin needed Danny for backup. But Danny wasn't there.

His mother gestured that Patrick was asleep, but Colin knew he must have been awake by then. With noise like that, anybody would have woken up, even the dead. He shook off his mother's grasp. Colin didn't need to be told anything. He knew what was going on. The chaos explained it all to him.

He kicked open the bedroom door and charged inside the room. He stopped in his tracks. Carmine. Carmine on top of Maureen. Carmine, large and heavy, moving on top of thin Maureen. Maureen, sobbing and tearing at the sheets, trying to claw Carmine off of her. She pounded at Carmine with her fists, but was held back by his greater strength every time. He slapped her face.

Carmine turned and saw Colin standing there. Colin was still frozen in shock at what he was witnessing. Colin could hear his mother shouting at him from the doorway. Her voice snapped him out of it. He shut the bedroom door and locked her out. Colin held the knife at his side as he stared at the back of Carmine's neck. Carmine looked over at Colin again with a smug grin. Maureen screamed out in pain and embarrassment. There was blood on the bedsheets. Colin recalled what Uncle Rick had done to him and thought how his sister had nothing to be ashamed about. Carmine was the bastard who was doing this to her.

Colin's mother banged on the locked door. He looked around the bedroom and didn't blink. Then in one sure motion, one quick second, he charged at Carmine's neck, stabbing him there multiple times before Carmine realized what was happening.

He pulled the knife out of Carmine's flesh a final time. Blood splattered across the wall and the sheets. Colin must have hit an artery. Carmine slid off the bed in crippling pain and crumpled to the floor. Colin stood over him. Carmine tried to hit up at Colin but his swing was useless and barely grazed Colin's ankle. Then he reached out and grabbed at Colin's shin.

"Help me, you motherfucker . . ."

His grasp around Colin's leg loosened as the life drained out of him. Carmine never said please. The floor and his pale flesh were covered in the blood leaking from his body. Colin was shocked when he didn't gag. He stared at the dead, bloody mess of a man on the floor. He had done this. He had killed a man. But it was over. And he knew Carmine would never hurt Maureen again.

Colin helped Maureen out of the bed and tried to hug her but she wouldn't let him near her. Colin understood. She had been through a lot, and it would take her time to heal.

"What are we going to do?" She stared at Carmine's body in shock.

Colin started to rub her shoulder then stopped when he saw it made her uncomfortable. "I'll think of something. Are you okay?"

Maureen shrugged, and then she slowly allowed him to dry her eyes.

Colin unlocked the door and Patrick ran in past him before Colin could stop him. Patrick stood over Carmine's body. His eyes widened and he started to cry before fleeing the room. Colin called out to him and tried to assure him everything would be okay. Maureen crossed her arms over the front of her nightgown, as if to guard herself from further harm. Their mother screamed and then refused to look.

"He needs to go to hospital," Colin's mother said.

She wanted to ring the police but Colin wouldn't let her near a phone. "He's dead, Mam. And I killed him. There's nothing we can do to help him now. Go comfort Maureen and Patrick. They're the ones who've been hurt by this. How could you just sit there while he was doing that to Maureen?"

There were tears in his mother's eyes but she looked away. "You weren't here to help me. I didn't know what to do."

Her words would always haunt Colin. He felt he'd failed his sister and his family. Colin washed his hands in hot water five times after killing Carmine. Yet for days after they were tinged with the man's blood.

Despite the corpse in the bedroom, he felt surprisingly calm, but he knew he needed a plan. After Maureen had changed, Colin ushered his family out of the apartment.

"I need time to think. Go catch a late movie. Come back in a couple of hours. And, Mam," he said, looking directly at her, "don't tell anyone about this."

When they were gone, and he was alone with Carmine's remains in a heap on the bedroom floor, he pondered what to do. He'd covered Carmine with a sheet. He sat at the table with a bottle of the Sambuca his mother had bought to celebrate her anniversary with Carmine in his hand. He pushed aside his father's ashtray and listened for sounds of interest, but the tenement was silent. He was thankful for the building they lived in and for the city. No one had called the police about the noise during the killing, no one had asked questions or intervened after. Mind your own business was the first city rule. Shut up was the second.

After his second gulp of the anise-infused Sambuca he came up with a solution. He grabbed a key, locked the door, and left the building. Colin wanted to look for a telephone, but it was late and no drugstores were open. He decided to walk the twenty blocks uptown to see Johnny. He walked at a brisk pace even as his stomach churned.

Colin stood outside of the building where Johnny lived on the second floor. No lights were on in Johnny's window.

"Johnny," he half shouted. Then he really shouted, "Johnny!" Johnny's window opened and he stuck his head out. "Colin?

What's..." He rubbed his eyes, and his hair was disheveled as he looked down at Colin standing on the sidewalk.

"I need to talk to you. It's important. Please open the door."

"It's not open?"

Colin tried the knob and then shook his head up at Johnny.

Johnny shut the window and emerged at the building's doorway in his undershirt a few minutes later. He gestured for Colin to follow him inside.

"What's going on?" asked Johnny as he made coffee. Colin sat at a card table in the middle of the kitchen.

"I've known you for a long time, and I need you to help me."

Johnny, hearing the urgency in Colin's voice, ceased making the coffee. He sat down at the table and looked across at Colin.

"What do you need me to do?"

Colin put his hand to his head. "This isn't good."

Johnny seemed to hesitate for a moment and then he nodded at Colin to talk.

Colin removed his hand from his head and looked Johnny straight in the eye. "I killed someone. I need your help getting rid of the body."

At first, Johnny didn't say anything. He just sat there, looking at Colin, as though he was dumbfounded. Colin and Johnny had gotten into some rough fights with other guys throughout the years, and they both had joked about running a 'criminal enterprise' as boys, and, sure, they'd picked pockets and stolen from shops, but they'd never discussed murder.

Johnny's face flushed. "What do you mean?"

"I killed Carmine."

"What... Why?"

Colin shut down. He knew Johnny respected Maureen but he didn't want anyone knowing what Carmine had done to her. Maureen had begged him not to tell a soul. "I don't want to talk about it. But I had a very good reason for doing what I did, and I know you'd agree with me if you knew why I did it."

Johnny nodded and his face relaxed a little. "Okay," he said quietly as though he was thinking. "Do the police know?"

Colin shook his head. "Only my family knows."

"Where did you do it? Where is he?"

"At my home. The body's still there. I need your help."

Colin stared at him and their eyes locked. Colin knew this was a moment that often occurred in the lives of men who lived by the rules of the streets, a grim moment when their friendship would be tested.

Johnny cleared his throat. Colin continued to stare at him. Johnny started to visibly sweat, and he couldn't look Colin in the eye.

"I don't know," Johnny said. "Murder? We could get into real trouble. That could get a guy locked away for life, or worse, sent to the electric chair. I can't end up in prison like my old man. I know it's been hard for you after your father… and you know I'd do anything for you, but… Do you know what my mother would do if she found out?"

"Your mother?" Colin said. "You aren't going to help me, are you?"

"I'm not saying that." Johnny sighed. "I have to think about it."

"I don't have time to think. I have to act now." Colin rose from the table. "Thanks, anyway. Thanks for nothing."

"Colin, wait—"

Colin left before Johnny could finish speaking.

Colin wandered the streets alone for a while and then he went into a pub on First Avenue he knew Danny frequented. Colin was familiar with the bartender from around the neighborhood and asked him if he'd seen his brother.

"Has Danny been around?"

"Yeah," the bartender, a tall and heavyset man, with combed-back hair and piercing green eyes, replied. "But he met up with some girl. They left about an hour ago."

"Do you know where he went?"

The bartender shook his head. "Want me to give him a message the next time I see him?"

Colin shook his head. "It'll be too late." He headed for the door, but before he left, he turned around and said to the bartender, "Actually, can you give him a message for me?"

"Sure. What is it?"

"Tell him I had no choice."

The bartender looked perplexed but he nodded. Colin walked outside.

Colin went home, hoping that maybe somehow through their family Danny had heard word about what had happened and would be there for him. But with the exception of Carmine's body, which was starting to turn rank, no one was home.

Colin decided there was only one possible solution left, and it was a solution he dreaded.

Uncle Rick had sold his pub a few years ago at a loss and had moved to Brooklyn. After Colin's father's death, Rick had hit rock bottom. He was divorced from Georgette and estranged from their daughter. All Uncle Rick did now was drink and struggle with debts. Colin hadn't seen his uncle in years, but he had heard of Rick's whereabouts from people in the Bowery.

First, he headed back to Johnny's place. Once again, he called up to Johnny's dark window from the sidewalk.

This time he didn't bother to whisper. "Johnny!"

It seemed as if Johnny had been expecting him because he turned a light on and immediately opened the window.

"I'll come downstairs."

A moment later, he appeared in the building's doorway. They went inside and headed up to Johnny's apartment again. They were quiet while they went up the steps and only spoke once they were inside the apartment and the door was shut.

"How can I help?" Johnny said.

"I need a car. I need to drive somewhere."

"The body—you need to drive the body somewhere?"

Colin shook his head. "I need to drive somewhere to talk to someone. The less you know, the better. I want to keep you out of this so you don't get into trouble if the shit hits the fan."

"I'll drive you." Johnny gave him a partial embrace.

Colin waited for Johnny to put a jacket on. Then Johnny locked his apartment and they went downstairs and outside the building. "Car's over there." Johnny nodded at a gleaming, red car across the street.

"You got a new car?"

"Yeah. My boss at the garage gave me this baby for almost nothing. I've been fixing her up myself."

"You did a great job. You're doing well for yourself. No wonder you were reluctant to help me."

"I'm sorry about that, but I'm helping you now. Right?"

"You are." Colin smiled at his friend.

Johnny didn't have a license and he drove at a slow speed, as though he didn't want to risk getting pulled over by the police. They spoke only a little during the drive to Brooklyn, and when they arrived in front of Uncle Rick's building, Colin suggested Johnny park and wait for him.

Colin let out a sigh as he opened the car door and stepped outside.

Uncle Rick lived in a fading red building. Colin braced himself before he went up the crumbling steps. He had to convince himself he was doing it for his own good, and for the good of Maureen and Patrick, whom he greatly loved; and even for his mother, though after this evening he wasn't too sure he still felt obligated to protect her. No matter what, he wouldn't drag them down with him. He couldn't land in prison. They needed his money and his help to get by. His mother wouldn't be able to support the family without him.

There was a large, wild dog roaming Rick's block, headed in Colin's direction. Johnny shouted to Colin and then rolled up his window. The dog drooled as it snarled at Colin, who sprinted up the steps and prayed that the front door would be unlocked. He struggled with the doorknob for a moment then it opened.

He raced inside and wandered the first floor where he knew Uncle Rick lived. But he didn't know which apartment belonged to his uncle. He found Rick after knocking on the wrong door twice. From the way Uncle Rick looked at Colin, Colin thought Rick didn't recognize him. Colin had changed since his uncle last saw him, but how could Rick not have known who he was? "Who are you?" Uncle Rick asked.

"It's Colin." When Rick shrugged, Colin said, "Your brother Michael's son."

Uncle Rick stared into his eyes. "Right, you are. You're almost as tall as me now."

"You'll never be able to hurt me again," Colin whispered.

"What was that you said?" Rick put his hand to his ear.

"I didn't say anything."

"Oh." Uncle Rick's brow furrowed. "I'll admit I knew who you were when I opened the door. I just didn't think you'd ever come here."

"I'm here."

"What do you want?" Rick's expression softened.

Colin had wanted to shed a few tears when he saw his uncle in front of him. Where had the time gone? He'd last seen Uncle Rick at his father's funeral. Had it really been that long since he lost his father? He hardly recognized his uncle now. Uncle Rick's skin had weathered. But his eyes were the same, those deceptive blue eyes that had looked down at him all those years ago on that horrible night when Danny had been shot and Colin had lost his childhood.

Colin cleared his throat to keep his emotions in check. "We need to talk. There's a problem."

Uncle Rick hesitated. Then he stuck his head out the door, as if to make sure no one was following Colin.

"All right. Come in."

He shut and locked the door behind Colin. Colin became on guard when Rick locked the door. Then he remembered he wasn't small anymore. There was an overpowering and unpleasant scent inside the apartment. Ripe sweat and cigarette smoke.

Rick took out a bottle of whiskey and a smudged glass from under a wooden chair. He didn't have much furniture in the room, just an end-table and that chair, which was missing a leg. Uncle Rick poured a shot and gulped it down. His hands shook as he made himself a second drink. Colin watched Rick's neck muscles tense before he swallowed.

"Want one?" Rick gestured with his glass. Colin shook his head.

Rick took two gulps then left the empty glass on the floor, and stepped into the kitchen. His body didn't sway as he walked. The kitchen was a separate room from the rest of the apartment but didn't have a door as an entranceway, rather just a frame to mark its place. "Come in here and sit," Uncle Rick called out to Colin, who was still staying close to the entrance door.

Colin could see Rick's back. He appeared to be making coffee. Colin hesitated but went in when his uncle called for him again. Colin was surprised to find that Uncle Rick had set out two cups of steaming coffee on the small kitchen table along with a pitcher of cream and a bowl of sugar.

"You act like you're afraid of me," Rick commented as he sat down at the table. "Don't you remember your father brought you to my pub almost every day?"

Colin nodded. He also remembered something else his uncle had done to him. Had Rick forgotten?

"Do you like cream and sugar?" Uncle Rick asked.

"Sure."

"I like my coffee black." Rick tried to smile but it looked wrong. Colin wanted to get down to business and then get out of there.

But he didn't know how or where to start. So he let his uncle do the talking.

"Your father was a great man," Rick said. Colin murmured in agreement.

"I can't get over how big you are. What are you, eighteen?"

"Sixteen," Colin corrected him.

"How did you get here?"

"A friend drove me."

"They're waiting outside?"

Colin nodded.

"You could've invited them in."

"I don't think so."

"If your father had lived longer, he would've been real grand in his old age. Do you know that?"

Colin didn't reply and just stared at his uncle.

"How's your mother?" Rick asked. "And your sister and brothers?"

"My mother's all right. They're..." Colin didn't finish answering the question.

"I'd like to get rid of David Burke and his whole blasted lot. Of course, it'll not happen."

"You're right. They'd probably kill you first."

Uncle Rick frowned at Colin and then chuckled in that awkward way one does when they've been insulted but don't know what to do about it.

Then for a while, they both said nothing. Colin looked down at his cup but didn't put in cream or sugar, or drink from it.

"I did something," Colin uttered as he glanced at Rick.

"What did you do?" Uncle Rick sounded concerned. "You can tell me, son." He reached out and patted Colin's shoulder.

"Don't touch me." Colin's body tensed and he shook off Rick's hand.

Rick sat there looking uncomfortable.

Colin began to talk. "My mother, she got herself involved

82

with this fellow, and he was a bastard. He messed with Maureen in the worst way and I caught him. I killed him."

Rick just sat there watching him. Then he rose from the table. "Get out of here." He had a revolted look in his eyes.

"Uncle Rick, please," Colin begged. "I need your help."

"I said get out of here!" Rick removed Colin from the chair by his sleeve and dragged him into the living room. "Leave. I don't need this shite." He shoved Colin toward the door.

Colin didn't comprehend what was happening, and he didn't fight back until Uncle Rick opened the door and pushed him out into the hallway. Rick was large himself, but Colin fought as his uncle slammed and locked the door behind him.

"You bastard. You damn bastard. After what you did to me, you owe me."

Then Colin fell silent. The hallway was still until someone, not Uncle Rick, shouted at Colin to be quiet. He left the building and didn't see the dog. Johnny waved to him and he got into the car.

"Everything okay?" Johnny asked.

Colin shook his head. He knew he would never go to the police and turn himself in for killing Carmine. They'd have to come for him first.

7

"Colin. How are you doing? How are you holding up?" Lucille said.

Colin looked over at her from where he rested on his back on his bed behind the jail bars. He smiled. It was good to hear her voice. "What do you think?" he said with sarcasm.

"That it's awful," she replied with a grin.

"You got that right." Colin put his head down on the bed again.

He stared at the decaying ceiling.

"Are you tired?" she asked

He shrugged.

"Want me to leave?" she said.

He thought about it for a moment. The prospect of being alone scared him even more than the possibility of her staying by his side bothered his dignity. He disliked sympathy from anyone, even from a woman he had feelings for.

"Stay." He glanced over at her beautiful lips. "I could use a distraction."

"Everyone's been asking about you."

"What did they say?" He was suddenly interested and sat up

and looked at her.

"They want to know how you're doing. My brother says he's going to give you free drinks for life when they dismiss this thing.

But they printed your real age in the newspapers so you're going to have to wait until you're older." She smiled. "It's not right you're in here. You were defending Maureen."

"It's nice they're asking about me. All the law seems to care about is Carmine's rights. It's like because Maureen's a poor woman, she doesn't count."

"The law doesn't care about women like me and her. They think we're nothing but garbage. It's good you saved your sister. You're her hero, Colin. I know she won't admit it out loud but that's what she's thinking. You're my hero as well."

Colin's face warmed from the compliment. "I'm no hero. And I don't need anything free from your brother. I always get whatever I want free when I drink at his pub with you." He smiled.

"You do." Lucille spoke as though she was reminiscing. Tears shone in her eyes.

Colin reached out for her but couldn't dry her eyes through the cell bars. "Please don't cry. I hate seeing you sad."

Lucille wiped her eyes with her hand and smiled at him, but her eyes had a heartbreaking look.

"I don't think I'm getting out of here," Colin said.

Lucille moved closer to his cell and touched the bars. "You can't think like that."

"I did it. And I get to go to jail for it. I knew what the consequences would be. I've accepted that. It's over."

"But you can't tell them that. You can't tell a judge that. You're so stubborn. Say you were overcome with anger at what he was doing to Maureen. That's what Johnny told me to tell you to say. Weren't you drunk?"

"I wasn't drunk. I knew what I was doing. Since when are you friends with Johnny?"

"Since you landed in here. Don't worry. It's not like *that*."

"Johnny's a good guy. You could do worse."

"He's too young. Like you." Lucille passed him rosary beads through the bars. "I was able to sneak these in."

Colin smiled and clutched the warm beads in his hand. "Do you need me to bring you anything else?" she asked.

"Like what?"

"I don't know. A magazine? A drink?" She laughed.

"A magazine would be nice. No newspapers, please." He couldn't stand how the tabloids referred to him as 'Killer Colin'. "Can't drink in here, not when they're watching me all the time. They think I'm a suicide risk because of my father. Can you believe it? What do they think I am?"

"My God." Lucille looked concerned. "You're not, are you?"

"Of course not. I'm not checking out of this world anytime soon. At least not by my own hand." He wanted to touch her face through the bars to reassure her but a prison officer was standing nearby.

"I'll bring you a magazine. Your mother's anxious."

"When isn't she?" Then Colin's tone became somber. "You've been to see her?"

Lucille shook her head. "Maureen said she was."

"How's Maureen?"

Colin thought about what had happened to his sister every time he lay staring at the ugly gray ceiling because he couldn't sleep. It made him angry to think about what had happened to her, and he tried to make himself forget, but it was hard to prevent his mind from wandering. At nighttime, when it was dark and quiet in the cold cellblock, the brutal memory of what she'd endured always returned to him.

"Maureen's doing all right considering. I heard she broke up with her boyfriend," Lucille said.

"Because of what happened?"

"I'm not sure. I don't think she likes me very much."

Colin smiled. "She never has. She thinks you're a bad influence on me." A couple of months had passed as Colin awaited his trial. He'd been denied bail, and even if the judge had granted it, there wasn't any money to pay for it. He missed the outside world. He'd been doing pushups in his cell in the afternoons to keep up his strength.

Lucille stepped so close to his cell her nose almost touched the bars. Colin's body shook with emotion. She tried to touch him but the prison officer intervened and stopped her.

Lucille shook the prison officer off her. "All right, I won't."

"Do you want to sit down?" Colin asked her when the prison officer had backed off. "Maybe they can give you a chair."

Lucille shrugged.

"Ask them," Colin said. "You should be able to sit down and rest."

"Who should I ask?"

Colin glanced at the prison officer, who was now speaking to a man behind bars a few cells down from them.

"Really?" Lucille said.

"Go on. You never were shy." He winked at her.

Colin watched Lucille as she walked over to the prison officer. She spoke with the slight man and he reluctantly brought a chair over to Colin's cell for her to use.

"You can sit down now," the prison officer said to Lucille.

Colin looked at Lucille. "You don't have to sit at his command. You sit when you want to, sweetheart."

The prison officer told Colin to shut up. Often the prison officers sounded like they came from the same street as him, and he felt this particular officer had it in for him because of his size.

"Please sit down, ma'am," the prison officer said to Lucille. "I have to keep an eye on you at all times, now that you have the chair."

Lucille glanced at Colin and then at the prison officer as though she hated choosing sides. "It's fine, Colin." She sat down.

The prison officer stepped farther back but still kept a close watch on them.

"You didn't have to listen to him," Colin said.

"Hush. My behind ass tired."

They both laughed.

"So, what have you been up to?" Colin asked.

"I got a real job."

"Congratulations. Where are you working?"

"At a button shop in the Garment District," Lucille said.

Colin started to laugh then realized she was serious. "You're not working for your brother anymore?"

"I'm still working at the pub sometimes. The button place is something to keep me... Now that we don't have our afternoons anymore, I needed something to keep me busy."

"To distract you?"

Lucille nodded. "It's getting harder though. Each day, I feel more and more like doing nothing."

Maybe she did have feelings for him after all. "I know what you mean." And Colin really did know. But he wanted to discuss more pleasant things. "Perhaps you can finally move out of the hotel." He smiled.

"I hope so."

"How's the Bowery?"

"Everyone asks about you, like I said. Maureen told the police what Carmine did to her, but she doesn't want the whole neighborhood knowing he hurt her. Turns out a lot of people didn't like Carmine regardless. They all want to know when you're getting out of here and coming home."

"I'm afraid you're going to have to break their hearts and tell them I'm never returning, at least not alive." Colin managed to smile.

"Don't talk like that." She paused. "I've been meaning to tell you something. It's about that night when you walked me home."

"We don't have to talk about that now. I understand, Lucille. I'm too young for you. We're friends, and I'm fine with that."

"Colin, let me finish."

He nodded at her to go ahead.

"When you walked with me to my place, and then when you asked if you could come inside and I wouldn't let you . . . I've been thinking a lot about that night. I like you, and if things were different, if you were older, I would've invited you to come in."

The prison officer informed them Colin's lawyer had arrived for a visit, and Colin didn't get a chance to tell Lucille how deeply he felt about her. Her voice held something back as she rose and said goodbye to him. Colin waved to her and hid his affection behind a serious expression.

Because Colin couldn't afford his own lawyer, the city of New York provided one for him. During their only prior meeting Emmett Hull told Colin he'd never handled a murder case before. "I'm going to be honest," Hull said to him today through the cell bars. "I don't have much background on your case. I was just recently assigned to you, and the trial is in a few days. And you won't tell me anything."

If he was looking for sympathy, he wasn't going to get it from Colin. "You're the lawyer. You figure it out. I've got enough to think about, like how the hell I'm going to get myself out of here after you don't."

"How am I supposed to help you when you won't help me?" Hull pleaded.

Colin didn't want to tell his lawyer all the details about that night with Carmine and risk upsetting Maureen in court. Her face bore marks from Carmine's fists, and the police thought Carmine had only beaten her and didn't know the whole story. All that mattered was that his sister was safe. If Colin had to go to jail forever then at least he knew Carmine could never harm Maureen again.

"I need more from you." Hull's voice rose with irritation.

"What do you need to know?"

"Well, why did it happen in the first place?"

"He angered me." Colin could sense Hull's lack of confidence being masked by his pedigree.

"Being a smart punk isn't going to help you in court. If you want to spend the least amount of time possible in prison then you better stop acting like one."

Colin smiled at him with sincerity. "I'm glad to see you're toughening up. We might actually get along."

"I know it's been difficult for you in here."

Colin found it amusing that Hull was trying to 'get through to him'. But Colin wanted to avoid prison as much as anyone confronted with the threat would, no matter how stubborn he was. "What do you need to know?"

"First of all, how long was your mother's boyfriend—"

"Carmine."

"Yes. Mr. Bianchi. How long was he living with you and your family?"

"About a year."

"He was abusive to your mother?"

"Not really."

"Does that mean a little?"

"It means not really. Sometimes. I don't know." Colin didn't want it to appear as though he couldn't defend his family.

"Did he hit you?"

"Not really. I just didn't like him. I didn't like him so I killed him. All right?"

"There was no reason?" Hull appeared puzzled.

Colin was too proud to admit to the fact that Carmine had mistreated him and his sister. He figured he'd already taken care of it by killing Carmine. What kind of man would the entire city think he was if it became known in the newspapers that he'd allowed Carmine to hurt him and his family for so many months before finally acting? It would make him look weak.

"There was no real reason," he told Hull.

His lawyer grimaced. "In that case, you're definitely not getting off easily. You're young, but you look older, and this isn't your first crime. I'm not sure you understand how serious this is. I'd like to put you up on the stand because I think you have a sympathetic face despite your imposing stature. But if you go into court and say you killed a man for no reason other than you felt like doing it then everyone in the room is going to despise you." Hull sighed. "If I'm even going to try to get you a lesser charge of manslaughter, there has to have been a justifiable reason for what you did. You know what manslaughter is, right? It's usually five to seven years—"

"I know what it is," Colin interrupted.

"Your crime has to have been unintentional. Not premeditated." He spoke as if Colin didn't understand him, which he did. "You have to have killed him by accident, not have planned it."

"I did it. He beat my sister, and he was . . ." Colin was about to tell his lawyer what Carmine had really done to Maureen but he stopped himself before he could.

"He was *what*? What were you going to say?" Hull's eyes lit up.

"He was a bastard."

Hull looked at Colin and shook his head. "You're up for murder. Did you know that?"

"I assumed it. I bet they can't wait to fry a poor bastard like me."

"I'm optimistic that you'll manage to avoid the electric chair because of your age."

"Maybe I'd rather be dead than rot in prison."

"I doubt that. And you're only hurting yourself by not telling me anything."

"Where do you live, Mr. Hull?"

"Me?"

"Yeah, you."

"Park Avenue."

"Of course you do." Colin chortled.

"What's that supposed to mean?"

"That you rich fellows run the show. Come on, you know as well as I do that the judge is going to hit me as hard as he can regardless of what I give as my reasons for killing. I'm an immigrant living in the Bowery. They love to make an example out of guys like me."

"I guess I can see your reasoning."

"Sure it's reasonable," Colin said.

"If you're really not going to help me, and yourself, I can try to make sure you serve no more than twenty years. I think you should reconsider though—"

"Swell. Where would I be serving? Ossining?" Colin tried to seem upbeat, but when Hull had said 'twenty years' he'd wanted to scream at the top of his lungs. That was more years than he was old.

"Yes, most likely it would be there."

"Upstate is damn pretty. I spent time in juvenile hall there."

"Right. I read that in your file. Don't curse. It doesn't look good in court."

~

In November, Colin appeared in front of a judge at court in Manhattan. Hull had informed him the minimum he could get was ten years. The judge presiding was Charles L. Stone. Colin thought the man's expression looked a lot like his last name.

The prosecution team, who wanted Colin charged as an adult, seemed a little too smug to him.

Carmine's decaying body had been found by a homeless man in an alleyway just outside of the Bowery. Colin had confessed at the police station when he was brought in by detectives – friends of Carmine's gave his name to them. He was surprised Uncle Rick hadn't snitched on him. Johnny had used his car to help Colin dispose of Carmine's body. Colin had insisted he keep Johnny out of it, and the police never knew of Johnny's involvement. He'd spent hours cleaning up Carmine's blood.

Colin confessed on the spot and said the crime was intentional. He admitted he'd had a problem with Carmine from the beginning of Carmine's relationship with his mother, because he was angry Carmine had become his mother's lover after his father's death.

He knew the more the detectives dug into the case the more details they'd find out, like the fact that Carmine had tormented him and abused Maureen. And Colin knew people would treat Maureen differently if the revelation went public and that they might even say horrible, untrue things, like she'd wanted Carmine to hurt her. He had to protect his sister, so he 'confessed' to the detectives immediately. He said he wanted Carmine dead, and he knew he wanted him dead. He signed a statement saying so.

Colin sat and listened to Hull's closing remarks. He hadn't been asked to testify. He watched the trial as though it was a play that had nothing to do with him.

Colin nodded at his family in the courtroom. He assumed a neighbor was watching Patrick at home. Maureen and Danny smiled at him. Their mother looked stoic as she sat there. Colin was surprised to see her. Lucille waved to him from the back row. The judge had ordered Carmine's family to leave the courtroom for yelling at Colin and cursing him.

"Your Honor, I ask you to be lenient," Hull said. "My sixteen-year-old client has led a difficult life. He is an immigrant and comes from an impoverished background. His father committed suicide when he was just a young boy."

Colin cringed inwardly when Hull said 'suicide'.

"He does not have the same advantages as our own children. Therefore, I ask you to consider that it was the circumstances of the life he's had to live, the life he was brought into, that caused him to commit this unfortunate act. He is young, and if he's sentenced reasonably, I am positive that after his release he will have the ability and the mindset to live a decent, productive life. Yes, he needs time to rehabilitate, but not his entire life."

Hull had asked Colin to make a statement, but Colin had declined because he wasn't sorry for what he'd done. Hull didn't call any witnesses on Colin's behalf, and even Colin knew that wasn't good.

Maureen had visited Colin in jail and she said she wanted him to tell the truth to save his life. But, in the end, nobody seemed interested in hearing what Carmine had really done to Maureen. That's what life was like for poor women. No one seemed to care that Colin had killed Carmine to protect his sister from repeated abuse.

Next came the prosecutor's concluding remarks.

"Your Honor, Colin O'Brien killed forty-year-old Carmine

Bianchi in cold blood. We've heard from a bartender who said Colin O'Brien told him he 'had no choice'. But did he really? We welcomed this immigrant into our great country, and this is how he returns our hospitality?" He spoke with outrage.

The prosecutor pointed Colin out to the courtroom as though he was a beast to behold.

"Mr. Bianchi led a productive life. He'd been working as a porter for one of our city's most respected hotels for many years. That is, until Colin O'Brien decided to brutally murder him."

Colin could feel all eyes in the courtroom on him.

"Although Mr. O'Brien is young, he has already been in and out of incarceration," the prosecutor said. "Clearly the time he has served in these institutions hasn't rehabilitated him. In fact, his delinquency is escalating, as his record shows he has gone from petty thievery and affray to now killing a man."

He'd stolen and fought to provide for his family, and he'd killed to save his sister. But he doubted even those reasons would be good enough for the morally upright.

"To release this criminal back into our city's streets too soon would be to do this good city a disservice, and it would be a great danger. This time it is the murder of one man, and then he is released in ten years; who is to say he won't go on to kill again, and again? The defendant has never apologized for killing Mr. Bianchi. He doesn't seem to feel any remorse for his actions."

He paused and stared at Colin for emphasis.

"This is a dangerous, unrepentant individual. We must be vigilant about releasing him into the same streets the many innocent citizens of this city walk," he continued. "He needs to pay for a long time for what he has done. We can't willingly expose our children and our families to the danger Mr. O'Brien presents. He is a menace to all that is decent."

Colin was convicted of murder and sentenced to fifteen years.

8

On Colin's departure from prison he was given fifty dollars from the state, which he had earned from making brooms while he was serving his prison sentence. No one was waiting for him when he left.

The war had ended while he was imprisoned, and the world around him had changed, but he hadn't changed very much. He returned to the city and lived on cheap, warm beer and New York City hotdogs for a few days. Then he moved into a flophouse in Chinatown for a week, and lived on delicious food.

One afternoon he returned to the Bowery and sought out his childhood home. But his family wasn't there. There would be no welcome home party for him. They hadn't even left his father's old ashtray behind for him. Instead an old, hunched-over Slavic woman resided in their apartment. He guessed the place wasn't reserved solely for the Irish anymore.

The building's landlord informed him he was in luck because the man who lived in the apartment above, Johnny's old place, was relocating downstairs to his son's apartment. And Colin could move into Johnny's old place if he wanted to. It was also from this landlord Colin had heard about Lucille Byrne getting married years ago and moving to Long Island. Lucille was the only person who knew his secret about Uncle Rick.

He had lost touch with the Bowery while in prison. His family hadn't visited him. Once, early in his sentence, Maureen had visited to thank him for saving her. Patrick had been too young to come, but Colin guessed the rest of his family were either ashamed of him or too busy. Lucille had never come. He wasn't angry with her. She had mentioned to him more than once how jails gave her the creeps since her father had died of tuberculosis in one.

Johnny's old apartment was available at fifteen dollars a month. Colin had spent ten of the fifty dollars at the flophouse and five on food. He put fifteen dollars down on the apartment, which now had a private bathroom, and had some left over for whatever else he would need until he found employment.

His first night in the apartment he missed noise. The prison had been noisy with conversation, screaming, and cursing. Before that, home had been noisy with all the children when he was young and then later on with Carmine.

It was strange how when you got on in your years, the things you once hated didn't seem so hateful anymore. Spite for them had lessened. As had Colin's hatred for Carmine. For the first term of his incarceration Colin thought constantly about his act of vengeance; but as the years passed his rage towards Carmine diminished. He had paid the price for his actions.

Colin was alone with the silence in the apartment. He had heard from the landlord that Colin's mother and Maureen and Patrick had gone to live with relatives in Wales. Colin remembered the current landlord's father. He had been the landlord for all the years when Colin had lived there with his family before prison. He was the one who had insisted the burning candles be removed from the entranceway the evening Colin's father's body had been discovered. Colin had once wanted to hurt the old landlord for that. Now he thought how young and foolish his feelings seemed.

Danny hadn't gone to Wales. He wasn't around the East Side, Colin was informed, or even still in the state of New York. He had been up until two years ago, but then he moved to Boston with his wife and children. Wife! Colin couldn't believe it. Grumpy Danny had actually gotten married. It caused Colin to think about all the years he had lost while in prison.

He didn't know how he felt about Danny these days. He had contemplated their relationship in prison. Danny wasn't there to help him deal with Carmine's body. But Colin wasn't ready for forgiveness just yet. Danny must have heard about Colin being released. If there was going to be an apology or reunion, Danny would have to be the one to initiate it.

His parole officer had instructed him to find lawful work. But the only work he could find paid poorly. He didn't want to be cleaning toilets. Many of his old friends and acquaintances were either dead or gone. Even the Dubliner had returned to Ireland. Most of the new people who had moved into the Bowery weren't keen on hiring convicted murderers. Not even the broom factory would take him. And he was too old to begin training as a boxer, although he had the genetics for it.

Then one night at the pub he heard of a job offer for any local who wanted it. There was no catch and no questions asked, just as long as you lived in the Bowery and were Irish. The job was for a sweeper at the small *Quinn's* drugstore in the heart of the Bowery, and Colin sought it out right away. He was hired by the owner and pharmacist, the aging Seamus Quinn, who had once employed Danny. Colin swept the floors, dusted the counters, and stocked the shelves. He worked mornings and nights.

It was there he met Tom McPhalen.

Tom was from Galway. He had come to the Bowery late in

life with his adult family, when he was sixty-one years old. His accent was still thick. Because his voice always sounded phlegmy, some poor bastard had once joked to him that 'he must've put too much cream in his tea'. But it wasn't wise to joke about Tom, and that was the last joke that man ever made.

In Ireland Tom had been released from prison for serving a ten-year sentence for bank robbery. Two days after he was released he'd joined a friend's gang. Then two years later he stabbed a rival gangster to death and served twenty more years in prison. He couldn't find work in Ireland after that because his crimes were so well-known – he was branded a 'murderer' and a 'gangster', and no one wanted to hire him. So he brought his family to the United States where he had ties to the Bowery.

Now Tom was a man stubbornly hanging on to life. He was now in his early seventies. He was around five-feet-ten inches tall. His face glowed from the years of a life well-lived, and the generous gut hanging over his belt signified a life well-fed. He took a shine to Colin because both were Irish, and because their stories were similar. Like Colin, Tom's father had died when Tom was young. And he had first killed young. After twelve years in prison, out three years early because of good behavior, Colin still knew the city better than Tom did.

When Colin told Tom the story of his father's accordion, Tom offered to ask around the Bowery to see if he could find out who had bought the instrument from the pawn shop. A few days later, Tom handed Colin his father's accordion still in its beautiful case.

Colin struggled not to cry. "How?" he'd asked Tom. Tom only smiled.

Colin felt indebted to Tom after that. Tom, who was good friends with Mr. Quinn, went to the drugstore almost every day. During this time, Colin came to know Tom very well. Tom made appearances in the early mornings and late evenings. Colin often wondered what he did with the rest of the day. Tom didn't seem to 'work', yet he talked about having plenty of money. Colin had a lot of time to wonder about Tom because all Colin did was work at the drugstore and then go to the pub after he finished his shift. Sometimes he'd visit cheap dance halls and meet girls.

Tom sat in the back of the shop with Mr. Quinn and 'the men's club', which consisted of men from the Bowery who were friends of both Tom and Quinn. They played dice for money. And bonded over alcohol, smoking pipes and fat cigars, while discussing wealth, sports and politics, and children, wives and girlfriends. They had set up their own bar in the basement, which was illegal because Quinn didn't have a liquor license. It didn't hurt, however, that one of the men who frequented the club was a prominent city detective. That was when Colin realized how connected the law and top criminals could be. Tom seemed to mostly respect policemen.

Once in a while, a few younger Irish men around Colin's age, would stop in and join the club for a couple of hours. These men, who almost always wore classy suits like Tom, only came once or twice a week, to drink and share tips about horse races and boxing matches. Sometimes they'd invite Colin to sit with them. They liked to sing after they had drunk a lot. Other times they got into trivial arguments and Tom tossed them out.

One evening after work Colin had a drink at Byrne's, which was still owned by Lucille's brother and didn't appear to be closing anytime soon. According to Lucille's brother, Tom was the top man in the Bowery. If you had a problem, you went to Tom. If you had suffered an injustice, Tom was the one to see. If you wanted to borrow money, you saw Tom.

"Tom's the guy," Joe Byrne said. "If you know what I mean. He makes the decisions around the Bowery."

"You mean like gangsters?" Colin laughed. He couldn't tell if

Joe was pulling his chain.

"Yes. And *he's* their boss. I wouldn't laugh at him if I were you."

"I'm not afraid of him."

"I mean it. He's the real deal. People around here call them the Salthill gang because of where they're from in Ireland."

"All right, Joe. Whatever you say."

Colin paid for his drink and left. At that point in his life he had little interest in gangsters or their lifestyle. He told himself he didn't like them because they had destroyed his father.

But Tom seemed different. He seemed like a gentleman. Colin grew to admire and even to like Tom. Mr. McPhalen, as Colin had called him until 'Mr. McPhalen' insisted Colin call him 'Tom' because all his friends did. Did that mean Tom considered him a friend?

Tom and the other Irishmen who hung around him weren't like the gangsters who had hassled Colin's father. They had class and were respectable and welcoming. Colin felt honored to have Tom consider him a friend. Colin liked the smell of the cigars Tom and Mr. Quinn smoked. He liked the way Tom talked, with a lilt that reminded him of his da. Tom intrigued Colin. Tom always wore good clothes and had money to spend. He wasn't struggling like Colin. Colin thought that must be a pleasant way to live. He reasoned that at twenty eight, he could be doing more than sweeping the floors of a Bowery drugstore.

On Tuesday morning Colin went to work at *Quinn's* as usual. But this time he went in reluctantly. He was nervous around Tom. Now that he knew Tom was an important person he wanted to make a good impression.

Tom sneaked up behind Colin. "Why are you being so quiet today?" he asked in a friendly tone.

Colin jumped with his broom in his hand. Tom stood very close to him. "No reason. I'm a little tired. That's all."

Tom stepped around to face him. Colin ceased sweeping. "Okay," Tom said. "If that's what it is. But is it really?"

Colin looked at Tom's glassy blue eyes. "That's all it is."

Tom nodded. He turned his back to Colin and was about to walk away, but then he stopped and faced Colin again.

"Maybe you're getting tired with your work here. Maybe it's not bringing in what you would like."

"No, that isn't it." He didn't want to insult Tom's friend Quinn.

"Are you sure?"

Colin leaned against the broom he grasped. He relaxed himself enough to shrug. "Maybe I am a little tired of it sometimes. But I don't want to offend Mr. Quinn."

Tom smiled. "I like your loyalty. I'll tell you what. You're a good worker. You've been working here for a while, and you've been good to Quinn, and to me as well. You always bring me the newspaper and my tea exactly when I want them without me having to remind you. You're a sharp, strapping young lad."

Colin smiled and waited for Tom to say what he had in mind. "I'm going to give you a chance."

Colin stared at Tom with his eyes wide. "A chance, sir?"

"Sir?" Tom grinned. "A chance to work for me. How about you come help me tomorrow evening? Come to Ronan's apartment. You know Ronan, right? He's been in here a few times for a drink." He gave Colin the address.

"Thanks, Mr. McPhalen—I mean, Tom. I'll be there. But what about Mr. Quinn? Won't he be angry if I quit?"

"Don't worry about Seamus. He won't harbor no dislike of you. I guarantee it."

Colin gulped because he sensed Tom was very serious.

Tom had just given him a chance, probably his only chance, to step up in the world. That night Colin strode home with an uplifting sense of pride, and he held his shoulders straight. He couldn't wait to call Lucille and tell her the news. He had no one else to share it with. Colin found a phone booth near his home. He wondered how much she'd changed and hoped she'd want to speak with him. He looked at the cocktail napkin her brother had given him. Colin gave the operator the number. It rang three or four times, and then a child answered.

"Hello?" It was a little girl. "Hello?"

"Is your mother home?" he said with patience.

"She's here. Who are you?"

"Tell her it's Colin."

He could hear the child shouting to someone. "Mom! Colin's on the phone."

"What?" Lucille spoke to the girl on the other end of the line. Lucille sounded the same to Colin. She came on the line. "Colin? Is this really you?"

"It's me, Lucille."

She breathed out. "Jesus Christ. How did you get my number?"

"Your brother gave it to me."

"You've been to the pub?"

"Yeah. I just got out of prison."

"I'm sorry I never visited you in there. You know how I feel about those places."

"I understand. It was good of you to visit me before my trial."

"Joe shouldn't have given you my number."

"Don't blame him. He knows I care about you. You're married now?"

"I am."

"I have to admit I was pretty disappointed when I heard that. How long have you been married for?"

"Seven years."

"And you have a child?"

"Yes. She's seven."

"Who'd you marry? Your brother wouldn't tell me."

"I married a detective."

"No wonder your brother didn't want to tell me. How did you meet this guy?"

"I met him when I was arrested. I'm sober now. I've been sober for years. I'm sure you don't want to hear the whole story—"

"I do. Please. You always told good stories."

After a moment of silence Lucille spoke. "Back when he was just a cop, he detained me for loitering a few weeks after you got sent away. I was in a bad way after you got sentenced and I lost my job at the button shop. I felt so terrible you were locked away. He took me to the station, but then he took pity on me when I sobered up and he let me go. I ran into him a few days later. He asked me to have dinner with him."

Colin noticed how she never gave him her husband's name, and he wondered if she was afraid to.

"I'm sorry you were in a bad way. I had no idea. The way you met your husband sort of sounds like a fairytale."

"I guess it sort of was a Bowery fairytale." Lucille laughed a little.

"You're living on Long Island now?"

"Yes."

"Can I come... visit you?" he asked quietly.

"Don't you have a family, Colin?"

"When I got out they were all gone."

Lucille sighed. "I think I heard about that. I'm sorry, but I don't think it would be a good idea for you to come here. My husband doesn't know I had a friend like you."

"Had?"

Lucille didn't elaborate.

"I found a good job." Colin hoped she'd be proud enough to let him visit her.

"Where?"

"I'm going to be working for this posh fellow named Tom McPhalen soon. I'm going to be making a lot of money, Lucille."

"Everyone knows he's a criminal," she said coolly.

"So am I. You know him?"

She cleared her throat. "No, but my brother told me all about him. You just got out of prison, Colin. Do you really think it's a good idea for you to be associating with criminals?"

"I need to make a living. Besides, I was a criminal even before I did that long stretch in prison."

"Get a regular job," she snapped back. "You're a big guy. I'm sure you can find work on the waterfront."

"I did have that kind of job for a while. I worked at a drugstore. It didn't pay enough. Nowhere that pays well enough to live will hire murderers. I thought you'd be proud. Working for Tom's still a job, just a different kind, and the money will be better."

She snorted and didn't say anything in response. After a minute she spoke again. "I need to go. I have food on the stove, and my daughter's going to wonder who I'm talking to."

"You sound different," Colin observed.

"A lot about me has changed."

"Lucille? I never got to thank you for the favor you did for me when I got myself into that tangle. Johnny and I wouldn't have been able to carry that bastard down the stairwell of my building and into the car if it wasn't for your help as our lookout."

"Oh, God. That was so long ago. Please don't talk about that. If my husband finds out, he'll take my daughter from me."

"That'd be terrible of him. He wouldn't dare. Anyway, you have nothing to worry about, sweetheart. I won't tell a soul. I didn't mean to upset you. Can I call you tomorrow? I like hearing your voice."

"God, Colin. You sound the same. You sound so young."

"I grew up fast in prison."

"I don't doubt that you did. And the answer is no. You can't call me tomorrow."

"The next day then?"

"No."

"The day after that maybe?" She hung up.

Ronan McDuff lived just outside of the Bowery. His home was a well-maintained apartment building with shiny brass doorknobs, clean window glass, and a regal entrance. Ronan was in his late thirties and had been released a year ago on probation after serving three years for perjury and bookmaking. He was a pleasant, red-haired man with a short, solid build.

Tom had bought Colin a suit to wear so he'd fit in with the other men. It was the finest building Colin had ever stepped into; it had an elevator, and the McDuffs had two entire floors to themselves. A woman answered the door. She used an elegant cane and in a subtle New York accent introduced herself to Colin as Ronan's wife.

Mrs. McDuff was a good-looking woman with green eyes and short brown hair. She was wearing a long black dress which was cinched at the waist. She had a lot of makeup caked on her pale face, and her lipstick was a bright red color. Her teeth were straight and very white.

Colin saw Errol, Tom's youngest son, inside the apartment. The barrel-chested Errol was below average height and all muscle with not an ounce of fat on him. From the drugstore, Colin recalled Errol as a short-tempered man who liked to start fights. He had the darkest eyes Colin had ever seen. He seemed around thirty years old.

Errol was married to Angela. 'Angie', as she asked Colin to call her, was a glamorous trophy wife with big, white-blonde hair and large breasts spilling out of her form-fitting pink dress. She kissed Colin on the cheek when he first met her, under the watch of Errol. Angela had a soft Irish accent and smelled wonderful, like mint and expensive tobacco. Colin would later find out Angie couldn't have children and Errol resented her for it. She seemed like a caring woman, and he didn't understand why she was married to a coldhearted man like Errol. But Colin guessed she, like many other women of her class, had probably married as a way to escape the circumstances of her upbringing. And Errol had money because of his father. The scenario made Colin think of Maureen, and he wondered how she was really doing. He planned to visit Maureen and Patrick someday; and his mother.

Errol wasn't Tom's only son. Tom had an older son, Joseph, who was somewhat of a phantom in the McPhalen family. Colin had heard he'd attended law school and didn't want anything to do with the family 'business'. Colin couldn't get a definite answer out of anyone he asked, but he managed to piece together that Joseph had worked for his father for around three and half years. Then, after he met and married a lovely Greek woman named Anna, he left the family business and moved out to Brooklyn to practice law. Joseph and Errol both had records, with Errol having the worst, for armed robbery, for which he'd served five and a half years. Joseph was only arrested once, for stealing a car, which Tom claimed tainted the family's reputation. From what Colin concluded, you had to have at least a perjury charge to seem acceptably 'tough' according to Tom's standards of masculinity.

Tom and his wife, and Errol and his wife, didn't like Joseph's Anna. Mrs. McPhalen disliked Anna the most. She claimed to Colin that the conservative woman kept Joseph away from his family because she thought the McPhalens were wicked. Colin didn't quite understand Mrs. McPhalen's complaint, because from what he'd heard around the Bowery, Anna seemed right.

"Have a seat," Tom said to Colin inside the McDuffs's apartment. He gestured toward one of the ornate high-backed chairs at the long dining room table.

Colin didn't know they would be having dinner first. "Thanks, Mister—I mean, Tom."

Tom gave him a wink.

Colin liked how they ate under a sparkling chandelier at a gleaming dark-wood table with a lace tablecloth that felt delicate under his hands. Everyone wore expensive-seeming clothes, and the women always smelled of perfume. They laughed a tremendous amount and drank fine Bushmills whiskey, and only Bushmills.

Tom's wife and Angela brought out the food because the McDuffs had sent their maid home for the night. Colin wondered why. He couldn't help notice how Tom seemed to stare at Angela's breasts and behind each time she walked, or rather sauntered, by. Good steak was served, then more whiskey and a coconut cake that Tom's wife had brought over for dessert. Errol had gotten drunk halfway through dinner, and now he raised his hands and went on a tangent about "those Cubans on the West Side".

Ronan corrected him and said, "I think you mean the East Side."

"I'm going to knock out your teeth," Errol said to him.

Tom spoke to Errol, "Calm down."

Angela glanced at her husband. "Be quiet," she muttered with a sigh.

Ronan's wife shook her head, and Colin just watched.

Errol got up from the table and walked around the vast dining room, still going on about the Cubans.

"Have some more cake." Ronan's wife gestured toward Colin, who was trying to ignore Errol staggering around the room.

Colin accepted another piece. "Thank you, Mrs. McDuff."

"*Mrs.* McDuff. So polite. I like this guy already. And he's tall and handsome, and has nice eyes." Angela smiled pleasantly.

"Do you usually begin work with dinner?" Colin asked Tom. He wasn't really curious, and the answer wouldn't have mattered to him one way or the other, but he wanted to make small talk.

Errol overheard and took it as something else. He walked to the table. Colin tried his best to avoid Errol's bloodshot eyes.

"You just come in here and think you're running things? I've been here my whole blasted life." Errol's breath reeked of booze.

Colin gradually looked over at Errol. "I'm not trying to run anything."

"Be quiet."

Colin remained seated and looked straight at Errol, which wasn't difficult because he was a lot shorter than Colin. "I should be quiet. Is that what you're trying to tell me? That I should be seen and not heard, like a child? As far as I can tell, you're not much older than me."

Colin knew he'd taken a risk by mouthing off to a hotheaded drunk, and one who probably had a loaded gun on him, but he wanted to make it clear from the start that he wasn't going to be intimidated by the boss's son just because he was the boss's son.

Tom interrupted them before Errol could retort or act. "Errol, sit down and shut your mouth. You're so fecking pissed there's no sense in your talking."

"He doesn't like change at first," Tom spoke to Colin when Errol was sleeping off the whiskey in a bedroom upstairs. "Give him a few weeks and he'll soften up."

Ronan nodded in agreement, but Angela laughed a little. Tom gave her a dark stare and Angie's face went blank. When Tom used *that* expression with someone, the expression where he didn't take his pale blue eyes off you for what seemed like minutes, you dared not question him. You watched your actions for the rest of the night and maybe even for the rest of the week. It didn't matter to Tom that Angela was his daughter-in-law. The 'business' always came first, and Tom was the boss. If Tom wanted Angela 'out' in any way, Errol wouldn't have a say.

Later, when he returned home, Colin made sure he practiced mimicking Tom's expression in the medicine cabinet mirror. He practiced for hours, and within a month he didn't need to mimic anymore. It had become second nature.

Someone knocked on the door and said in an Irish accent, "East beats west."

Colin watched the other men chuckling at the table. Was this some sort of code?

"Come in," Tom called out.

Colin wondered who these people were that they felt so untouchable they left their apartment door unlocked during the night in what was then a dangerous city. Soon it became apparent to him that they weren't afraid of the city. The city was afraid of them. They made the city quiver and then gobbled it up with their passion and their greed.

A man wearing a tan suit and a flat cap stepped into the apartment and glanced over at Colin and then at Tom, as if to ask Tom, "Can he be trusted?" He was a tall, thin, middle-aged man with curly brown hair, a stern face, and light brown eyes.

Tom shot him a look that said, "Better than anyone." Colin smiled a little.

The man who'd entered introduced himself to Colin as "Bill". But everyone in the room called the man 'Little Bill', which was strange because, like Colin, he was very tall.

Tom rose from the dining table. "Colin, come into the kitchen to help me."

Colin excused himself from the table and Tom walked ahead

of him. The kitchen was to the right of the dining room and Colin could see Tom stand on a wooden stool, push aside boxes and reach into the very back of a closet shelf. Colin hurried in, not wanting Tom to have to wait for him a second longer than was necessary.

"You're a tall lad. Here, take this." Tom handed Colin a large, heavy box.

"What's in it?"

Tom looked over at the doorway.

"Tell him," Errol said from behind him. "You've already told him fecking everything else."

Colin jumped a little.

Tom looked at Colin. "It's a counterfeiting machine. We keep it up there in case there's a raid."

A raid? That worried Colin. He didn't want to return to prison anytime soon. "Has there ever been a raid?"

"No," Errol said. "And I don't expect they'll ever be one as long as everyone does what's best for them and stays quiet."

Was that a veiled threat? Colin knew he'd somehow have to get on Errol's good side if he was going to work for Tom – if Errol even had a good side.

Colin looked at Errol. "You can trust me."

"We better be able to."

Tom stepped off the stool and patted his son's shoulder. "Of course we can trust him." He smiled at Colin.

Colin followed the other men through a secret door, and down in the dim recreation room Errol, who had sobered up, opened the large box. Tom sat down on one of the folding chairs gathered around a plain table. Little Bill was eating dinner upstairs. Ronan was somewhere talking with his wife.

Errol bragged to Colin how he was, "Going to screw Angie tonight."

Errol still had tired eyes. Colin thought Errol probably didn't know, or care, how to please a woman in bed and he felt sorry for Errol's wife.

"Watch your filthy mouth in the presence of a cross," Tom said to his son.

Errol glanced at Jesus hanging from the small wooden cross on the corroding brick wall. He laughed and sarcastically uttered a Hail Mary. Colin was going to let out a laugh, not because he thought what Errol was doing was funny, but because he wanted to get on Errol's better side. But then he remembered the presence of Tom, who clearly objected to Errol's actions, and so he didn't even smile. Except for the machine and another box, a small one, the aluminum table downstairs was empty. Colin sat on the very last wood step leading into the recreation room. He didn't feel comfortable enough to sit on one of the chairs until he was invited, which he hadn't been yet. He wondered if they were being inconsiderate or were just oblivious. His gaze wandered from the table to Errol standing in a corner of the room. Errol was lighting a cigarette with a match. The small matchbook said *Deegan's* in neat, black cursive.

Colin came to understand that there were no women allowed in the recreation room during operation hours, not even to bring down refreshments. Tom asked Errol to get them drinks.

"No booze," Tom instructed his son. "You've already had enough and we need our heads clear for this."

Ronan came down the stairs, stepping past Colin, and sat on one of the chairs. He said nothing to anyone, and he didn't seem to have noticed that Colin was sitting on the last step. But it was Ronan who finally gestured for Colin to take a seat at the table.

"Tom told me you just got out of prison," Ronan said as Colin sat down in the surprisingly comfortable chair.

There was an unwritten rule among the men that you didn't

ask for details about a man's crime unless he divulged them.

"I did twelve years," Colin said.

Ronan whistled. "I could tell. You have that thing about you." Colin looked at him.

"You're a big bloke so people notice you, but you have this quiet thing about you. You need to get used to the outside again. It was the same with me when I got out last year. And now," he said, looking around the room, "it's like I never left."

Ronan explained they counterfeited identification for the immigrant community.

"Our fee is modest because it's a good cause," he said.

Errol returned with five glasses of cola on a tray. It was assumed that Little Bill would be down soon to join them. Colin held the glass Errol had carelessly thrust his way, and some of the cola had spilled on the floor. Tom gave Errol an annoyed look. Errol shrugged and glared at Colin, as if it was his fault. Colin started to wipe the floor with his handkerchief but Tom stopped him.

"You don't have to do that, Colin. You're our guest. We'll clean it later."

A guest. Colin's heart sank a little because he'd thought he was becoming one of them.

"You don't like cola?" Errol asked Colin after a half an hour.

The three others had finished their drinks, but Colin hadn't touched his.

"I do. But I'm not thirsty right now. I'll drink it later." Errol smirked at Colin's obstinacy.

Tom chuckled.

Several hours later Errol leaned against the wall in the corner. Colin felt Errol watching him and he finally had some of his drink. He wondered if Errol disliked him because he didn't consider him a genuine Irishman, being as he was mostly raised in the States.

Before Colin left that night Tom embraced him and instructed him to return to Ronan's tomorrow at the same time, promising the same occurrences would take place. They would have dinner and then counterfeit and bullshit. Colin exited Ronan's building feeling overjoyed.

He went straight to Byrne's where he had a pint of Guinness, bragged to Joe about his new career, and broke up a heated argument between a foul-mouthed drunk who reminded him of Errol and a helpless, scrawny younger guy. The angry drunk man's more sober friend was a boxer and gave Colin a purple-black eye for intervening. Colin didn't want any trouble so he remained calm. Men seemed to like to start quarrels with him because of his great height, well over six feet, and his large frame, as though beating him would boost their egos. It had happened to him frequently in prison. Sometimes the prison officers would even make the inmates fight for entertainment.

Joe told Colin to let Tom McPhalen know what had happened and how the man had blackened his eye just for trying to make peace. Colin told Joe he didn't know if he should take it that far, and then he calmly left the pub with a sore eye and a cut lip.

But Errol wanted to know what had happened when Colin came by Ronan's the next evening. And Errol wouldn't stop asking until he obtained the specifics.

Errol gave him a grin. "What the hell happened to your eye? Did you get into bed with the wrong woman?"

Colin laughed although he didn't find Errol's brand of humor particularly amusing. "It was nothing. I tried to stop a pub fight, that's all. And I ended up being the one beaten."

"Who did it?" Errol persisted. "*You* got beat up?"

"He was no one special. Just some local asshole."

"Who the feck is he?"

Colin didn't answer him.

"Why won't you tell me the name? I'm sure getting beaten by a woman is nothing to be embarrassed about." Errol snickered.

Colin straightened his shoulders. "It was a guy named Daniels. He's a boxer. Are you happy now?"

"Paul Daniels?"

"That's him."

"He owes." Errol spoke as if learning the name was so exciting to him that he couldn't manage words.

"What?" Colin said.

"He owes me over four thousand dollars, which the bastard borrowed and never paid back. You see, my father likes you. He thinks you aren't a screw up like me. Your beating gives me an excuse to finally do something about this Daniels bloke. Thanks, kid." Errol grinned. "My father's picky about taking lives. But I say if they don't pay then destroy them, or at least put them in a coma." Colin knew Errol didn't care Paul Daniels had messed up his eye. Errol was just glad because Colin getting hurt gave Errol a chance to retaliate against Daniels for personal reasons. Colin felt sympathetic toward Daniels's situation because it reminded him of his late father's plight. Tom had told him he'd have to lose those feelings if he wanted to work for him, but Colin wasn't sure if he'd ever lose them. He could disguise them perhaps, but he could never forget why his father had died. Colin still thought of David Burke sometimes, but his hatred of the man had diminished over the years and Colin no longer dreamed about killing him.

Colin knew it wasn't a coincidence when at six o'clock in the evening a few days later the police found Paul Daniels shot in the head in his car outside of the boxing gym. No arrests were made.

After that every man at Byrne's walked on eggshells around Colin, trying to not so much as brush his shoulder when they passed by him.

9

"Can you fecking believe it?" Errol said about the horse race.

It was October. Autumn had always been Colin's favorite season, and October his favorite month. It was the month of his birthday, and he recalled fond memories from his childhood. Getting a red toy train from his parents, and Patrick's smiling face when Colin had bought him a similar present years later; a pair of mittens and a kiss from Maureen; and a bottle of beer from Danny as a present when Colin was a teenager. He had always loved October.

Colin had been working for Tom McPhalen for two months. "Lucky Red came in first," Errol said. "Blue Moon was supposed to win."

"Maybe you got the wrong information," Colin said.

"What are you saying? I always get the horses right."

"Maybe you heard it wrong or your father told it to you wrong."

"If I wanted your fecking opinion, I'd ask for it. Sometimes I don't know why we even hold on to you, kid. You bother me sometimes."

Colin disliked being called a kid when he was only two years younger than Errol. But he didn't say anything in reply. Errol was a genuine asshole, and there wasn't anything Colin could do to change that. So Colin changed the subject.

"Your father asked us to work tonight."

"He asked you to tell me?"

"Yeah. What's wrong?"

"It's interesting, that's all. What time?"

"Six o'clock."

"That's a little early because I have plans tonight. Angie's parents. They just moved here from Galway. I bought them a house on Long Island. We're supposed to go there for dinner."

"Where on Long Island?"

"It's near Levittown. Why?"

"Nothing. I got a friend out there on Long Island, that's all."

"A girl?" Errol smiled.

"Yeah."

"Why don't you come along with us? I'll drive, drop you off at your lady's place then head over to Angie's parents."

"Thanks, but I don't know the address."

"Do you mean she doesn't want you to have it?"

"Yeah, that's about right."

Errol chuckled. "My father will get the girl's address for you."

"He can do that?"

"Sure he will. You feel like getting lunch?"

"Sure."

"*Deegan's?*"

Colin nodded. *Deegan's* was one of the favorite, more elegant pubs of Tom's men.

Besides Colin, Errol, Ronan, and Little Bill, there were always other men who worked for Tom socializing at *Deegan's*. Most of them were men who had followed Tom to America from Ireland, either at the prospect of hitting it big with Tom in the

United States, or to avoid prosecution for their crimes in Ireland.

Jarlath Dougherty was among the most distinguished of the men who had followed Tom to America. Jarlath had fair looks and appeared only a little older than Colin. He was a hard hitter who did the toughest jobs for Tom, yet he'd managed to avoid serving time in prison. Like Colin and Tom, his father had died when he was young. Colin looked up to Tom, but he looked up to Jarlath as well. He felt a bond with the clever young man from Ballinasloe who stood out among the others. Tom was always ribbing Jarlath for dressing hip. But Colin liked Jarlath's motorcycle jacket, the same kind Brando had worn in *The Wild One*. They had shown the inmates that film in prison. Colin didn't mind when Jarlath called him 'kid'.

Steve and a man nicknamed 'Tats' were yellow-haired identical twin brothers who occasionally worked for Tom. They held other, real jobs, as policemen. Tats—who got his nickname from the tattoos he had from being in the Navy—and Steve owned *Deegan's* pub, where Steve played the piano on some nights. They were married to women who were both named Rose. They grew up in the Bowery, a street away from Colin. Colin had seen Steve and Tats around the neighborhood as a boy, and they had made jokes with him in the pews at church. His father had known their father.

"Someday I want to be running something myself," Jarlath mentioned at Byrne's pub a few hours after lunch. "I have big plans of my own."

Colin was set to leave for Long Island with Errol and Angela in an hour. Jarlath had started going to Byrne's with Colin a few weeks ago.

Colin was drinking Guinness but Jarlath was having a cola. He claimed he was trying to ease up on his drinking because now that he was getting on in his years, it could do harm to his bones. Colin was almost as old as Jarlath, but he wasn't planning to quit having a drink once in a while anytime soon.

"You want to be the boss?" Colin asked with a smile.

Jarlath chuckled. "Yeah, that's it. You've put it in simple terms, fella. What I want is to be the top man someday."

"Anything's possible. And if anyone can do it, I think you can. You're sharp and you know the game. Of course you'll have to worry about Errol because he's surely going to want to take over once his old man's in the ground."

Both laughed at the thought of the stubborn and irrational Errol as their boss, but it frightened Colin a little.

"Another Guinness?" Joe interrupted them.

Colin peered into his empty glass and shook his head. Then he turned to Jarlath. "Do you know what's funny?"

"What?"

"You giving up drinking. I never pegged you for a square." Jarlath laughed.

They hadn't known each other for more than two months, yet they communicated with each other like old friends.

"The question is, how long can I last?" Jarlath thought out loud.

Then he put his hand in the air. "Joe, bring me a Guinness."

When Errol pulled up to Lucille's house on Long Island Colin felt as if he'd been driven to another world. Everything, from the manicured garden, to the white mailbox with *The O'Gradys* written on it in swirling blue letters, seemed exotic to him. A child's small red bicycle rested on the front porch.

"Go on," Errol encouraged Colin from the driver's seat. "We don't have all day."

Angela nodded and smiled at Colin from the passenger's seat, as if to encourage him to step out.

Colin opened the car door and left the backseat. He carried a bouquet of yellow flowers in one hand, and a red-haired, freckle-cheeked doll in his other hand, a present for Lucille's daughter. When he reached the steps to the house, Errol had already sped away.

Colin stood outside for a moment in silence, then he knocked and could hear footsteps.

"Who is it?" Lucille asked from behind the door.

"Flower delivery," Colin said on impulse. He feared that if he said who he really was, she might not open the door.

Lucille opened the door and stared into his eyes. She had changed her appearance. Her blonde hair was shorter and coiffed, and she wore a respectable housedress with simple black shoes.

"What are you doing here?" she whispered as though he was someone she wanted to hide from her family. "Do you need something?"

"No, of course not. I came for a visit."

"Did my brother give you my address? I wish he wouldn't encourage you."

"Your brother knows I care about you, but he didn't give me your address. I have ways."

"Ways?"

"I know people."

"You mean, Tom McPhalen?"

Colin nodded. "They aren't such bad fellows."

Lucille scoffed. "How could you, after what men like them did to your father?"

"They're nothing like them. They assist the immigrant community." He handed her the flowers and the doll. "Here, I brought you these." Colin pointed at the toy. "That's for your daughter."

Lucille held the gifts limply in her hands. "My daughter's not home. She's out with her father. They're visiting his parents. I don't get along with them."

Colin was glad to hear that her husband wasn't home despite it being a Saturday.

"Can I come in for a moment?" he asked.

Lucille stepped out of the doorway and glanced around the neighborhood, as if she was checking to make sure no one was watching them.

"You can come in for a moment. Just for a moment."

He followed Lucille inside and she shut the door. She put the gifts down on a table and Colin wondered if she'd throw them away after he left.

"Aren't you going to put the flowers in water?" he asked.

"I will when you leave."

"Why don't you get along with your husband's parents?" She didn't answer him.

"Your home is beautiful. How long have you lived here?" Colin envied how Lucille's husband could provide her with the luxuries he couldn't yet.

"Since after my wedding," she said.

"To escape the Bowery?" He smiled.

"My husband got a better job offer here. He's the chief of police in our town."

"I'm impressed." Lucille frowned.

The house had peach-colored carpeting and tasteful furniture. On the fireplace mantel there were photographs of Lucille's husband and daughter. Her husband had a chubby face, and he looked like a decent man, but Colin thought that he was better looking. Lucille's blonde daughter looked a lot like her.

"Your daughter looks like you," he commented to Lucille. She murmured thanks.

Colin pulled the rosary beads she'd given him out of his pocket. "I still have these. Looking at them in prison and thinking about you helped me survive in there."

Lucille's face flushed. "Would you like a drink?"

He put the beads in his pocket. "Yeah. Thanks. Scotch or whatever you have is fine."

"We don't keep any of that in the house. My husband's very religious. We don't drink."

Colin was about to make a joke then he noticed a picture of Jesus on the wall and realized Lucille was serious.

"We have cola," she said.

"That's fine. Thank you."

Lucille nodded and left the room in a hurry, as though his presence tempted her and she was happy to get away.

Colin looked over the photographs of Lucille's family at the beach while she was in the kitchen. He stared at the pictures of her husband particularly hard. From what he could see in the photos, her husband was tall, clean-shaven, and had dark hair, just like him. He looked around forty years old. Lucille's daughter had the same bright green eyes as her.

Lucille returned and gave Colin the drink. He set the glass down on the mantel. He grabbed her hand and looked her over. "Let me have a look at you. Beautiful. You don't look a day older than when I last saw you."

She pulled away. "Colin, stop. What do you want?"

He looked into her eyes. "I don't want anything. I wanted to see you."

Lucille looked away from him. "You're lucky my husband isn't home. What makes you think you can just show up at my house?"

"If he had been home, who would you tell him I was?" Colin smiled. "An old friend?"

"He's a good man. I love him."

"You love him," Colin echoed.

Lucille stared at Colin. "I love him very much."

"I'm starting to feel like I'm not welcome here."

"You aren't. Please go. And don't call me."

Colin drank his cola and handed her the glass. "Okay, I'll leave. But I'll call you."

Johnny still worked at the auto mechanic's shop. Colin knew this and he avoided walking near the place. It's not that he didn't want to see Johnny. In fact, they had seen each other. They ran into one another a few days after Colin had been released from prison and returned to the Bowery. Johnny was now shorter than him. They'd made small talk for a couple of minutes and Colin had thanked Johnny for his help with Carmine, and then they'd parted ways, as though they'd seen each other only yesterday, when it had been years. When Colin got sent to prison they had been friends, but the lost years had created an awkwardness between them. Johnny hadn't written to him in prison. And it was as though they noticed their skin color more now that they were older.

Johnny was twenty-nine years old. He sometimes stole and resold cars, but the aspirations of Johnny and Colin's boyhood 'criminal enterprise' had fallen through over a decade ago. Johnny was divorced from Donna, with a young son and daughter who lived with their mother in Brooklyn. Johnny made it a point to see his children often because he didn't want them to grow up without a father like he had.

Like some of the other boys in the Bowery, Johnny had

wanted to be a gangster when he grew up. Because, after all, gangsters made a lot of money and often came from nothing; but unlike most of the other boys in the Bowery, Johnny had both Cuban and Irish blood. Gangsters were sometimes of mixed blood, but there were certain boundaries. If you were Italian and Irish you could work for the Irish or the Italians as an associate, but you could never become a made member of either. Things went the same way if you were Cuban. But there weren't any Cuban-Irish gangs in the Bowery. So Johnny was left hanging.

Tito Bernal was a Lower East Side guy himself. He came to the US as a twelve-year-old. He grew up on Fifteenth Street, and he led a small gang there called the *Tigres*, who stole cars and sold the parts, and broke into stores at night to take appliances, which they'd resell. They weren't anything big, but Tom McPhalen was becoming more aware of them.

In the 1950s more Cuban families started moving into the Lower East Side because of the armed revolt led by Castro. Some of the older residents resented the new families coming in and acted out their dislike. Some Bowery landlords wouldn't lease apartments to Cuban families, and some local employers wouldn't hire them for jobs. Others took out their resentment with violence, as though they'd forgotten the similar treatment their ancestors had faced years before. They beat up the Cuban men with metal pipes, and their wives threw lye at the Cuban women and tripped them as they walked in the street. Offensive graffiti began to appear on the outsides of Cuban-owned shops.

Tito Bernal watched this happening to his people and he didn't like what he saw.

Johnny met Tito at the garage when the older man came in for new car tires.

"Are you Cuban?" Tito asked Johnny as he changed his tires.

Johnny stared at the stocky man in the fedora who'd introduced himself as Tito Bernal. "Yeah. My father was."

"Was?"

"He died a few years ago. Right after he got out of prison." Johnny had never reconnected with his father.

"I'm sorry to hear that." Tito gave him a sympathetic smile. "It's good to meet a fellow brother." He read Johnny's nametag and shook his hand. "Johnny."

"Johnny Garcia."

"So it was your father's side?" Johnny nodded.

"It must not have been easy being only a half-gringo in this neighborhood."

"It's not. Your car's ready." Tito nodded but didn't move.

Johnny couldn't tell what Tito Bernal wanted. He knew that Tito's car was done and he could take his car and leave the garage whenever he wanted to.

"I can only imagine how hard it was for you to grow up here," Tito said, glancing around the garage. "And it still is hard."

"Your car's ready," Johnny said to get things moving. Tito nodded.

"You can pay at the front," Johnny said when Tito didn't budge. "The guy up there will take care of you."

Johnny left Tito and walked over to a side project he was working on that involved fixing up an old car for his mother to use someday. He kept an eye on Tito Bernal as Tito made his way up to the front counter to pay. Tito must have felt Johnny's gaze on him because he smiled at Johnny. Johnny looked the other way and continued working.

Tito stepped into his car and Johnny heard him start the engine. But then Tito opened the car door and came outside again. He walked toward where Johnny knelt on the floor working. Johnny saw Tito's shiny black shoes near him and looked up at the older man's smiling face.

"Here's a card for our club," Tito said.

LESCA

143 East Fifteenth Street

Johnny stared at the card. "Lesca? What's it mean?"

"Lower East Side Cuban Americans. Do you speak Spanish?"

Johnny shook his head and accepted the card and shoved it into the pocket of his mechanic's suit without looking at it again.

"You should learn," Tito said.

"Maybe."

"We're having a gathering tomorrow night. There will be music, dancing, refreshments, and lots of pretty girls." Tito smiled.

"Thanks. I'll think about it."

"Six o'clock."

"I said I'll think about it."

Tito nodded. He turned away and went back to his car with the engine still running. He opened the door and stepped inside. Johnny watched him drive slowly away.

When Tito was gone Johnny took the card he'd given him out of his pocket. He didn't know why but he spent more than five minutes looking at it. He wondered if he had thought the texture, the letters, the ink, would be different because a Cuban had ordered them, maybe even printed them. Did they do things differently? Did he do things differently? And did people notice? People around the Bowery? How about across the rest of the city?

Besides heritage, what really made a Cuban a Cuban, and an Irish an Irish? And, since he was both, where did he belong?

"You can go home now, Johnny," his manager called out.

"It six o'clock already?"

"Yeah."

Johnny slipped out of his mechanic's suit. He looked at his reflection in the grimy mirror on the wall as he washed his hands. Cuban. Irish. A little bit of each.

He walked out of the mechanic's shop in his jeans and t-shirt, but he'd forgotten the denim jacket he had arrived to work wearing. He remembered about the jacket when he was on the subway and halfway uptown on his way to see his mother. He knew he wouldn't be returning to the garage to get his jacket, but he would be going to that party tomorrow night.

Tom was in the middle of cutting a deal with the Woodlawn gang on the Lower West Side, and he appeared quite worked up about it. Sweat glistened on his forehead when he told Colin the news. The deal involved opening a nightclub and restaurant that would be a front for a gambling operation.

The leaders of the Woodlawn gang (the 'Two Declans', as they were dubbed) – Declan Burke, who was not related to David Burke as far as Colin knew, and his underboss, Declan O'Connor – were Irish-American. Most of their men were second or third generation. Tom's gang consisted of men directly from the old country. Men like Colin, who, although he'd grown up in the US, still thought of himself as Irish, despite having lost his Northern brogue and many of his memories of home.

No-Last-Name Max, a notable hitman and a captain for Declan Burke, and a few years his senior, was thought to be more of a gentleman on the inside than Declan Burke ever could be, but not as sharp business-or-dress-wise. Tom told Colin that was why Max wasn't the boss or even the underboss.

Tom chose Colin to cut the deal, even though Colin had been in the organization for less than a year.

"All you have to do is tell them the plan to open up the nightclub is moving along as scheduled, and that we're all excited about working together on it. How finally after all these years we're joining up, and it's fantastic. Shite like that," Errol told Colin outside of Tom's large brownstone house. "Saying shite, that'll make them grin. Make sure they know we're all so fecking happy about working with them on this. That's what my father wants you to say. Okay? He thinks they'll like you because you're a giant but you have an honest face. He thinks they'll take you very seriously. I don't agree about your face but that's what he thinks." Errol smiled. "The most important thing, and the real purpose of this meeting, is that we need the five thousand instalment from them. They should have the money with them. Bring it back here, and be careful that nothing happens to it. If you lose it then you're not alive anymore. Understand? And if for some reason they don't have it with them then you need to ask them where the feck it is, but in a nicer way."

Colin wanted to tell Errol to fuck off for threatening him, but at the last minute he thought better of it. "I understand."

Errol handed Colin some keys. "Here's the keys for the car. It'd be too risky walking or taking a taxi with all that money. You can park at the pub."

"Okay, Errol." Colin stared at the black car parked in the street. The car was a sleek beauty that Tom loaned to all of his men for important meetings and errands so they could travel in style.

Errol peered at him. "You'll do well."

His kind words reminded Colin of his da. That surprised Colin, but it didn't surprise him as much as when Errol patted him on the back. Errol wasn't a warm person, and he never made gestures like that unless he meant them. Colin knew he should be honored so he thanked Errol.

There were three members of the Woodlawn gang waiting for Colin at *Dowd's* pub on the Lower West Side at around one in the afternoon. The men all had dark hair and brown eyes. In appearance two of them seemed grittier than Tom's men and didn't look like sophisticated gangsters. Those two wore old denim jackets and cigarettes dangled from their lips. Colin had once worn a denim jacket, but that was when he was a teenager. Now he wore good suits.

They appeared a little insulted that Tom hadn't sent a top man to discuss the deal. But after Colin sat down and spoke for Tom, they seemed to accept him.

No-Last-Name Max, Dean Fitzpatrick, and Gerry Thomas were the Woodlawn gang members seated at the booth in the pub. Their leaders weren't present. That angered Tom when Colin told him afterwards. Tom saw it as a sign of disrespect that the 'big men' hadn't bothered to take the time to come. Colin then pointed out to Tom that he hadn't sent his top men either. He had sent him.

"About the nightclub, we've decided we don't have to spend that much more money getting it ready," Colin said to the men. "The neighborhood it's in isn't very nice. If the place looked too classy, it'd stand out too much."

The three men hadn't taken their eyes off him during the conversation. Then they nodded almost all at once.

"That's what the Declans thought as well," Max, the only one wearing a suit, albeit one too small for his chunky figure, said.

"It's settled then," Colin said, and Max nodded. "Tom's very enthusiastic about working together."

Dean Fitzpatrick, the largest of the three, smirked. "Is something wrong?" Colin asked.

Dean shrugged.

"About the payment arrangement," Colin continued.

"We have the money on us," Dean cut him off.

Colin could tell that Dean, a tall, gaunt man with piercing dark eyes, hadn't liked him from the beginning. He didn't smile like the others had when Colin entered and introduced himself. Dean had sat there and glared.

Dean took a stuffed packet out of his denim jacket pocket and tossed it on the table. Colin picked the packet up and held it in his hand. He was about to count the money inside.

"What? You don't trust us?" Dean said.

Colin put the packet back down on the table. All four men stared at it. There was silence at the table for a moment, with Dean glancing at Colin every so often, and Colin trying to ignore him.

Working for Tom had tamed Colin. "We're not boys," Tom was always telling the gang. "And we need to control ourselves during business. Guns aren't necessary unless you have no other choice."

Max broke the tense silence. "Come on, Fitz." He chuckled.

"There's no harm in it."

Colin didn't dare call Dean 'Fitz'. "Except he don't trust us," Dean said.

Dean picked the packet up from the table and held it in his thin, veiny hand. He was like a child who was unwilling to share his toy with another boy.

Max shot Dean a glare.

"Okay. Okay. Let him fucking count it if he wants to." Dean tossed the packet on the table again.

Colin picked it up and counted the money.

Dean remained difficult for most of the night, until after he had a couple of pints, and then he settled down a little. But he still didn't talk to or acknowledge Colin's presence much. He kept to himself, and he sat there with his arms crossed and an uninterested expression on his face.

Max said he was impressed with Colin and then tried to coax him into working for their organization, but Colin insisted he had already made a commitment to Tom.

"Tell me, I heard through my boss that your family comes from the North. Is that correct?" Max asked him.

"Yeah, from Kilrea."

"A while back our families came from the North. So what are you doing working for the Southern Irish then?"

"I live in the Bowery. And I have a relative or two in the South."

"So does Gerry." Max nodded at Gerry, who was seated across from them next to Dean.

"I got a great-uncle there," Gerry said.

Max ordered a whiskey. "Anyway," he said to Colin. "Just having a 'relative or two' there don't make you a South. I'm surprised Tom's letting you work for him. Usually, they're pretty strict with their rules. South ancestry and Irish-born only. All of their fellas are South and directly from Ireland. You ain't."

"But I was born in Kilrea," Colin said. "I came here with my family when I was a boy."

Max nodded his head in approval. "So, you came here a while ago, then. Guess that's why you lost your accent." But he seemed unable to change the topic. "Still, why do you think they chose you out of all the South guys they got over there in the Bowery?"

"I don't know. I guess Tom thinks I have something to offer. He saw past everything else."

"You'll see, Colin. When you're there long enough and it's about time they moved you up, you'll realize then that you don't belong. You're a Northerner. Sure, they might let you move up a little, but they'll never let you go as high as a sharp Northern guy like you could." Max pointed at him with his finger to emphasize his point. "Our boss will let you in, I'm sure of it. If you want a shot at becoming something big, you need to work with us." He smiled. "Besides, McPhalen's all about making himself and his son rich."

Colin glanced at Max's unkempt associates.

"They can afford suits, but they dress that way because they want to," Max said.

"Ronan McDuff's got money," Colin countered.

"His wife's father's a politician. She's the one with the dough."

"What's in it for you?"

"I'd like to help out a fellow Northerner."

Colin nodded. Tom had trusted him enough to attend the meeting despite his Northern heritage, and he wasn't going to downright agree with Max, although it seemed like a fair offer and he felt he could deal with Dean Fitzpatrick. His family was from the North, and he had always felt a bond with the few other Northern Irish in the Bowery. Now a powerful Northern-affiliated organization had given him an offer to join them, with what he assumed would be a promotion to captain.

Colin left the meeting still uncertain. He wondered during the drive home if he should have said yes to Max's offer and then he could have been rising to the top over time, and maybe he'd even be running an organization someday.

He dropped the car, keys, and money off at Tom's and reported the details of the meeting to him, minus Max's clandestine offer. Then he went to Ronan's building because Tom had mentioned Ronan needed Colin to do a favor for him. When he knocked on Ronan's apartment door and was greeted by a pretty young woman, he forgot about Max's offer for the moment.

Her name was Margaret and she looked around eighteen

years old. She had luminous skin and soft-looking brown hair. Her eyes shone with kindness. She introduced herself as Ronan's niece. The wife's side, obviously, based on her looks. She explained she was visiting her aunt and uncle on a rare visit. Her mother had dropped her off on her way uptown to see her divorce lawyer.

Margaret would be spending the afternoon in the city. She lived in Yonkers and didn't know Manhattan well. Colin was instructed by Ronan to show Margaret around and make sure she was safe. Ronan made it clear that nothing was to happen to his lovely, sweet niece, and that Colin was to protect her with his life. Colin knew that wouldn't be a problem because just by looking at her, he already wanted to protect her.

"How old are you?" she asked him as he drove her around the city.

"I'm almost thirty."

"You're over a decade older than me. That's a long time. But not too bad. Some girls I know would marry fellows that old."

"We're engaged now?" he joked. Margaret laughed.

"Maggie—is it all right if I call you that? Your uncle said your name's Margaret so I wasn't sure what I'm supposed to call you."

"Call me Maggie, please. Nobody calls me Margaret except for my mother when she's angry with me."

Colin smiled. "Okay, Maggie. Do you want to get some ice cream? Your uncle Ronan said he wanted you to have fun."

"I'm not a child, but, sure, let's go."

"I'll take you over to Little Italy. Ever been there? Of course you have."

He navigated through the traffic to *Paulie's Gelateria*, because every Irishman in the Bowery knew the Italians made the best ice cream, only they called it *gelato*. You went to the Bowery for a stout, and you went to Mulberry Street for food. A cone or a milkshake from *Paulie's* cost almost as much as three cones or two shakes from other places. But Maggie wasn't like many of the other girls in the Lower East Side. She was the niece of Ronan McDuff, who was Tom McPhalen's underboss, and was royalty there.

Colin double-parked and got out of the car to move the milk crate blockade in one of the parking spaces in front of the shop. Paulie illegally reserved a private space for his loyal customers – mostly the mafia, and a few Irish guys they sometimes collaborated with, like Tom and his men – to use. So of course no one in the neighborhood dared to complain to the police. Colin got into the car again and parked. Maggie seemed amused by the milk crate barrier.

"Is that so no one else can park here?" she asked.

"It is. The fellow who owns the shop, Paulie, only lets his favorite customers park here."

"You mean criminals?" Maggie snorted.

Colin didn't know how much Ronan had told his niece about his line of work so Colin didn't answer the question.

He got out of the car and opened Maggie's door and led the way inside the sun-filled shop toward a small corner table. Maggie sat down and Colin asked her what she wanted. He walked to the serving counter and ordered a chocolate milkshake for her and a vanilla cone for himself. Colin knew Paulie through Tom.

Paulie glanced over at Maggie seated at the white table. "I see you have a date, Colin. She's very pretty."

Colin nodded at Maggie, who was gazing out the window. "She's just a young girl," he said to Paulie. "Too young for me."

Paulie continued to smile.

"That's Ronan McDuff's niece. He asked me to chauffeur her around the city and keep an eye on her."

"Why, is she a troublemaker?"

"I'm not sure, but I better return to the table soon just in case she tries to sneak out."

Paulie chuckled. "It must not be that tough of a job because at least she's cute. Right?"

Colin laughed.

"Is she Robert's daughter?" Paulie asked.

"I don't know. She's from Yonkers. McLean Avenue, probably. The wife's side, I guess."

"I forgot she had a sister. It's on the house."

"What?"

"Your sweets, they're on the house."

Colin looked at Paulie like he was playing a trick on him. "They're free. Understand?" Paulie said.

"They never were free before."

"You come in here all the time. You give me business. I give a little something back. Okay?"

Colin nodded slowly. He understood Paulie's point, but, still, Paulie was Sicilian. He knew mafia guys. What did he really care about pleasing one of Tom's Irish hoods? Colin knew better than to ask Paulie to explain. Tom expected his men to accept the gratitude that was offered to them if it was genuine and Colin felt Paulie's was. Colin thanked Paulie and took the ice cream cone and the milkshake to the table. He set Maggie's shake in front of her and she smiled up at him.

"You're tall," she said.

He could feel himself blushing as he sat down. He put his hat on the table and licked his cone carefully so as not to appear vulgar in front of the girl.

He thought about what Paulie had said about Maggie's beauty. Of course, Colin was interested in pretty, fascinating women. And right then he thought that he would like to lean across the table and kiss Maggie's soft, red lips, but he didn't dare go beyond dreaming. Ronan would maim him if Colin put the moves on his innocent niece.

"Have you lived in the Bowery for all your life?" she asked him. Colin noticed that despite having grown up in Yonkers, Maggie had no trace of an accent. The way she twirled her red-and-white straw between her fingers made him smile.

"No." He tried not to stare at her long, dark eyelashes and tempting lips.

"Where did you live before you came here?"

"I was born in Kilrea."

"Where's that? Ireland or somewhere?"

"Northern Ireland."

Maggie's eyes widened. "You aren't kidding, are you?"

"I'm not."

"Where's your accent?" she teased.

"I came here when I was a very young boy. I lost it over time."

"I've been to Europe. Once. A few years ago."

"Did you like it?"

"Oh, yes." She beamed. "I loved it. I'm going again someday. My parents are getting divorced so we won't be going anytime soon."

He didn't want to admit the longest time he'd been away from the city was prison. "I'm sorry to hear about your parents."

"It's better for them. They can't stand each other, and they'll be happier apart. They only stayed together for me, but now that I've finished high school they don't have to anymore."

Colin glanced at the crowded sidewalk. He looked at Maggie again and she had already finished her shake. "You know, you're going to get a stomach ache."

"What?" She frowned.

"Your shake. You drank it so fast you could get a stomach ache because it's cold. It happens to me all the time, especially with the milkshakes from this place because they're so good." He didn't want her to think he was criticizing her so he smiled.

After a second she said, "I don't mind."

"How did you like high school?"

"How did you like it?"

"I never went."

"Really? It was nothing special. You didn't miss anything. We read. We wrote. We did math. Learned history. The girls had to learn home economics." Maggie made a face. "It's nothing as exciting as being a gangster."

"How much do you know about what your uncle does?" Colin asked carefully.

"Enough to know that you're probably a gangster like him." She grinned.

When the day was over he brought Maggie back to Ronan's building. She secretly gave him a quick peck on the cheek and thanked him for the good time she'd had. He sensed she wanted to see him again, and he wouldn't have minded seeing her either. But she had held herself back. Perhaps she didn't want to encourage him because she knew that as a pair they would have almost no chance at a real relationship or even a friendship. It was sound advice not to romance a gangster's female relative, and even more sound advice for lower-ranked men in an organization not to seduce the women who belonged to the upper echelon. And if one did foolishly step over that line, he'd spend nearly every moment with the woman taking care not to upset her, or push her to do things she wasn't ready to do, because if he did, he'd get maimed or killed, or both, by her father or her brother or her uncle.

Colin swore to himself he'd never wash that cheek again, but he did, eventually.

But he kept after Ronan, using good judgment, asking him when Maggie might be back in town. Ronan always said he didn't know, and after Colin had asked him a fourth time, Ronan snapped, "Why the feck are you so curious about her?" Colin knew from then on there'd be no more asking.

∼

Johnny stepped toward 143 East Fifteenth Street at five-fifty on Friday night. Ten minutes early. But he couldn't wait inside the coffee shop across the street, where he'd been slowly drinking a cup, for any longer than he already had. He knew he had to get himself out of there and across the street right then or he might never go.

Already he could hear the music booming from inside of the building. He pondered if he should wait outside for another few minutes or just go in.

He went inside.

Tito Bernal greeted him at the door. "I am glad you've made it." He smiled.

"Thanks for inviting me."

To Johnny's surprise, the room was already packed. People were scattered across the gymnasium of the local school, where Tito had mentioned club meetings of LESCA were held. The people were seated in folding chairs at the tables around the dance floor or leaning against the walls in groups or by the refreshments table. They were chatting, laughing, and moving to the sound of the musicians warming up on the stage. Colorful ribbons hung from the ceiling.

"You can take off your coat and give it to the lady over there." Tito pointed to a small woman with white hair who was managing the coat-check. "The music will begin shortly. Please grab a drink for yourself."

Johnny thanked him again and then looked around the bright room. His shoes squeaked on the waxed wooden gym floor as he walked to the coat-check area. Everyone in the room looked like him. After he handed his coat to the woman and received his ticket, another woman accosted him from behind.

"I don't think I've ever seen you before. What street do you live on?"

Johnny turned around to see a young woman standing behind him. She had short, curly black hair and deep brown eyes. She appeared to be no more than eighteen or nineteen years old, with a body still that of a girl's, straight and thin. She had on a simple black dress embroidered with small white flowers.

"I don't live in this neighborhood. I live a few streets away."

"So do I. You were born in New York?"

"Yeah." Johnny started to walk away from the girl—she seemed too young for him—but she called after him.

"Same here. My parents are Cuban, though."

He turned around. Johnny rarely met somebody growing up whose parents weren't from Ireland or Italy. "Really?"

She walked to where he now stood a little farther from her. "Yes. You sound surprised. Why are you surprised?" Her eyes brightened with curiosity.

"To tell you the truth, I grew up in a mostly Irish and Italian neighborhood, and my mother, she's Irish. My father was the one who was . . ." He struggled to finish the sentence.

"Cuban?"

Johnny nodded. "I didn't grow up around Cubans."

"Now you are with us." She finally smiled. "What's your name?"

"Johnny Garcia."

"I'm Lila." She held out a delicate hand.

Johnny took her smooth hand and didn't ask for her surname. "Would you like a cola?" She stared at him with her pretty eyes. "Sure." He looked away and let go of her hand. She still seemed too young for him.

Lila didn't give up. She grabbed his hand and led him to the refreshments table. Johnny didn't dare glance down to check out her backside as they walked. She probably didn't have much there, anyway.

"Have you ever been to the homeland?" Lila asked Johnny while they waited for their drinks.

"To where?"

"I said, have you ever been to where your father was from?"

"No, I've never been there."

"Me either. Maybe we'll be able to go together in the future."

"What?" His mouth hung open.

Lila laughed. "I was kidding."

"Oh."

"You're a very serious person."

"Being the only Cuban kid on the street, means you have to be serious."

"That must have been hard."

"It was. Still is."

"Even now?" Then she answered her own question. "Don't worry. There's many more of us moving in now. Soon we will have our own force." She gestured to the people socializing in the crowded room.

"You sound like a gangster," Johnny teased.

"Yes, I'm the Cuban mafia," she teased him back.

He stopped chuckling when Tito quietly approached them. "Johnny. I was going to introduce you but I see you've already met this enchanting young lady." He gestured to Lila.

Johnny tensed up a little, then he smiled and nodded. "I introduced myself to him first," Lila said to Tito.

"That's good, my dear. It's good of you to be friendly to our guests."

Johnny gave him a perplexed look.

Tito continued to speak to Lila, "But it's eight o'clock, my dear." Then he said to Johnny, "If you'll please excuse her, my daughter has to leave now with her mama. Lila has school early tomorrow. But she'll be at our festivities again two evenings from now. Perhaps you will be there as well, Mr. Garcia?"

"Maybe." Johnny glanced at Lila. He'd assumed she was young but he didn't know she was young enough to still be in school.

Lila frowned and set down her soda.

Tito Bernal put his arm around his daughter and they walked away. Johnny stood still and then drank his cola.

10

————

"Hi," Colin said.

"It's you," Lucille whispered on the phone.

"What happened to us?"

"Us?"

"You know what I mean. We used to be friends, and we could've been more someday. That's what I thought, anyway."

"You went to jail. I moved on. I'm sorry but I had to."

"I understand that. But now you act like you hate me."

She sighed. "I don't hate you. I'm married now. I don't know, it's different."

"Won't you have dinner with me? Or we could grab drinks?"

"I don't drink anymore."

"Then we can grab a soda. My boss is having a party for me tonight. Maybe you can stop by."

"Is that what you called me for?" Lucille snapped at him. "You want to invite me to your gangster party? Don't you have a date you can bring?"

"I want you to come."

"I'm not going to go. Thanks anyway. I have to pick my

daughter up from school soon, and then I'm making dinner for my family. I love them."

"I know you do." Colin sighed.

Lucille hung up the phone.

Six beautiful girls danced in a long, straight line across the elegant hotel's stage. Their hair was done up high on their heads. The *bodhrán* drums thundered, players strummed guitars fast, and the notes leapt from flutes and fiddles. The girls' upper bodies never moved as all of them kicked into the air and then back down again. Their shoes hit the glossy wood stage. The light of the brilliant glass-and-gold chandeliers shone on their red hair and made their skin pink with youth.

Colin watched them from his table. Their traditional Irish dance was for him, a gift from Tom. Colin sat back in his new tuxedo and new shiny, black shoes. He was thirty years old.

The day Colin turned thirty Tom threw him a huge party out in the quaint New York countryside. Tom gave him a brand-new silver gun as a gift. Everyone at the party, which consisted of the organization and their families and friends, clapped and smiled when Colin opened the present. Up until then Colin had been using one of Errol's old Colts. Tom bragged to the room that Colin was a natural when it came to shooting, but Colin hadn't divulged that his granny had taught him in Kilrea. He also received a box of solid gold bullets and an elegant leather carrying case that would hold his new gun.

From Jarlath he received a motorcycle jacket, identical to Jarlath's own.

And from Errol he got a modern black telephone. "We've arranged for you to have your own line, so that now we can ring you for business, instead of you always having to stop by."

Tom's wife presented him with a masculine gold ring. She gently put the heavy ring over his finger. When he felt the warmth of her closeness, heard the comforting lilt in her voice, and smelt her lingering perfume, like lilacs, he closed his eyes. She reminded him of his mother, who was now faraway and might be long gone, for all he knew.

"Now you are truly family," she said.

Family, because Tom and Errol, and every man in the gang, wore the same gold ring. Colin finally belonged somewhere again.

"Let's toast!" Tom said to the guests in his thunderous voice.

All of the guests clapped and a few of the men whistled. Tom had arranged for good wine to be served throughout the evening. The men at the party were too polite to mention that all most of them really wanted was a pint of Guinness.

"What's he trying to do? Is he trying to be like the Italians?" Ronan joked to Colin.

The women liked the wine, but most of the men, including Colin, couldn't wait until the cake was served and eaten so they could head over to the pubs in the city for the remainder of the night. But they would stay for Tom's toast and the cake.

The headwaiter, a tall, thin man, carried out a bottle of *Taittinger*. He opened the bottle, the cork flew off, and then he shot Errol in the chest.

It happened so fast Colin didn't know what was going on until it was almost over. At first, he couldn't tell the difference between the sound of the cork popping off the bottle and the gunshots being fired. The headwaiter uncorked the champagne and as it overflowed from the bottle, he drew a black gun out of his waiter's jacket. He dropped the bottle on the table and it shattered some of the crystal glasses. The champagne streamed down to the carpet. Then he turned to Tom's left, where Errol sat gulping wine and laughing with sensuous Angela.

And maybe Angie really did love Errol, because when Errol collapsed to the floor after the headwaiter fired the bullets, she cried as she held his head in her hands. Blood ran down both sides of Errol's chest and turned the hotel's white carpet bright red. Bubbles of blood popped around his mouth. Errol's eyelids fluttered.

Angie must have kissed Errol on his face a dozen times, and she kept wailing, "Please, Lord, make him be okay. He's only thirty-two."

By then everyone who had gathered in the ballroom for Colin's birthday stood around the couple and tried to help Errol.

The headwaiter dropped his gun in panic as though he wasn't a professional killer, and Colin chased him through the red-carpeted lobby, past the shocked hotel workers, and outside to the dark expanse of the parking lot. Colin glanced over his shoulder and saw Ronan and Jarlath close behind him. He ripped off his bowtie and loaded his new gun as he ran. He cursed when a few of the expensive bullets fell to the ground.

The cold air bit into his skin and pushed on his lungs. He glanced at the sky and could see stars, which he rarely saw in the city.

Jarlath and Ronan caught up to him.

"Why did this bloke shoot Errol?" Ronan said.

"Maybe he didn't like the way Errol looked," Jarlath replied not without sarcasm.

"Think Errol will make it?" Colin asked.

"He's been shot before and made it," Ronan said. "He can be an arse sometimes, but I hope he makes it. Tom won't be the same if he doesn't. At least you get to try out your new gun."

Jarlath gestured toward the direction of the man they were chasing. "That bastard is determined."

Colin and Ronan grunted in agreement.

The only light was from the stars and it was difficult to see the headwaiter as he ran into the woods that surrounded the parking lot. Colin cursed under his breath. His chest felt heavy as they continued to run after the man. The icy air kept pressing on his lungs. He had already drunk a lot at the party, as had the other two, and the presumably sober waiter had an extra advantage over all of them.

Colin was determined as well, and not because he was in a hurry to retaliate for Errol, but more so because he feared anyone getting away from him. He broke into a sprint and lost sight of Ronan and Jarlath as he exited the parking lot and entered the woods after the waiter. He could hardly see well enough to move freely among the thick, sharp mass of trees.

"Even if I don't catch you tonight, you're a dead man anyway," he shouted out to the darkness. "We'll find you no matter what, especially if you've killed our friend."

Colin didn't consider Errol a friend, but he considered Tom one, and Errol was Tom's son. The headwaiter didn't answer, but Colin thought he could hear him panting up ahead. Colin could see a bright highway in the distance, and the waiter had stopped at the side of the road. There must have been dozens of cars driving fast along the highway. The headwaiter wouldn't be able to get across without being hit by one of them. Colin ceased running as he waited for the man to decide what to do next. He turned in Colin's direction and Colin went closer and aimed his gun at the man's head.

The waiter's eyes went wide as he looked at Colin and then at the gun. Then he charged straight into the traffic. Horns blared and cars swerved. Metal hit and crushed his body.

The headwaiter was sprawled and bloody in the center of the highway. The cars had come to a halt around the man with their lights shining on his mangled remains. They beeped their horns and a few people screamed inside their cars.

Ronan and Jarlath reached Colin.

"What the hell happened?" Jarlath asked.

Colin explained. "I didn't even have to shoot him. He ran out into the road."

"He did himself in," Ronan said.

Blood trickled out of the man's mouth. His eyes had rolled back into his head, and it looked like pieces of his brain were coming out of him. There were large bloody gashes all over his face. His arm had become detached from the rest of his body during the accident and had landed a few feet from him on the road. When people started exiting their cars, Colin knew it was time to leave.

"Tom will want proof he's dead," Ronan said.

"What should we do? Run into the highway and carry him back in pieces?" Jarlath joked.

"I think we ought to leave him," Colin said. "He's dead, and he's not going to get any deader than this. The police are going to come any second, and I wouldn't want Tom and his family dragged into this. Tom will have to take our word for it."

Jarlath let out a low whistle. "Look at you, lording over our man Tom." He grinned at Colin.

Ronan didn't say anything but raised an eyebrow at Colin. "Are we going to have trouble later, Ronan?" Colin asked.

"No. Let's go back."

They took their time returning to the upscale hotel.

"I'm fecking tired from all that running," Jarlath commented on the way.

"I could use a drink," Ronan said. "It's too bad we never got to have your cake, Colin."

"I could use a drink as well," Jarlath said. "How about you, Colin? Could you use a drink? How about we return to the city and go to *Byrne's*? Sorry your party ended like shite."

Colin nodded. "But first we have to make sure Errol isn't

dead. And if he isn't, we're going to the hospital to see how his family is. And if he is then we're going to the pub."

The two other men nodded in agreement at his simple reasoning.

The ambulance had already taken Errol away, and his family had followed in their cars. None of the three men would admit it aloud, but Colin sensed they were all a little disappointed that Errol wasn't dead when they heard the news. Not because they despised him, but because now they'd be stuck at some rural hospital for the rest of the evening with an emotional and unpredictable Angela and a temperamental Tom, and the three of them still sobering up and weary.

Colin, Ronan, and Jarlath rode in Ronan's car, which smelled like new leather, to the hospital. Ronan parked in the tree-lined visitor's lot. Errol had been pronounced dead by a doctor a few minutes before they arrived. But Colin knew Errol's fate as soon as he stepped into the waiting room. Sensing tragedy had become natural to him over the years. Angela sat on a chair, crying softly, being comforted by Ronan's wife. Tom was slumped over in his chair with his arm around his wife, who sobbed. Tom stared straight ahead. He wasn't crying, and he didn't look broken but rather hungry for revenge. Ronan, who had known Tom the longest, embraced Tom and his wife.

Angela looked up at Colin. "He's dead. My Errol's dead."

"I'm so sorry, Angie." Colin patted her shoulder.

Colin stepped over to Tom and gave him his condolences. He reported on the shooter's demise. "Ronan, Jarlath and me took care of the bastard who did this. We chased him to the expressway, and the coward ran out and got hit by a car rather than having us shoot him. He was torn to shreds, Tom. He suffered greatly."

The family, including the women, smiled at the news.

The hard look on Tom's face softened a little. "Thank you."

An hour later, Colin looked at the seated mourners and didn't know where he belonged, perhaps at the pub. The strange odors of the hospital bothered him.

"*Byrne's?*" Colin said to Jarlath as they stood by the coffee machine in the hallway.

"Sure." Jarlath knocked back the remainder of his coffee and threw the cup into the garbage can.

Jarlath nudged Ronan who was leaning against the wall. "Want to go to the pub?"

"Let's go."

They went outside to Ronan's car in the parking lot. "I feel terrible for Tom and his family, but I'm glad we're finally leaving. I didn't think I could stand being around all that death much longer. If my old lady wants to stay, she can, but I said to her, *I'm* taking the car. I'll pick her up later and take her home."

"I know what you mean. It gets to your head." Jarlath looked over at Colin who had been quiet.

Colin didn't respond. He couldn't get enough of the stars in the sky.

They returned to the hotel to collect Colin's gifts. Colin had felt comfortable leaving them there because he knew no one would dare steal from Tom's party.

They spent an hour at Byrne's that night. Colin called Lucille from the phone booth near his apartment.

"Lucille," he said when she answered.

"Colin, it's two o'clock in the morning," she whispered.

"I know. I'm sorry."

"I asked you not to call me again."

"I didn't have anyone else to call. It's my birthday."

She sighed. "Happy birthday."

"I killed somebody."

"What do you mean you 'killed' . . ."

"I got them killed. Did you hear the news about Tom McPhalen's son, Errol?"

"No. What about him?"

"He was killed tonight. We chased after the fellow who shot Errol, and the guy ran into traffic and was killed."

"If he hadn't done that then you would've shot him, wouldn't you?"

"Yeah, I would have had to."

"Please don't tell me more. I shouldn't know more. God knows I know too much already."

"I was thinking of you earlier."

"While this man was dying?" she snapped at him.

"No. At the party Tom gave me. You weren't there to celebrate with me. I missed you."

"Are you drunk?"

"Of course I am. It's my birthday." He chuckled a little. "Can I see you?"

"Now?"

"I'll come to where you are, or meet you halfway."

"No. No. It's two in the morning. My husband is sleeping. Oh, no. He's awake. I have to go. Don't call me again. I won't answer the phone. You're a good man, Colin, get away from Tom McPhalen."

He spoke as if he hadn't heard her. "Will your husband answer if I call again? I'll talk to him if he does. I'll let him know how much I care about you. Why doesn't he ever answer the phone? Is he afraid of me?"

"Colin, don't." Lucille ended the call.

A year went by and Errol's death still hung in the air. The police had treated Errol as simply a victim, and since the headwaiter had died in what they deemed a suicide, the case wasn't being actively investigated. Errol's mother made an elaborate shrine to him in the living room. Colin couldn't step inside Tom's house without encountering the gold-framed photograph of Errol surrounded by tall red candles, which smelled like cheap perfume. Every time Colin visited Tom's house, the scent of the candles caught in his throat. Errol's favorite black hat rested on top of the picture frame, and a dried four-leaf clover that his mother had saved from Ireland was displayed in front of the photograph. After Errol's death, traditional Irish music played on and off from a record player in the house.

It turned out that the headwaiter and Errol had a past. The man's brother had owed Tom money, and the brother had been killed by Errol. So the man had arranged to work at the party in order to shoot Errol for revenge.

Colin thought a lot about Johnny after the deaths. Once in a while he'd see Johnny on the street and they'd say hello, but otherwise they didn't acknowledge that years ago they had been good friends. They still hadn't had a real conversation.

Colin had heard Johnny quit the mechanic's shop and was now working with an up-and-coming street gangster named Tito Bernal – who had become a hero of sorts for the Bowery's Cuban residents. Johnny was running a gambling operation for Bernal and enforcing. He had married Bernal's daughter, Lila, a few months ago, and they had a baby girl. Johnny was living with Lila and her mother farther up on the East Side. The mother was divorced from Tito Bernal, who had remarried.

Colin stopped by the pier that ran along the East River one Friday evening in September to see if Johnny might be there. They had frequented the pier as children, and Colin heard Johnny still visited the now decaying place to fish or smoke a cigarette and escape his mother-in-law. Tom was worried about Tito Bernal moving in on the Bowery, and Colin had told Tom one of his childhood friends worked with Bernal. He promised he'd have a chat with the friend to see if he could obtain information on Bernal's motives.

The air wasn't quite cool. A damp smell, which Colin liked, came from the river. It reminded him of the old days before his father died. For a while he sat on a thick piece of rotting wood stained green with algae close to the water's edge and looked across at Brooklyn. Then he rose from the log and sat on the dirty ground cross-legged, like he had done as a boy. Out of the corner of his eye he thought he saw a shadow. He looked sideways and saw nothing. Brooklyn seemed so close that he tried to reach out and hold it, but he couldn't. The bright city shone on the gentle, flowing water.

"Colin?"

He turned around.

"Colin?" Johnny stood a few feet behind him.

Colin rose and tried to act surprised to see his old friend. "Johnny. What are you doing here?" He smiled.

"I come here a lot to escape the chaos in my home. If you haven't already heard, I got married again." Johnny walked closer.

He sounded upbeat, he sounded the same, but Colin hardly recognized his old friend. Johnny dressed just like him. He had styled hair and wore a gold watch, and he seemed wealthier and more sophisticated. Colin couldn't recall his childhood friend wearing anything except jeans but now he wore a suit.

"I did hear, actually. Congratulations." Colin stood up to shake Johnny's hand. They embraced and Colin patted his back. "I wanted to send you a gift for this one, but I didn't know the address."

"Thanks, but don't worry about it."

Colin downplayed his friend's insult with a chuckle. "Come on, you don't want a gift? That's not like you. Maybe it is like you now. I don't really know you anymore." He tried to keep his emotions in check. "Congratulations on the new baby as well."

"Thanks." Johnny glanced at the river. "So how come you're out here?"

Colin shrugged and looked at the river. "Just sitting, thinking. I haven't been here in a long time, not since we were boys. I wanted to see how it looked these days. Remember we used to come here as boys?"

"I do. Thinking. That's a good thing to do. I ought to try that myself sometime." He laughed.

Colin laughed along with him. "Are you going to go on home to your woman now or what?" he teased.

Johnny smiled and played along. "Are you trying to tell me something? You trying to kick me out?"

"I'm not sure yet." Colin grinned.

"I was going to stay here for a bit, if that's all right. Sorry if you wanted to be alone. I can go somewhere else if you want to be alone."

"I don't mind the company. We haven't spoken in a long time. How are you?"

Johnny gestured to the ground. "Actually, can we sit down?" Colin nodded and sat with him as they had done as boys. "I'm doing all right," Johnny said.

Colin wasn't going to ask him to elaborate. He concluded, as he sat on the sand-and-rock ground with shards of old broken glass, Johnny wasn't going to give him much else. They had been boyhood friends, great friends, but that didn't mean they were friends now.

Instead, Colin remarked, "Isn't this peculiar? Here we are, both in suits, and we're sitting in the dirt."

Johnny smiled. "How've you been?" he asked after a moment.

"I'm all right. I'm not married."

"I remember when we were younger how you were always after older women. Remember Lucille?"

"I can't believe you remember her name."

"She helped us that night so it's not like I'll ever forget her."

"That stays between us." Colin used a serious tone.

Johnny nodded. "Of course."

"I appreciate that."

"Have you spoken to her since your release? She married a cop."

"I have," Colin said. "The guy's now the chief of police where they live. They have a daughter."

Johnny whistled.

"I've spoken to her only a little," Colin said. "She doesn't really want to talk to me. She said I should move on."

"I'm sorry to hear that. What about other women? Anything good to tell me?"

There seemed to be a tinge of longing in Johnny's voice, as if he wanted to live the unmarried life again, and not be tied down by a wife and child, no matter how pretty and adoring his wife was and how sweet his child.

"There's this one, she works as a cigarette girl at one of the nightclubs we do business with..." Colin stopped when he realized it wouldn't be appropriate to brag about a particular woman's assets, because if he told Johnny then Johnny might tell someone else, and so on. "She's very sweet. Cute, you know."

"She's sweet? Cute? That's all you're going to tell me? You know who you're talking to, right?"

"I sure do. All right. I'll tell you. But don't go spreading it around to everyone."

Johnny crossed his fingers. "*Scout's honor.*"

Colin smiled and crossed his fingers. Scout's honor. Like when they were boys. Colin hadn't said that in a long time. He hadn't been making many innocent promises lately.

Colin told Johnny about some of the women he'd been with in the past year.

"I'd like to try that sometime." Johnny grinned.

"But don't you have a pretty wife now? I heard she's very pretty."

"She is. But it's hard to be with the same woman every night. That's not something you would understand."

Colin laughed a little then became somber. "We never got to know each other again after I got out."

"You regret it?"

"I do. You?"

"Yeah."

"Are you happy? I mean, not just with your lady, but do you like the way things are shaping up with Bernal?" Colin asked delicately.

"Of course I'm happy. I make good money, and I'm respected. It's what I've wanted forever, and what I deserve."

Johnny's tone surprised Colin but he admired his confidence. "I spent my youth ashamed of who I am. But now I'm—we, my people—are finally getting some of the respect we deserve around here." Johnny held his head high.

"You should come work with me," Colin suggested. He feared that if Tom went to war with Tito Bernal, something could befall Johnny, and not something good. It'd be easier on Colin's conscience for him to work with Johnny rather than spy on him. Johnny had helped him with Carmine, and Colin cared what happened to him. "It would be like the old times. Remember the enterprise we were going to start? With McPhalen, we can—"

"Our enterprise was the dream of boys," Johnny said. "It was a joke."

Colin hadn't viewed their plans that way.

"Anyway, I'm Cuban," Johnny said. "You know I'll get nowhere with the Irish."

"I'll talk to Tom. I'll see what I can do. You're half Irish."

"The only difference is your Irish will never see me as Irish enough. It's the same as you could never work for Tito."

"But I'm not Cuban."

"Well, I'm not Irish. At least, not Irish enough for Tom McPhalen. Don't bother talking to him. Guys like him will never be convinced. My Cuban brothers have accepted me despite my Irish half. I am glad to see you seem to like working for McPhalen."

"I love working for Tom."

"Love. That's a strong word."

Colin couldn't tell if Johnny was trying to pick a fight. The gangster in him thought so, but the good friend wanted not to believe it.

"I do love it."

"All right."

"You don't believe me?"

Johnny faced the river instead of Colin. "No, I believe you. But they're not Northern Irish like you. And how happy can you be if you're still living in our old building and you're still drinking at *Byrne's*? Yeah, I know these things, Colin."

"I like *Byrne's*. I'm not married like you so I don't mind living where I do. I like living in the Bowery. Anyway, I'm just one of Tom's soldiers. There are other guys who work for him who are ranked higher than me. I'll get promoted someday. You're married to Bernal's daughter, so of course you're living better than me," Colin challenged. "It must be fun living with your wife's mother," he joked.

Colin didn't want a fight, and Johnny must have sensed it because he laughed.

Johnny shrugged. "She's got nowhere else to go. I don't want to talk business anymore. Do you want to come over to my place for dinner? You can meet my wife. Just keep your charm to yourself." He grinned. "Her mother's a mean bitch sometimes, but she's also a mean cook."

Colin chuckled. "When am I invited?"

"Tonight. You're free?"

"I'm always free to eat."

They got up to walk to Johnny's place and passed by *McShane's* bakery on the way. The McShanes didn't own it anymore, the Santiagos did. The McShane family had sold the business to them last year. The Irish and the Italians in the Bowery were dispersing to places such as Long Island, Queens, and Staten Island.

Johnny nudged Colin out of his daydream. "Do you remember Mrs. McShane?"

"How could I forget her? She was beautiful. We were practically in love with her."

"*You* were in love with her. Remember being a boy? Seems like such a long time ago, doesn't it? We had some hard times then, too, for sure, but less to worry about then."

Colin had a feeling Johnny meant their fathers, and Carmine. "Remember when we'd get beer and then sell it to the rich kids in Murray Hill for double the price?"

Colin laughed. "I remember." Then he said, "She moved away, didn't she?"

"Who did?"

"Mrs. McShane."

"I think she and her husband moved to Staten Island."

"Lots of the Irish and Italians moved away."

"To make room for us."

Colin ignored his comment. "How's your mother doing?"

"She's doing good. She still lives on the same street in the same apartment even though I gave her money so she could move into a nicer place. She likes things to stay the same, kind of like you."

Johnny smiled. "I know your family moved away. Sorry about that."

"Do you know what happened to them after I left?"

"Danny helped them. And I pitched in when I could."

"Thanks, Johnny."

"But I think it was still hard for them. I think it was just easier for them to leave. Do you think you'll visit them?"

"I've thought about it, and I'd like to. I know Danny still lives in the States. But I'm so busy now. I'd like to send Maureen, Patrick, and my mother money."

"You can never be too busy for family, or for friends." Johnny glanced at him.

"Sometimes I feel like an old man. I don't even have a steady girl yet, but maybe I want to be a family man. I feel like I have to rush everything because I missed out on what could've been my best years. Did I ever tell you I wanted to be a policeman when I was little? Maybe I can get a job as a cop someday."

"So that Lucille might leave her husband for you?" Johnny had seen right through him. "What about her kid?"

"I'd raise her child as my own."

"You're not planning on killing her husband, are you?" Johnny said seriously.

"No, of course not." Then Colin grinned. "At least, I don't think so."

Johnny shook his head and chuckled. "Anyway, you don't want to rush into marriage. I know from experience. And with your murder conviction, you can't be a cop. It's nothing to be ashamed of. I got one for thieving."

"I don't get what happened to Lucille. She's a completely different person."

"I heard her husband introduced her to religion."

"I know plenty of people who are religious and they still drink."

"The difference is most of them can stop drinking when they want to, like us. It's different for an alcoholic. She didn't know when to stop. She couldn't stop."

"Religion helped her stop?"

"Something like that."

"I visited Lucille right after I got out of prison. She didn't like seeing me."

"I'm sorry to hear that."

"She said she'd moved on. Did I already tell you that?"

Johnny nodded. "Speaking of moving, I've been thinking about relocating. Lila wants to move to Long Island."

Had Johnny changed the subject to lighten the mood?

"Do you really think it's a good idea to move all the way out there? You'd be stuck out there. At least in the city you can escape once in a while."

"Women like houses. We'd still keep our apartment in the city."

Johnny must have been making more money than him. Colin kept talking as though he hadn't heard Johnny. "When I visited Lucille on the Island, I felt trapped, and I was only there for a little while. It seems like it'd be hard to sneak out of the house to clear your head."

"I kind of am already trapped. She's my wife. The mother of my child. She's always going to be there. Anyway, she's dead set on going."

Colin spoke more about his visit to Lucille.

"Funny how she's married to the chief of police, especially how she helped us with that thing with Carmine," Johnny said.

"What's that supposed to mean?" Colin said.

"It means she probably hasn't been honest with her husband."

"Or she has and he stays silent to protect her."

"Because he loves her?"

"Yeah, maybe he really does. I don't think he knows about that night though."

"Why do you think that?"

"Something she said. I hope he does love her."

"But not like you loved her, from what I remember."

"That was a long time ago."

"Some feelings don't change."

As they got closer to Johnny's apartment, Johnny seemed to hold his breath. Colin watched his childhood friend and wondered, when had he become such a man? When had they both become such men? Was it from hearing and seeing all that they had so early on in life? Or had the pollution from the river seeped into their blood over time and ruined them like it had ruined all the fish?

Colin sighed.

"What's the matter?" Johnny asked.

"Ah, nothing. I just need some escaping, that's all."

Two pretty young women went by and their hips swayed as they strolled.

"Is that what you need escaping from?" Johnny said.

Colin smiled. "That's it." Johnny could always make him feel better.

Johnny lived in a well-maintained red-brick building. Despite Colin's past friendship with Johnny, he kept his fingers lightly touching the gun in his camel-hair coat's pocket as they went upstairs to the third floor. After all, Johnny worked with Bernal.

Lila's mother answered the door. It was then that Colin took his hand off his gun. The woman was small, a good foot shorter than him, with a neat bun of gray-brown hair. She looked younger than Colin had imagined, and she wore a plain housedress and flat black shoes. Her eyes were bright and kind.

Lila didn't surprise him. She was petite, sweet-natured and pretty, just the kind of girl he knew Johnny, who could be soft at heart, would eventually marry. She had short hair, cut almost all the way to her ears, and beautiful bone structure. Her skin glowed, and her large brown eyes were framed by very long lashes. She had a patient smile.

Colin had thanked Lila's mother for letting him have dinner with her family, but he spent a little more time speaking with Lila. "Johnny is a lucky man." He looked at Johnny, and when his friend gave him permission he kissed Lila's soft hand.

She blushed. "It's good to finally meet you. Johnny speaks fondly of you."

That surprised Colin. He couldn't tell if she was being polite or if Johnny did talk about him at home.

Lila stood on her toes and kissed Johnny in the doorway. She gestured for them to enter the home.

"The baby's asleep in the bedroom," she whispered.

Johnny told Colin that his daughter shared a name with her mother.

The large, tidy apartment, a big upgrade from Johnny's childhood home, smelled of food, and Colin's nose went wild. He smelled spices he'd never come across before.

Lila's mother beckoned them to the table. "Please, have a seat." She spoke English with a heavy accent.

A colorful array of food had been set out on the kitchen table overcrowded with chairs. Yellow rice and chicken with what looked like red peppers.

"The saffron makes it yellow," Johnny explained. "Just take what I take and you'll do fine." He handed Colin a plate.

When Lila's mother sat it appeared as if there'd be no room

for anyone to move even an inch. Colin watched as Johnny ladled chicken from the largest dish first, and he took a generous helping after Johnny. After Johnny scooped the yellow rice onto his plate, Colin followed.

"Ready to eat?" Johnny said.

Colin stared at his plate and nodded.

"Drink?" Lila's mother asked Colin. "Yeah, thanks."

"Rum or cola?"

"I guess I'll have rum, please."

Lila smiled at him. "Are you uncertain, Colin?"

Colin couldn't help but warm a little on the inside. It had been a long time since a girl had teased him.

"He's not used to rum," Johnny said. "The Irish don't drink it very much. Isn't that right, Colin?"

He laughed at his friend's joke.

Many glasses of rum were served. Colin drank his first glass, and had another, and another and then another, to prove he wasn't ignorant. He lost count of how many glasses he'd had. Lila congratulated him on having such a high tolerance. Colin insisted the Irish were born with that. Johnny laughed and said if that was true, then he must have had only half of the tolerance. Before Colin knew it, he was joking with Lila's mother.

"Eat, handsome." She put more chicken on his plate and patted his shoulder.

Colin beamed at her. He hadn't shared a meal with Johnny in forever, and he hadn't been this complacent since they were boys. Perhaps it wasn't a coincidence that the two events were occurring together.

"Colin," Lila said. "I thought I loved you."

The room spun around Colin. Had he really had that much rum? He laughed at her joke.

"I'm not kidding. I thought I loved you," she said, again.

Colin laughed again. "That's very funny. I don't think Johnny will be very happy to hear that though."

"I'm not joking," she said, and he realized she wasn't. Colin didn't say anything and glanced at Johnny.

"I don't love you now, but when Johnny talked about you I loved you based on his description." Lila's eyes lit up, and she giggled and kissed Johnny's face.

Johnny seemed flushed with anger. He put his arm around his wife. "That's enough, baby. You've had too much to drink. You should go to bed now."

Lila pushed Johnny off her. "Don't touch me. Damn you. I didn't want to marry you. I don't even think of you as my husband. If you hadn't gotten me pregnant, I wouldn't have married you. Don't boss me around, I don't like it."

Without warning, and to the surprise of Colin, but not Lila's mother, Johnny reached out and smacked Lila. In silence he rose from the table, trembling. Colin wondered if he would leave the apartment and slam the door. Lila put her hand to her face and cursed Johnny. Their child started crying in the bedroom.

Colin sobered up quickly. He had never seen his old friend so angry at a woman, and he couldn't help but feeling at fault. After all, the cause of the slap had been over something Lila had said to him.

Colin got up and went over to Johnny. He lightly touched his shoulder. "I think I should leave now."

"No, stay. She always gets like this when she drinks. She says strange things." His voice was higher than it had been, and he sounded like a boy again.

Colin gave an excuse. "It's getting late. I have to go to Brooklyn early tomorrow for business."

He thanked the women for hosting him. Johnny's mother-in-law got up and went into the bedroom to check on the crying child. Then Colin looked at Johnny again. "You take care of yourself. If you ever need anything, or change your mind about what I suggested, come see me." He hadn't mentioned Tom again until then because he didn't want to seem like he had ulterior motives for their reunion.

Johnny nodded but didn't say anything.

Colin put on his hat and coat and walked out of the apartment. He went down the stairway without his hand on his gun. He remembered when they were boys but knew everything had changed. They were no longer carefree, wild boys but hardened men. If only they could start over.

11

Everything changed again in December when Ronan McDuff got killed. There had been a war a month before, a month after Colin had dinner at Johnny's. Tito Bernal and his Tigers versus Tom and his Salthill men. Ronan got caught up in the middle. One night he was drinking with Colin and Jarlath at *Deegan's*, and the next night he was found face-down on the sidewalk in front of the place. Six bullets in the back. Only cowards shot someone in the back.

Tom and everyone else in the gang swore revenge so Colin did too. Colin wondered how Johnny could have let something like that happen. They'd had a drink together only last week at Colin's apartment, and Johnny hadn't mentioned anything telling. Colin questioned his own allegiance. If Tom sent out an order that might get Johnny killed or harm him or his family in some way, would Colin warn him beforehand? Johnny had been his childhood friend, but that was long ago. Still, they had been close. On the other hand, Tom was Colin's boss, and the man he aspired to be someday.

Ronan's niece Maggie was at her uncle's funeral, cute Maggie from back when Colin had shown her around the Bowery when she was an eighteen-year-old girl. Colin talked to her for a while at the reception, and she mentioned she was attending college in Yonkers. But she had become conceited and wasn't interested in him or his life anymore. She made Colin feel like an old man. He gave her his condolences and offered to buy her a cup of coffee later in the week, and she declined and said she "didn't get into Manhattan much anymore."

He told her she never had.

"We're going to get them." Tom pounded his fist on the table at the funeral reception at the McDuffs' building, causing the delicate Waterford crystal bowl filled with white-and-red mints to move. He steadied the bowl with his hand.

Both had liked Ronan, but while Jarlath grunted in approval, Colin remained quiet in his seat.

Tom looked around at his men seated at the table in the private room. "Things shouldn't have ended like this for Ronan." His face flushed a deep red, and his blue eyes were aflame. "It starts tomorrow."

When Tom dismissed the men from the meeting, Colin stood in a corner with Jarlath at the reception. Mrs McDuff bawled on the couch, and everyone else got drunk, including Colin and Jarlath, who drank from the flasks of scotch they'd brought with them.

"I always knew something like this would happen to Ronan," Mrs McDuff told the woman comforting her. "This is why we never had children. I didn't want them to have to go through this."

"What'll happen to Ronan's wife?" Colin asked Jarlath.

"Her family's well off. Still, Tom will look out for her. We all will. That's usually how things are done when one of us dies. Can you imagine she survived polio as a child and now this?" Jarlath paused. "You're friends with that Garcia bloke who leads with Bernal, aren't you?"

"Many years ago we were friends."

"Is that going to be hard for you?"

What choice did Colin have but to say no? It wasn't as if he could opt out on this one. "No. You guys come first. Always."

"Thanks, Colin. You know, Tom's pretty much a mess over this whole thing. In our life this shite happens but I guess he never thought Ronan would, you know."

"I know."

"Of course, Ronan was his top man. That's bound to have him mad as hell. Ronan was a top man in spirit too."

"He was."

"Still, it's not so surprising how it ended for him. It's not like this is the kind of business most are able to retire from."

Colin wondered about their own fates and was glad he had the scotch to take the edge off.

Someone's glass fell to the floor. Jarlath and Colin both turned around at the same time. For a moment Colin had thought it was Errol, because he'd always dropped things when he was drunk. Then he remembered Errol was dead as well. The man who had dropped the glass got on his knees and picked up the pieces.

Later, as Colin left the reception with Jarlath and Little Bill, Tom followed them outside and said, "I want to see you all at ten in the morning. Come at ten or don't bother to ever come near me again."

"Is that ten tomorrow or ten today?" An intoxicated Little Bill joked.

Tom glared at him. "Ten today."

Tom called Colin aside on the street. Colin watched Jarlath and Little Bill as they started to walk downtown in the middle of the quiet, dark road, not bothering to check for cars, their bodies swaying with the power of the drink.

Colin hesitated then faced his boss under the streetlamp's

glare. Even in his drunken haze he sensed Tom wanted to discuss Johnny, and it filled him with dread. He had been anticipating the talk for the entire day. He knew Tom might make him prove his devotion.

Tom didn't want to talk on the sidewalk or on the steps of the McDuffs' building so they went back inside where it was warm, and cigarette smoke and anxious chatter permeated the room. Liquor didn't stay long in glasses before it was swallowed. The reception had been tense the entire night, but Colin recognized it even more so now that he'd gone outside and then returned.

"Want another drink?" Tom asked.

"I'm all right, thanks."

"I'm going to get one for myself."

Tom's eyes seemed kind but Colin knew better than to fall for that.

As he waited, he looked around the reception at those who remained. Were they the dedicated few? Were they the ones who had loved Ronan McDuff the most, and that's why they'd stayed? Or just the souls who wanted more free booze? Were they the ones who didn't have friends or family to go to the pub with, the ones who wanted someone to drink with?

A girl in a dark blue dress stared at him. She looked very young, around fifteen or sixteen years old. She had curly dark hair and soft green eyes. Colin winked at her and she frowned. Then he was disgusted with himself, and he wondered if he should go over and apologize to her, explain his behavior was due to his drunkenness.

Tom returned with a glass of what looked like whiskey. "Were you dreaming?" He smiled.

"No."

Tom seemed like he didn't believe him. "I'm sure you can catch up with the other lads at the pub later. The reason I asked you to stay behind is I understand one of Bernal's top men is an old friend of yours, the one you told me about. A while back, you mentioned him and I asked you to try to get information out of him."

"I'm sorry I wasn't able to get anything substantial for you. This fellow is smart. He caught on to me. About this guy, we were friends a long time ago when we were boys. Like I said, that was a long time ago." It stung for him to refer to Johnny with such indifference.

Tom drank from his glass. "Is this going to be an issue for you? This is a war, and people die in wars."

Colin felt Tom watching him and started to sweat. He cleared his throat and closed his eyes for a moment. Was this a war? It wasn't the same war Danny had been so eager to fight in Europe and the Pacific. What really defined a war, and if Tom's war wasn't a war then what was it? A game?

Colin opened his eyes to find Tom staring at him. "There'll be no trouble from me. I'm with you and that comes first."

Tom nodded and patted his back. "It's settled, then. You're going to the pub now, like the rest of the lads?"

"Yeah."

Tom chuckled. "I don't know how you young lads can drink that much well into the morning."

"It isn't too hard," Colin said under his breath.

Snowflakes fell outside on the sidewalk. Ten days until Christmas. Colin remembered how before he'd gone to prison he'd walk past the Christmas trees for sale in the street and smell the pine. His family never had a tree because there wasn't enough money to buy something non-essential, and he vowed the family he'd start someday would have a tall tree every year. Would he ever start that family?

When was the last time Colin had celebrated Christmas? His first year with Tom they'd had a Christmas party. Tom had given everyone at the party an entire crate of English cigarettes.

That crate was long gone now. It had only lasted Colin a few months.

He didn't head to the pub but he didn't return home. It seemed pointless sleeping when he'd be working so soon. He contemplated seeking the services of a prostitute then he chuckled to himself when he remembered how many numbers he had. He could call any of those girls from a drugstore phone booth, and he knew five who'd come there that instant to meet him in the middle of the street. But he didn't want that tonight. Maybe he just wanted to go to the pub after all, where those who had gone earlier would be more than drunk by now, and slurring and ranting, and maybe even crying about the death of Ronan McDuff. But he couldn't imagine any of those guys with tears.

"Hello? Hello, I'm talking to you!"

Colin turned around to see who'd shouted at him. Johnny's wife stood behind him on the sidewalk. "What are you doing in this neighborhood?" he asked.

"I'm going home," Lila said.

"From where? It's dangerous to walk around here at night. Does Johnny know you're here?"

"What are you, some kind of detective? I didn't follow you so don't worry." She smirked. "Johnny doesn't get to keep a leash on me."

Colin winked at her. "I don't doubt it."

"I've been out, trying to escape the commotion in my apartment with my mother and kid in there. Do you know what I mean?"

"I don't have children, and I haven't seen my mother in years, but if I had, I think I'd understand."

"I'm sure the right woman for you will come along soon and you'll have kids someday."

Colin smiled.

"I'm sorry to hear about your mother," Lila said. "Where is she?"

"I heard she returned home, but I'm not sure. When I got out of prison, she was gone. The rest of my family were gone too."

"Johnny mentioned you were in prison for a long time."

"I was. Did you leave Johnny at home?" Colin didn't want to get too personal with Johnny's wife.

"Heck no. My mother's watching little Lila. Johnny doesn't come home much anymore, and when he is home, he doesn't stay long."

"I'm sorry, Lila."

She shrugged. "We weren't in love. We never should have gotten married. My father pushed us into it."

He noticed her beauty more in the night, highlighted by the dim lights of the quiet city. Her wide-set brown eyes, and full lips painted the color of deep red. Her dark hair. When he first saw her he'd thought she was pretty, but tonight she looked beautiful.

"Do you feel like getting a drink?" Getting to know Johnny's wife wouldn't help Colin make peace with what might happen to Johnny, but he reasoned he'd look after her and her child if something happened to Johnny, and it wouldn't hurt to know her better.

"Right now? With you?"

"Sure. Why not?"

"Are you hitting on me, Colin O'Brien?"

"Of course not. You're Johnny's wife."

"And that's all I'll ever be anymore, Johnny's wife," Lila said bitterly.

"Don't think that way. It'll only make you sad. You can be whatever you want."

She smiled up at him and entwined his large arm with hers. "Which bar are you taking me to?"

Colin tried to think of a good place to take Johnny's wife for a drink. There weren't many pubs open at this hour and he didn't want to take her some place too dodgy. He glanced up at the sky and the stars were blocked by the tall buildings of midtown in the distance. "Have you ever been to *The Siren*?"

"No, I haven't."

"It's the most decent place that will be open at this hour."

"Decent? You sound like an old lady."

Colin chuckled.

"Is it in the Bowery?" she asked.

Colin shook his head. "It's on Fifteenth Street. Is that too close to where you live?"

"It isn't too close. We're just two friends getting a drink, right? We don't have anything to hide." She winked at him and he knew he was blushing.

They walked the rest of the way in silence. Given the hour, inside *The Siren* was quiet.

"We're closing in ten minutes," a woman called out without looking up from cleaning a table.

"How about we stay for one drink?" Colin asked her.

The woman sighed, but when Colin smiled at her, she said, "Hold on a second. Let me check." She went into a back room and Colin could hear her talking to someone.

"Should we leave?" Lila asked him.

Colin patted her hand. "Let's see what she says."

The woman returned. "The owner says you can stay for a little while." She finally smiled.

The bar was close to the door but she sat them at a private table in the corner. They were the only customers in the place. She gave them drink menus and then left the table.

"This must be a 'decent' place if they have menus for drinks," Lila commented with a smile on her lips.

"I'm buying so please get whatever you want." Colin put his

menu down and watched her read her small menu with her beautiful eyes. He already knew what he wanted to drink.

He ordered a martini, and Lila asked the waitress for a sangria.

When they were alone once again, Lila smiled at him and he wondered what she was thinking. She didn't speak.

Lila was still quiet when the drinks arrived. "How is yours?" Colin asked as she sipped.

"Wonderful. Thanks. Where were you coming from tonight when I ran into you?"

"I was at a reception for a funeral I attended this afternoon."

"I'm sorry to hear that. Was it for a relative? I hope not."

"No." Colin drank his gin martini. He didn't want to drag Lila into the troubles between Tom and her father. "It was for a friend named Ronan McDuff. You or Johnny might've known him from around the Bowery. Johnny knew of him, I'm sure."

"He was Irish?"

Colin nodded. "He worked for Tom McPhalen."

"Like you do."

"Johnny told you?"

Lila shrugged. "Everyone knows."

"How are things between you and Johnny these days?"

"What do you mean?"

"That time I went to your place for dinner—"

"Do you mean, does my husband still hit me? What do you think?"

"I hope he doesn't."

"Your hope is incorrect."

"I'm so sorry, Lila."

"He wasn't like that when I first married him. You should've seen him when he begged me to teach him Spanish. He was a sweet man. Working for my father changed him. Maybe he's been using some of the drugs they sell."

"I'm sorry to hear that." Colin signaled for the waitress to come to their table. He ordered another martini. "Do you want another?" he asked Lila.

"Weren't we only supposed to stay for one?" she whispered to him.

Colin shrugged. "They don't seem to mind."

The waitress smiled at him and lingered for too long. "She likes you," Lila said after the waitress had left.

"Who?"

"Our waitress, she likes you. You don't seem to notice." Lila laughed.

"She doesn't."

"Then why has she been smiling at you the whole time we've been seated?"

"She hasn't been."

"She has. Every time she's come to the table, she's smiled at you. She's never smiled at me once. You can't see her now, but she's smiling at you now too, behind you. You're blushing. I bet a lot of women feel that way about you. You're tall, strong, and handsome, and I'm sure you won't like me saying this, but you're kind of sweet sometimes, like a tall, lumbering boy."

Colin chuckled and imagined he was blushing quite a bit more. "I mean that in a good way," Lila said. "I'm sure you have had— have—lots of women. But here I am, thinking what an interesting man you are and how if I wasn't married, maybe we'd . . ."

"Maybe you'd date me?"

"Yes."

"What's wrong with now?" he teased.

"You're kidding? I'm married to your friend."

"You know more than anyone that Johnny and me aren't friends these days."

"You must be a lonely man, handsome, but lonely, to be chasing after a woman who is married to your boyhood friend."

Colin shrugged because he couldn't admit she was right about him.

"Are you lonely?" she persisted.

"I'm not."

"It can't be easy leaving prison and coming back to everyday life. I would imagine it's quite difficult."

Lila talked smart, and Colin felt like he could actually talk to her.

"It is," he admitted after a while.

"My younger brother got out last year. He's had similar problems."

"Problems?"

"Problems interacting with women."

Colin laughed. "I don't mean to sound rude, but I have no problems interacting with women."

"Sorry, but you do. You're with me, and I can tell."

"You're a lovely woman."

"You've already told me that. Tell me something else."

"Like what?"

"Something other than about my looks."

He stared at her for a moment. "When I'm with you, I'm fine. When I'm not, it's like I have a terrible headache."

Lila watched him in silence as she smiled. "Colin, you hardly know me. You're hardly *with* me."

"I know. That's why most of the time I have a headache." She laughed. Then she glanced at her watch.

"Do you need to go home? It's getting late," he said. "I think they probably want us out of here so they can leave." The waitress had stopped smiling at him.

"Yes. I didn't realize how late it was. I've been having such a good time with you."

"And I'm having a good time with you. Let me walk you home. It's late. It isn't safe." Colin got up after Lila had.

"No."

He took a step back and tried not to look hurt.

"No, because if I let you do that, Colin, I might be tempted to go home with you instead."

"I'm honored. Let me just walk you home. I'll make sure you don't end up with me." He smiled at her. "Please?"

She didn't reply.

"It's dangerous this time of the night." He gently touched her arm.

"All right."

He put money down on the table and they collected their coats. Halfway to Lila's apartment, she made him turn around. They hadn't discussed where they were headed next. But Colin led, and she never objected. He put his coat around her shoulders when he noticed her shivering. It was so big on her small frame it dragged on the sidewalk. They walked the thirteen blocks to his apartment in silence, as if each of them knew they were committing a sin that would secretly brand them forever. They might go their separate ways afterward, and they would certainly go on with their lives, but they'd always be marked. Because what they did with each other, to each other, would be remembered.

They hurried up the stairs and Colin shut the door to his apartment. Lila checked twice to make sure the lock was secure.

"Come here," he whispered.

She stepped close to him. He could feel her warm breath, sweet with the drink. The phone rang.

She jumped in his arms. "That scared the heck out of me." She trembled against him.

Colin rubbed her shoulders. "Don't worry, it's okay." He glanced at the phone as it continued to ring. He didn't answer it.

The phone stopped ringing. Colin wrapped his arms around Lila. "Do you love Johnny?"

"No."

He nodded as he kissed her on the forehead.

Her body was very warm when she undressed, and when he first touched her skin he wondered if she had a fever. Then he realized she was anxious.

"Lila." He softly touched her neck and her face. "It's going to be all right."

After their lovemaking, Colin smiled at her small, tan body next to his larger, paler one. He reclined on his side in bed, leaning on his elbow, with his head resting in his hand, watching her sleep. Their bodies were covered by a sheet.

Lila woke up. "Colin?" He smiled at her. "Have you..."

"Yeah, have I?"

"Have you ever wondered why you can say you love somebody, convince yourself so much that you marry them, and then one day you ask yourself why you did it when you knew all along that you never loved them?"

Colin didn't reply. He kissed her tenderly on the face.

Colin glanced out his bedroom window after she had drifted off to sleep again. A firetruck barreled down the street. He saw a corner of the pale moon but no stars, and he thought he saw Johnny walking the streets, searching for his wife.

A few hours later, after Lila had taken a cab home, Colin stood in front of Lucille's house. It was eight in the morning. He didn't know if Lucille's husband would be home, but he didn't care anymore. He'd told Lila that if she didn't at least call him once in a while to confirm she was getting on okay, he'd stop by her apartment to make sure she was all right. Although she wouldn't want to have anything to do with him again after today.

He knocked on Lucille's door and heavy footfall approached. A man answered.

"Yes?" The man, Lucille's husband, wore dark pants and a green golf shirt. Colin recognized him from the photographs he had seen in the house. He was actually taller than Colin had thought, but not as tall as him.

For a moment they stared at each other in silence. "What do you want?" The man sounded alarmed.

Colin felt that Lucille's husband sensed who he was. "Is Lucille home?"

"She is. Who are you?"

"I'm an old friend of hers from the Bowery, but I think you already know that."

"I'm sorry?" When Colin didn't elaborate, he said, "Wait a moment." He didn't invite Colin inside the house. He walked away with the door halfway open.

Colin could hear Lucille whispering from inside the house as he waited on the front porch.

"Get rid of him," her husband said.

Lucille stepped outside wearing a blue cooking apron. She shut the door behind her and wiped her hands on the edge of the apron. "What are you doing here? I asked you not to come here again."

"Are you all right? Your husband shouldn't speak to you that way."

"I was fine until you showed up."

"I had to see you." He moved closer. "What's your husband's name anyway? You never gave it to me. What's your daughter's name? You never told me that either."

She retreated to the side of the porch like she feared him, and it wounded him.

Colin followed her. "Please don't be afraid. I didn't mean to frighten you. That isn't what I wanted to do at all."

"I'm not afraid of you, Colin, but my husband is not going to like that you were here."

"He doesn't hurt you, does he? Because if he does—"

"No, he doesn't."

"Good." Colin smiled. "You'd tell me if he did, wouldn't you?"

"*Yes*. Why are you here?"

"I came here because I have to tell you something."

"You couldn't do it over the telephone or in a letter like a normal person would?"

"It's not the same. Besides, you asked me not to call you."

"So you thought showing up at my house would be better?" Lucille put her hand to her face and shook her head. When she looked at him again, her skin was flushed and there were tears in her eyes. "My God, why can't you leave me alone?"

"I'm sorry. I'm not trying to upset you." Colin tried to touch her arm but she moved farther to the side. "I've always cared about you." He lowered his voice. "From the first time we met at your brother's pub, to the first time we drank together—"

Lucille shook her head. "That's called drunk, not caring about someone."

"I cared about you when I wasn't drunk." He attempted to take her in his arms. "I know the timing wasn't right before. I'm older now."

She pushed him away. "You had a crush. That's all it was."

"You asked me to marry you."

"I was a drunken fool." She glanced at the curtained windows behind them.

"You were never a fool."

Lucille wiped away a tear. Her husband called for her from inside. She gave Colin a firm look. "Go. Leave now."

He headed down the porch steps and then turned around to

look at her one last time. "I'm sorry for disturbing your new life. But I came to tell you I remember our old times and I loved having you in my life."

～

Café Acebo and Social Club on the corner of East Third Street was owned by a friend of Tito Bernal's named Manuel Acebo. Johnny, now called José by his cohorts because he had taken up his father's name, frequented the café with Bernal and the Tigers. They liked the Cuban beer Acebo served and the food his loquacious wife dished out, food from their native land.

Since joining Bernal's rackets, Johnny had also moved up in the ranks of the Bowery streets. The gringos didn't mock him anymore. Johnny and Tito were gradually pushing the Irish out of the Bowery betting and loaning trades and the drug business. But they weren't successful infiltrating the local pubs and nightclubs, and the dock unions and construction companies. Those were still dominated by Tom McPhalen.

The afternoon at the café was like any other. The men sat around discussing the things that men of a certain age sitting around often discuss – women, sports, cars, money, and their children. Outside the sun shone in the cloudless sky. The cool breeze of the mid-morning had stopped. It was the wintertime, but it was very warm out.

"This weather, I feel like I'm back in Cuba," Tito Bernal joked to the men around him at the indoor tables.

Johnny looked up from reading his Cuban newspaper and smiled.

"If only we were," Tito said, reminiscing. "José, you must go someday soon with Lila, and take the little one with you."

"We plan to."

"Yes, and maybe the new Mrs. Bernal and I will go with you. A family holiday, *si*? Wouldn't that be nice?"

"I'm sure the first Mrs. Bernal would love that," Johnny said in jest.

"Who cares what she thinks?" Tito frowned. "How is my daughter doing these days? I haven't seen her for a few weeks."

"She's doing good."

"How is the marriage?"

"It's going well."

Tito chuckled. "You don't have to pretend with me. I know how Lila can be sometimes."

Johnny felt uncomfortable laughing about Tito's daughter with him, but he pretended to laugh.

"Lila is a wonderful woman," Carlos, who had sharp, light eyes, said.

Johnny glared at him. Carlos had newly been initiated into the Tigers, was thirty years old and American-born like Johnny.

Bernal winked at Carlos. "Thank you." Carlos smiled at Johnny as if to act smug.

Johnny continued to stare at him as he picked up his beer from the table and drank fast.

Jarlath smoked a cigarette in an alleyway close to East Second Street. When he finished he threw the butt down to the ground and asked Colin if he had another smoke. Colin handed him a pack of cigarettes.

"Thanks." Jarlath took one out and returned the pack to Colin, who nodded in acknowledgment.

"When are Bill and the others coming?" Jarlath glanced at his watch.

"Should be any minute now."

Jarlath looked at his watch again.

"They'll be here."

Jarlath lit the cigarette. "You never came to Byrne's last night. Did you meet up with one of your ladies?"

"Sure. Marilyn Monroe."

"No. Who is she?"

"Do you really want to know? You really want me to tell you? Because I don't think you want to know."

"Now I do. Who is she?"

Colin knew his friend wouldn't stop asking until he told him. "Lila Bernal."

"Bernal's daughter?" Jarlath shouted.

Colin nodded and gestured for him to keep it down.

"No one's around." Jarlath's eyes widened. "I can't believe it. Tom is going to explode if he finds out."

"He's not going to find out."

"Of course not, Colin. I won't say anything." Jarlath smiled.

"What's so amusing?"

"You sleeping with that man's daughter. Sweet revenge, right?"

Colin didn't want to discuss Lila in a crass manner. She deserved better. "Sure."

"Is she good?"

"What?"

"Bernal's daughter."

"In bed?"

"Yeah, where else?"

"She's a good person."

"Despite her father. And what else is she good at?"

"Nothing I'm going to tell you."

Jarlath smiled as if he could picture Lila Bernal nude. "I bet she is good. She's not going to like you very much after today."

"I know."

"After you kill both her husband and her father, she's going to hate you."

"Maybe I don't care."

"You do. I can tell by your face."

"Here's Bill," Colin said to change the subject.

Little Bill had stepped out of a yellow taxicab lugging a large, nondescript black case.

"Do you see the size of that case?" Jarlath said. "Those feckers don't stand a chance."

Bill's case contained machine guns. Tom's local mafia connections wanted the Cuban problem solved as well and had supplied the weapons.

Colin didn't reply to Jarlath. They greeted Little Bill on the sidewalk. Yesterday it had been snowing. Now it felt like the late spring. The snow had melted, causing an unpleasant watery slush, which had turned black from the grime of the city streets.

"It's so bloody warm out," Bill said.

"Nice shoes." Colin glanced at Little Bill's white shoes, which were smeared with street muck.

Little Bill looked at his shoes and shrugged.

"Who else did Tom send?" Jarlath asked Bill.

"Mikey M and O'Neill."

"Frank O'Neill?"

"Yes, him."

"Terrific," Jarlath said with sarcasm. "The bloke can't keep his blasted mouth shut. I can't stand him."

Bill laughed. "Who knows, maybe he'll die today?" Jarlath chuckled but Colin didn't.

"Here comes Mikey," Jarlath gestured up the street.

Michael M, a tall Irishman in his late twenties, took his time as he strolled. When Colin saw Mikey, with the black hair and the wild blue eyes, he saw a slightly younger version of himself.

"Hey! Hey!"

Frank O'Neill trailed after Michael M. 'Fried Frankie' was just one of a dozen unflattering nicknames for the man from Connemara. The men waved to Michael M and grunted in Frank's direction. Michael M always had plenty of cigarettes to offer those who needed one.

"How come Mikey gets such a nice greeting but I don't?" Frank frowned.

"Why do you think?" Jarlath said. "No one can stand you."

All of the men laughed, including Frank, who didn't understand the insult.

"You lads want to know something else funny? Colin fecked Tito Bernal's daughter. His mate's wife." Jarlath laughed and shook his head.

"Holy shite." Frank grinned. "We won't tell anyone, but tell us, Colin, how was she—"

Colin's skin heated and he glared at Jarlath. "You promised me you wouldn't say anything. You're starting to act like Errol, do you know that?"

"Colin," Frank and Michael M. said at the same time.

Jarlath's eyes darkened. To be compared to a dead man before a shootout foretold misfortune, and Colin knew that.

"You shouldn't have said that, Colin."

"What am I supposed to say? You're the one who spilled my secret . . . Ah, forget this. We have a task to do for Tom and that's what we're going to do. Let's head over there."

The men around him nodded in agreement. Jarlath stomped out his cigarette.

∾

"What time is it?" Tito Bernal asked.

Johnny looked up from his newspaper. "Noon," Carlos said.

"Who's hungry?" Tito looked around at his men.

They all nodded. When Tito Bernal spoke it was never a question, it was an order. *Acebo* had no menu. The men could say what they wanted to eat and the café would make it.

As the men discussed what they would order, someone kicked open the door and five men with machine guns rushed inside. These men weren't wearing disguises to conceal their faces. Their anger and passion was evident in their features. Johnny thought he recognized one of them.

"All right, you feckers," a man wearing a dark jacket spoke directly to Tito's table. "Drop your guns. Old man, drop that gun. And you over there, put that knife the hell down. Put it down. This is for Ronan—"

Bang. Bang. Manuel Acebo burst from the kitchen firing a black pistol.

Colin yelled as he fired point blank into the men at the café, but it was Jarlath who had spoken the words to Tito Bernal's table. Bullets flew from the guns of both sides, and seconds later Jarlath was on the ground, his blood pooling around him. Glass had been shattered, and chairs and tables split in two from the force of the bullets.

"Jarlath." Colin stood above him.

"I'm doing fecking grand. How about them?"

"They're all gone. We got them all."

"So you did it. You helped us kill that friend of yours," Jarlath whispered.

Old friend, Colin thought.

Jarlath smiled and his teeth were stained with blood. Spit and blood dribbled out of his mouth as he started choking. Then Jarlath's chest heaved and he shut his eyes for the last time.

Colin was glad Jarlath had closed his eyes so he wouldn't have to do it for him. He didn't think he could have touched a dead man's eyes, for he knew someday that might be his fate also.

"Jarlath's fecked up?" Little Bill was slumped in the corner. He kissed his machine gun. He didn't appear wounded but exhausted. The front of his blue shirt was speckled with the blood of those they had killed, and his white shoes glistened red.

"He's dead."

"Shite."

Colin looked around the room littered with the bodies of Tito Bernal and his men.

To his right was the body of his childhood friend, Johnny Garcia. He was a Cuban, but Irish too. When they were boys they had talked of being friends forever. Now Johnny had fallen over in his chair, bleeding from his head onto the table. It was the last time he'd ever be whole. Soon he'd be buried in the ground, and over time his flesh would cave in and his body would rot. He'd never think again, laugh, hold his child, or kiss his pretty wife. Johnny Garcia, thirty-two years old, half-Cuban, half-Irish, raised in the Bowery with Colin as his boyhood friend, was dead.

But Colin hadn't shot Johnny, though Tom had wanted him to as a show of devotion. Jarlath had, Colin was sure of it. It was good of Jarlath to have done that despite their earlier quarrel.

Little Bill surveyed the dead men in front of them. "I can't remember which ones I shot."

Colin pointed at Johnny. "Do you know who shot him?"

"The truth is, there were so many bullets flying, I don't know what I saw."

Colin's secret was safe.

"Scout's honor," Colin whispered under his breath, because that was what he had promised Johnny when they were boys.

He had seen the dead before, he had been seeing the dead ever since he was a boy. But to know someone so well, as he had known Jarlath – or Johnny when they were children – and to see them slumped in front of his eyes, their bodies perfectly still it still shocked him. The smell of it all. The fluids they emitted after they had died because the body's entire system had collapsed . . . it remained in Colin's senses for many days after.

Colin could hear police sirens in the distance. "Scout's honor."

"What?" Little Bill said. He motioned to Frank and Mikey.

"Let's get out of here. Tom has a car waiting at the corner."

C olin put the glass on the end-table in his bedroom, stared at it for a moment and then pressed it to his lips again. The warm scotch slipped down his throat. It no longer burned as it went down, and there were no headaches in the mornings anymore.

One night in a dream he imagined Johnny was still alive. In this particular dream he hadn't seen Johnny in what felt like years, and while he had been busy establishing his reputation, Johnny had quit the Tigers all-together and moved out of Manhattan into the suburbs with Lila and their daughter.

"So you're a Long Island guy now?" Colin joked in the dream.

Johnny smiled. In Colin's dream they stood next to the crumbling pier by the East River. Johnny reached out to hug him and he accepted the embrace.

"You were my boyhood pal and then you killed me. I saw you."

Colin stepped out of the embrace. "It wasn't me. It was Jarlath."

"Jarlath?"

"Yeah. Do you know him in heaven?"

"What makes you think men like us end up in heaven?"

"Because we go to church. Sometimes."

"Getting into heaven is not all about going to church, Colin. You shouldn't have seduced my wife even if she and I didn't love each other."

"I'm sorry, Johnny. How do you know about that?"

"I know everything where I am."

They began to walk in the dream, away from the pier and into the streets of the Bowery, only it was the streets of their youth, the old Bowery. They waved to the people on the sidewalk because they knew all of their faces. As it got dark outside they returned to the pier. The water moved faster than it had before.

"We had some good times, Colin."

"We sure did."

"Have you ever thought about leaving this place?"

"Sometimes, but I don't know where I'd go to."

"You could come to Long Island, stay with us. We could get real jobs at the same place. The way I figure it, working for Tom could get you killed someday. Look what happened to me working for Tito."

"But we killed you. I didn't stop them. Can you forgive me?"

"I do."

There were tears in Colin's eyes.

And then he woke up alone and damp with sweat.

Colin would sometimes still privately weep over Johnny's demise. It had been a few years since Johnny had died, yet Colin still sent money to his family every month.

Colin began to associate himself with a young woman named Beatrice who lived on the other side of the Hudson River in Hoboken, where Frank Sinatra grew up. She was petite with short blonde hair and green eyes. Her family were respectable people, and she was studying to be a nurse. Colin bought Beatrice things like a fur stole and a gold bracelet. He enjoyed her companionship but he never had sex with her because he felt she was too young. He used other women, older women, for such pleasurable experiences.

Sheila Finlay was from Queens, just outside Manhattan. She was twenty-seven years old, worked as a sales girl at a famous department store, came from a middle-class Italian and Irish family, and was more than determined to make a name for herself. Her older sister was a proper schoolteacher.

If Beatrice was cute and traditional, Sheila was beautiful and glamorous. Taller than most women, she had long, red hair, and a face that was reminiscent of the actress Rita Hayworth. She knew how to dress to show off her long legs, 'wasp' waist, and ample chest.

Colin met Sheila through Beatrice. The girls' parents knew one another. It was no coincidence that the gorgeous, exciting Sheila, who frequented the nightclubs in Manhattan and dated affluent men twice her age, who had once snubbed the younger and somewhat ordinary Beatrice, began to invite her to go shopping and out to lunch once she heard the girl was dating Colin. And it was no surprise that Beatrice, being the naïf she was, accepted the invitations.

Colin first encountered Sheila at Beatrice's nineteenth birthday party. The large party was held at Beatrice's family's home, and it was the last time Colin ever spoke to Beatrice.

When Sheila arrived, all the guests in the grand living room turned to stare at her, but Colin barely noticed her at first. Sheila had been voted Miss Atlantic City as a teenager, and she could have been a showgirl. At the party she wore a close-fitting dark dress with billowy sleeves, and her red hair spilled down her back. Colin was surrounded by Beatrice and her friends, all girls, who were eager to speak to him.

Sure, Colin loved women, and Sheila looked fantastic, but he wasn't going to run and trip all over himself just to talk with her. First and foremost he wanted to make the line of work he had going successful for him. He was focused on attaining power.

He had glanced at Sheila once or twice throughout the evening as she hovered by the bar, flirting and drinking. He was impressed by her temerity.

Then she came up to him and grabbed his arm. Colin could tell she'd had too much to drink.

"Do you like dancing?" She beamed.

"It's all right."

"I love it." She pulled him onto the dance floor before he could stop her.

She was a terrific dancer, and they danced together for every song, and when they weren't dancing they were drinking. Sheila and Colin discovered they had something in common: they both liked to have a good time.

When Colin glanced at Beatrice she was chatting away a young man with eyeglasses, and she didn't seem angry at Colin.

Colin and Sheila danced even when the party had wound down and their bodies dripped with sweat. They danced as everyone else began to collect their coats and started to walk out of the front door.

Colin and Tom and Angela had arrived at the party together. Tom and Colin had business to take care of in Jersey City after the party, and Angela had friends in Hoboken.

When Colin finally left the party with Tom and Angela and Sheila's phone number, Tom warned Colin that Sheila could be a problem. She had dated Italian mob guys and had a reputation. He'd said all she wanted was to get close to power and would attach herself to any man she thought could get her that power. When the Italian guys couldn't give her what she sought, she'd moved on. Colin later found out Tom himself had messed around with Sheila years ago, and was pretty much still fixated with her. After all, she had that face and those legs. But Colin had a feeling Tom was taking care of Angela on the side these days.

Colin got caught up in Sheila's beauty. Colin hadn't had serious feelings like this for a woman since Lucille, and it scared him and excited him. Sheila seemed to show up at the same restaurants and nightclubs as him, and they always ended up spending the evening together.

Sheila told Colin she believed she was the result of her mother's affair with another man because no one else in her family had red hair. She expected things in return when they began to see each other. Each time they set foot inside a shop or in a pub in the Bowery, Sheila made it clear she was 'Colin O'Brien's girl' even before she officially was, as if she expected to be treated like a star. Soon she no longer paid for her perfume and clothing, or her liquor and meals.

Despite Colin reminding Sheila of the organization's structure, she pushed him to ask Tom for a higher-ranking position. Tom said no, that had to be earned over time, and questioned whether Colin or Sheila was asking for this. When Colin admitted it was Sheila's doing, Tom tried to convince Colin to ditch her. Only one thing came out of their conversation: the fact that Sheila was going to be sticking around.

"I've dated a lot of fellas like you," Sheila told Colin one day. "You have guts, baby, but I know the only way you're going to rise to the top is if you make that clear to others."

One time when they were at a bar inside a recently opened

hotel, they overheard a man make a snide comment about Sheila's laugh, and she begged Colin to "get him."

Colin thought it was a joke at first. Then he realized she was quite serious. He didn't want to lose Sheila. If he'd been sober, he would have reasoned he didn't want to be sent away for another twelve years. But he was pretty drunk, and when drunk, there seemed little to lose except Sheila.

"Colin," she purred into his ear. She thrust her chest into his side and fingered the outline of his gun through his suit jacket.

Colin remained frozen. "Come on, baby!" Shiela shouted.

People inside the bar ceased their conversations and stared at them.

Colin placed his hand over his gun. The man who'd offended Sheila ran for cover. People rushed to remove themselves from Colin's path, and tables and chairs were knocked to the floor. Sheila kissed his face.

Colin took his gun out and didn't bother to perfect his aim as he pulled the trigger. It took him less than a second.

Sheila screamed in glee.

But Colin hadn't shot the man. The bullet hadn't even grazed the guy's shoulder. Colin knew right away after he fired that he had missed and hit the decorative mirror instead as he'd intended. But he didn't tell Sheila that.

Colin put his gun away and clutched her hand. "Let's go. I'm not waiting around until the police come."

"Tom will handle it." Sheila grabbed his face and kissed him.

Colin wasn't as sure. "Let's go. *Now*." He pulled out of her hold and gripped her arm.

"I haven't finished my drink."

"Leave it." Colin dragged her outside to the sidewalk.

Sheila attempted to pull Colin close to her as he tried to walk down the street.

"No." He gently pushed her away. "We have to get out of here."

"Just one kiss. I'm so proud of you." She put her arms around his neck.

Colin pried her warm body off him.

Sheila backed way. "Fine. Have it your way."

He could tell she was angry because she insisted on sleeping on the couch in his living room that night instead of in his bed.

Early the next morning Colin woke up to Tom shouting in his face. "What the feck did you do it for?"

Tom had somehow gotten into the apartment. Colin could hear Sheila yelling and banging on the bedroom door, which Tom had shut and must have locked.

Colin got out of bed and put on his pants. "What's going on?" The light pouring in through the curtains burned his eyes.

"You know what the hell I'm talking about." Tom grabbed and shook Colin's arm.

Colin didn't pull away. "I didn't actually shoot the guy." Colin put his sweaty palms to his face and rubbed his eyes. "We'd been drinking."

"You should drink less, or else I won't be able to keep you on board."

Had Tom threatened him? He and Sheila didn't consider what they did boozing. They simply considered it having a good time. But Colin didn't want to end up like his father. He stopped yawning, and Tom's remark made him wake right up. He might be out of a job, or worse, Tom would eliminate him.

"You got lucky this time," Tom said. "The publican is a good friend of mine. He called me instead of the police. But some people who were inside the place talked, and now the police are asking questions. I'm going to have to pay off the cops who matter to keep them quiet. It doesn't matter that no one was hurt. You can't fire a gun inside a luxury hotel. That place isn't some Bowery flophouse. Hasn't working for me taught you anything? I expected better from you. You need to get some more class, Colin. We waste money because of this kind of foolishness. Things like this make us look like *eejits* in the newspapers. I'm going to need you to pay me back. And Liam, the man who owns the hotel, he's going to have trouble too, and he's a friend of mine also. He's a good man and his business has never had any trouble until now."

"Sheila—"

"You stay away from that bitch."

"She's not like that."

"No." Tom's face reddened. "You stay away from her. You're young still, you don't know anything about women like her, so I'm telling you, stay the hell away from her kind because they're not good for business or for you." Tom pointed his finger in Colin's face.

Colin silently looked Tom in the eyes.

Tom sighed. "What are you trying to prove, that you're fecking invincible?"

"I don't know," Colin answered honestly.

"That's what I thought." Tom unlocked the door and let the screaming Sheila in.

It wasn't until Tom asked him to cut another deal with the Irish over on the Lower West Side that Colin thought he might just be invincible. Colin and Sheila had scaled back on their drinking but were still seeing each other.

Colin remembered Max and Gerry from when he'd finalized the deal at *Dowd's* pub, back when Max and Gerry had worked for the Two Declans. When Colin inquired about Dean Fitzpatrick's whereabouts, he'd been told the man was in prison and would be there for a long time. The Two Declans had long since died. They were shot one dreary night on the West Side. Now Max and Gerry worked for a man named Sean McCarthy.

McCarthy was the son of an immigrant from Castlewellan, who had become a prosperous wool merchant in New York, and a Scottish-American woman. This had always been an issue for Sean since all of the Woodlawn gang boasted seventy-five percent Irish ancestry or more. After completing college, an unusual feat for someone in his line of business, he'd decided a traditional upper-class existence didn't interest him. He was as an astute student of corruption and learned the 'trade' quickly.

'No-Last-Name' Max was sitting with Gerry and Ed Dowd when Colin stepped inside the pub. All of the men now wore suits, which must have been Sean McCarthy's influence, and Colin assumed McCarthy had more control over his men than their previous boss.

"Colin." Then Max looked at Ed and gestured to Colin. "This is the fella I've been telling you about. He sealed that deal with me and Gerry back when we worked for the Declans."

It didn't seem to matter to Max and Gerry that they were now working for Sean McCarthy, who had gunned down their previous boss and underboss in cold blood. They followed whoever had earned control.

Ed Dowd only glanced up from his Guinness. He was younger than Max and Gerry. Colin said hello to the men and sat down. He ordered a half pint.

"Are you Irish or not?" Ed Dowd questioned Colin, after what had to have been Ed's fourth round.

"I am."

"Then why did you only order half then?"

"I don't drink to get smashed, buddy. I drink because I like the taste." Colin smiled as he concentrated on Ed's eyes.

Ed laughed and continued to drink. "Why are you working for the Bowery guys?"

"Why are you cutting deals with them?"

"My boss wants to. I don't make the rules." Ed smirked at him.

Colin watched the drunken Ed Dowd. Ed's hair was a shiny black but if he looked closely enough he could see a few gray strands. Ed had intense brown eyes. The deep scar on his face had to have been from a knife wound. He looked tall, even when seated. Ed was about to say something else, or take out his gun.

"Don't mind him. He's smashed," Max interrupted and lessened the tension in the bar room.

"He is," Gerry said.

"I ain't drunk." Ed slumped down in the booth and took another gulp.

"Don't worry about it. Sometimes he gets all fucked up in his head when he drinks." Max put his finger to his head when Ed wasn't looking and gestured. "You can talk to me and Gerry."

Colin nodded. "Tom wanted to let your boss know that if he'd like to contribute to the place in Harlem, it'd be best to do so immediately."

The Harlem building, an old coffee factory, would be renovated and used for one of the largest money laundering schemes Tom had ever devised. It needed partners and resources. Tom was asking every monied top man he knew to contribute, and, in turn, was promising them a share of the profits. Tom and Sean McCarthy attended the same church, and since Sean was the very 'top man' of all the Irish gangs in New York, and maybe on the East Coast, everyone consulted with him.

Tom was now a very old man, and after the deaths of Tom's top men, including Errol, Ronan, and Jarlath, Colin had once believed that when Tom left this earth he'd be the one to move up and lead because he was brighter and more doted on than Little Bill. But a few weeks ago Colin received some unpleasant news.

"Tell him we're not sure if we're interested. Tell him next time he should send one of the policemen he has on his payroll." Ed's eyes looked bloodshot.

Max cleared his throat and smiled at Colin. Gerry shrugged and then stared at the table. Colin didn't say anything. All he could think about was how much Ed reminded him of Dean Fitzpatrick from his first meeting with these guys. He later found out that they were cousins.

Ed pounded his fist on the table. "Why are you working for Tom McPhalen? You haven't answered me."

Colin chose to ignore him.

"Take it easy, Ed. Colin's a big guy. I'd be careful if I were you." Then Max smiled at Colin. "Don't listen to him. He can't handle his booze."

"No. He'll listen to me or I'll make him. I ain't afraid." Ed rose from the booth, and he probably would have reached for his gun and pointed it at Colin, but when he got up he was so drunk he crashed to the floor.

Gerry and Max laughed, and Colin did as well but it shocked him when not much did anymore.

Max looked at the floor where Ed was snoring, and tossing every so often. "He looks like a damn baby in a suit sleeping there. He's going to need to get that suit dry cleaned."

The men laughed again.

None of them went to lift Ed from the floor. The bartender, a large man around sixty-five with curly white hair, told them to pick Ed up.

Max grinned at the man. "His grandparents own this place. Remember?"

The bartender hesitated for less than half a second and then went back to buffing the glasses with a white cloth. It reminded Colin of the way Uncle Rick had cleaned his pub glasses. It seemed Colin had all but forgotten about those times these days, when he was always busy with so much else. Colin didn't know what became of his uncle and he didn't care. But he shivered at the memory of Uncle Rick's cold hands.

They carried out the rest of the conversation with Ed passed out on the floor. Max and Gerry were curious about Colin and were welcoming toward him. They wanted to know everything about him, from how he began working for Tom to what his family had been like and if he had a girl.

"You know," Max said after a while. "You can do doubles."

"Yeah, that's a good idea," Gerry said.

"What's that?" Colin asked.

"Doubles. You're with Tom, but you're also with us." Max leaned in toward Colin from across the booth.

Colin liked these men, but he didn't know them well so he wasn't sure if he could trust them. Were they playing a trick on him? "I don't know if that would be a good idea. What if Tom found out?"

Max stared at him for a moment, as if he thought Colin might have been daydreaming when he replied and wasn't paying attention. "He won't. You know, it's a good way to make additional money. Sean pays great."

Gerry agreed.

"We pay you to keep an eye on them and their friends for us." Max stared at Colin and beamed. "It'd give you a chance to get out of the Bowery, and, as a Northerner, you'll make more money with McCarthy than with anyone else. Sean's a good man."

Colin doubted that from what he'd heard about Sean McCarthy. McCarthy had once slit a man's throat for accidentally spilling a drink on his shoe in the pub.

"Every guy from the Bowery wants to get out of the Bowery," Gerry said.

"I've known Tom for a long time."

"But they aren't your people." When Colin didn't reply, Max said, "What do you say to we buy you another drink and you can sit on the idea?"

"Yes to the drink, and I'll think about it."

"Good. Let's go to the pub down the block for that drink. It's a great place. Better than here."

Colin knew it wasn't smart to move to another location during a meeting. Tom had warned him that was a good way to get killed. "Are we walking or driving?"

"Colin, we're not going to harm you." Max looked him in the eye. "The place is called *McBurney's* and it's owned by Mr. McCarthy. It's named after his grandmother."

Colin nodded. Maybe he was still intimidated. He convinced himself otherwise and agreed to go.

Gerry began to lift Ed off the floor. Ed was bigger than Gerry in girth and stature, and so the process was amusing to watch. Max laughed as Gerry struggled. Colin offered to help but Max dissuaded him.

"You're our guest. Stay inside and have a drink on the house while we get him into a cab."

Colin watched Gerry and Max assisting the wobbling Ed as they left through the front door. A burst of cold air flew into the pub. A few minutes later Max came back inside without Gerry. Colin had sat and waited and hadn't ordered a drink. Max gestured for him to follow him outside. Colin patted his gun to reassure himself.

"Gerry rode home with Ed," Max explained. "Sorry about Ed. Don't let him bother you."

"He doesn't."

"The only reason Sean keeps him and his cousin around is because they're safecrackers."

"Safecrackers? That's surprising." Max chuckled.

Outside the air was even colder than Colin had remembered. Colin thought the scent of alcohol from the pub seemed to drift off and surround them as they left. As they walked, Max explained that McCarthy's pub was a notch above most in the area. Colin still wasn't sure if he wanted to involve himself with these men, but he was willing to test it out. It wouldn't hurt, he reasoned, to see what the Northern guys had to offer.

Despite Colin's seeming faithfulness to Tom, he wasn't planning to bequeath Colin the throne. Until then Colin had felt that, regardless of his Northern ancestry, Tom and him had a silent understanding. But a man named Jack O'Clery, a second cousin of Tom's in New York, would be getting the throne when the time came. Tom, who had once appeared to be grooming Colin for the position since the deaths of Errol, Ronan, and Jarlath, now not only wanted to keep things South, but also 'in the blood'. And since Tom's son Joseph had removed himself, Tom chose O'Clery. From the little Colin knew of Tom's second cousin, Colin didn't respect him and wasn't confident in his leadership and Colin couldn't work for someone he didn't respect or trust.

Colin listened to what Max had to say. As a Northerner, he'd never go far in the new ranks of McPhalen's racket, according to Max. But working for Sean McCarthy and his fellow Northerners would guarantee Colin respect and a promotion.

"So who does old Tom have with him these days?" Max asked.

"He's got some of the same guys, like Little Bill," Colin replied. "You know him?"

"Yeah. Not the brightest fella."

Colin murmured in agreement. "Some of the others died, like Errol."

"Yeah, I heard about him." Max didn't shake his head.

Colin wondered if Errol's death had pleased Max. He wouldn't be surprised because Errol had made more enemies than friends during his short life.

"And I'm sure you know about Jarlath," Colin said. "Yeah. Jarlath was a good man."

"He was."

"I knew him well because he used to date my sister."

"And Ronan McDuff."

"Crazy son of a bitch, but smart. Now that was a loss." Max shook his head. "Here we are."

Colin glanced at the pub's sign.

McBurney's Fine Drinking Establishment & Restaurant

"Do you know why I wanted to come here?" Max said. "I want you to meet McCarthy. And I think you're going to be glad you came."

The large oak front door had a shiny brass knob. Max led the way inside. The pub was redolent of cigarette smoke and the wood floors shone. The bar itself was a beautiful, immaculate dark wood. To Colin the bar taps looked like they were made of bright gold. The Irish flag was plastered everywhere, in the form of cloth flags on the walls and a painted flag on each of the back tables. It seemed to Colin that the further removed from the ancestry people were, the harder they tried to prove they belonged.

"Max," a chubby red-haired man called out from the rear of the pub where he sat drinking from a tall, foamy mug.

"Robbie!" Then Max looked over at Colin. "His wife's very ill. I gave him some money to help with the bills. Do them one favor and then they all think you're their best friend."

Colin smiled in agreement. He wasn't paying much attention

to Max because he was too busy taking the place in. And there was something that stood out. Probably because she was one of only two women in the place, but more so because she was the most elegant looking girl Colin had ever seen. She looked a class above any other woman he'd met in his life, and he decided that someday he would make her his.

"I take it you've noticed Catherine?" Max smiled at Colin.

"Who is she?"

"Sean's daughter."

"Mr. McCarthy's daughter?"

"Yeah."

Catherine McCarthy was a raven-haired beauty with porcelain skin and light eyes. In stature she was average. She had a defined waist and slender hips and a chest that Colin thought looked perfect in proportion to her body. She carried herself with a debutante's air of grace. She was wearing a blue dress and was quietly reading at one of the tables at the back of the pub.

The bartender, an old man with a white beard and spectacles, said something to her and she laughed. When she laughed the dimples of her otherwise elegant face were evident. Colin loved that, and he also loved how she laughed with her entire body. He wanted to make her laugh and cause those dimples to appear. Kiss those lips.

Colin gasped at the sight of her.

"I'll introduce you before we meet her father," Max said with a wink. "You should see her mother. She's part French or something. A real looker like her daughter."

"I'm not interested in her mother."

Max laughed. "Be careful, she's only seventeen."

"Unbelievable. She looks older. I can wait a few years."

"McCarthy would kill you even if you did wait a few years." Max laughed again, but Colin sensed he was serious.

"She's worth the risk."

"Her mother's off on a cruise somewhere. She wanted Sean to go with her but he wouldn't hear it. He's very business focused. The only things Sean loves are Cathy, his businesses, and his doves."

Max told him that McCarthy kept doves in a large cage on the rooftop of his pub. He fed and took care of them, and no one was allowed up there except for his daughter and him.

Colin nodded but he wasn't paying much attention to what Max was saying, although he did notice Max hadn't mentioned Sean's wife being one of the things he loved. Colin's gaze and thoughts were on Catherine. He glanced at the cover of her book. *Pride and Prejudice.*

"My smart girl," Max said.

Catherine looked up from her book and beamed. "Max! Where have you been? I haven't seen you around for a while."

"Oh, you know me, I went to Paris for fun."

Catherine laughed, and when Max didn't smile, she said, "Really?"

Max grinned and shook his head.

Catherine laughed again. "Stop teasing me, Max." A white cat peeked up from her lap.

Colin stood to Max's right and smiled at the cat.

"This is Theodore," she said to Colin in a warm voice. Colin kept her soft vowels in his mind for days after. "I'm Catherine." She offered her hand to him. Her manner was polite, not too friendly, but not cold.

"Colin O'Brien." He took her soft, delicate hand and held it for too long. "What are you reading?"

She waved the book in the air. "Austen. You've read her?" Colin's face heated and he shook his head.

Catherine laughed and pulled her hand away. She looked at

Max and tilted her head in Colin's direction. "So, what's he doing here?"

Colin thought it was a bit rude she was conversing with Max as if he wasn't standing there. But he watched her animated eyes, plump lips, her flawless skin, heard the warm tone of her voice, and her manners seemed to matter less to him.

"He's from the Bowery," Max said.

Catherine seemed amused. "How did he end up here?"

"He was meeting with me and a few of the fellas for business, darling. And he might come to work for your father so be sweet to him." Max winked at her.

"Don't worry. I will." She glanced at Colin. "I'm sure it won't be too hard."

Colin felt himself blushing. "Is your father upstairs?" Max asked.

"Yes." Catherine spoke in a hushed tone, as if her father's whereabouts were a secret.

Max touched Colin's arm and guided him toward a staircase at the far left. Colin stared at Max's hand on his arm. Almost no one he ever knew well had done that to him. And he wasn't sure if he liked it from an almost stranger. Still, he allowed Max to keep his hand there.

Catherine called out goodbye to them and gave Colin a smile when he glanced at her. He smiled a little in return.

Max led him up a winding staircase. No one watched them as they ascended the elaborate stairs. Colin wondered why no one would be curious. But maybe they already knew – or perhaps in this pub they just didn't look.

Max started to search him for weapons outside a door to what seemed like an office.

"What are you doing?" Colin asked.

"Mr. McCarthy doesn't want anyone who doesn't work for him to enter his office with a gun. Sorry."

Colin handed him his gun. "You could've just asked for it, you know."

"Thanks. Most fellas aren't as cooperative."

Younger than Tom, Sean McCarthy had graying brown hair and piercing brown eyes. He looked nothing like his daughter, and his skin was somewhat weathered, but he must have been considered handsome in his younger days, icily handsome, with those sharp eyes, chiseled jawline, and iniquitous grin. McCarthy's eyes and demeanor conveyed to Colin that he was the most intelligent criminal Colin had ever encountered. The office smelled of his spicy aftershave. He was shorter than Colin when he rose from the large wood desk he sat behind. The lustrous desk had his surname engraved in gold on the front. His dark suit looked expensive. Colin glanced at McCarthy's diamond cufflinks and then at his own more modest ones.

"Max." McCarthy seemed surprised to see Colin there. "Who are you bringing me at this hour? Is he behind on a payment?"

"No, no, this is Colin O'Brien," Max quickly said. "He's with McPhalen in the Bowery."

"Old Tom?" Sean's tone wasn't any kinder. "Yes," Colin said.

"Is that so? Does Tom have something he wants to say to me?"

He sounded defensive.

Max still appeared nervous. "No, Mr. McCarthy. Colin's thinking about joining us."

The fact that Max had called his boss 'Mr.' hadn't been lost on Colin.

Sean laughed and apologized to Colin. "I didn't mean to scare you, it's just that when you have another boss's henchman in your presence, you tend to get a little tense."

"Sure, I understand."

"Are you going to be joining us, or are you only thinking about it?"

Colin stepped forward. "I am." He had made his final decision. After dealing with Errol's animosity for years, he figured he could handle Ed Dowd.

"Good. It'll be useful to have a giant like you on board for muscle." Sean gave him a firm handshake. "O'Brien, right?"

"Yeah." Colin glanced at a strange, colorful painting hanging above Sean's desk.

"I bought that recently." Sean gestured at the painting. "It's a Pollock."

The name meant nothing to Colin but he complimented the artwork.

"Where's your family from in Ireland, O'Brien?" Sean asked.

"The North mostly. I was born there."

"That's right. Max told me. Then what are you doing working for the Souths?"

"Right place, right time."

"How well did you know Tom's guy Jarlath?"

"I knew him well enough."

"I bet you didn't know Jarlath did some side work for me a while ago when I was in Woodlawn in the Bronx, where our organization originated. Of course, Tom doesn't know about Jarlath." He chuckled at Colin's shock. "Everyone has an amount they'd accept to betray their own. Tom has made the mistake of using too many men to keep an eye on."

"Mr. McCarthy—"

"Call me Sean." There was something about his smile. It seemed emotionless, as if it was expressed by a dead man without a functioning brain.

"I don't want you to think I'm betraying Tom. It's just that I'm from the North like you guys..." He also knew Sheila would be pleased about the additional money.

Sean chuckled again and then looked at him closely. "You're trying to make yourself feel better. I understand. But being here in the first place is betrayal. In fact, even thinking about joining us would be betrayal. But all is good. Tom won't find out."

Sean's harsh laugh agitated Colin, but he smiled although he knew Tom wasn't a fool.

"Let's talk details." Sean sounded even smarter. He sat down in the chair behind his desk.

Colin remained standing.

"Have a seat." Sean gestured toward a chair at Colin's right. Colin sat across from him. Even staring face to face with Sean made Colin nervous because he couldn't tell what Sean was thinking. That trait must have made Sean a very good liar. He confused Colin. His grin was unnerving, yet his eyes had an approachable glimmer in them.

"How are things in the Bowery?"

"Not bad, sir."

Sean chuckled. "Call me Sean."

Colin shifted in his chair. "They're not bad, Sean."

"You're going to have to tell me more than that." Sean folded his hands on the desk. "Are McPhalen's guys still raking in big money like they were a few years ago?"

"No. Profits have been decreasing ever since..."

"Ever since when?" Sean sounded impatient.

"I'm sure you already know a lot of Tom's top men were killed." He glanced at Max, who stood waiting in the corner. "After those guys died, some of the other guys got jittery. They said Tom was going down and that we'd all be knocked out sooner or later, or jailed. Some of them returned to Ireland. Even the ones who are wanted by the law there, they said they'd take the consequences and they went back. I don't know, maybe they couldn't take all the heat that had been going on with Tito Bernal and his Tigers. It was bad for a while. Those guys who left, they said they'd form their own organization back home."

"Bernal was cut. Is anyone else still causing trouble there?"

"Not yet."

Sean grinned. "Maybe we can get your friends in Ireland to help us if the time comes. It would be good to have a current connection to there."

Colin nodded but he didn't make any promises because many of those men were still loyal to Tom from afar.

"What do you think, do you think Tom's going down?" Sean asked.

"I wouldn't say he's going down at the moment, but he's coming closer to it every day." Colin couldn't tell whether Sean was pleased. "Can I ask you a question?"

"What is it?" Sean sat way back in his chair but didn't put his feet up on the desk.

"Your daughter, Catherine, is she really seventeen?"

"She is. Why are you asking?"

"She looks older."

"She's seventeen."

"So, she's still in school?"

"No."

Sean wasn't leaning back in the chair anymore and seemed less relaxed. He sat erect as he read a paper on his desk. It looked like a bill for the pub. But Colin sensed he was still paying attention to him.

"She graduated from private school early this past May," Sean said. "She's smart like her father."

"She does seem like a smart girl. What's she doing now?"

"She's living with her family." Sean used a brusque tone. He moved the bill aside and stared at him.

Colin could tell it would be best to drop the subject now.

Sean raised his eyebrows. "She's younger than you are." He lit a cigarette and leaned back into his chair as he smoked. "Colin, tell me something. Why are you so interested in my daughter?"

"I'm not. I met her downstairs and was curious. I didn't mean to offend you."

"You haven't. I'm not surprised you noticed her. Everyone notices Cathy. She takes after her mother."

Colin nodded. He didn't want to speak and put his foot in his mouth more than he already had.

"Let me tell you something, O'Brien, since you're going to be joining us." Sean put out his cigarette in an elegant glass ashtray. "Catherine is unique. She's my daughter, my only daughter, my only child. She's the most important thing in the world, the thing that I live for. And because she is what I live for, I want the very best for her. Cathy is off limits. You shouldn't be interested in her. I don't want you talking about her to me or anyone else. I don't even want you thinking about her. All my men know that, and now you know it too. I want the best for my baby, I want her to have it all, a businessman or a politician, not some crook from the Bowery."

Colin's mouth hung open. He didn't know what to say so he remained silent. Sean's eyes froze in a resolute stare. Then he politely excused himself and rose from his desk. He went over to Max and whispered something. Then he closed the door quietly as he exited his office. Colin was left motionless in his chair.

Max patted Colin on the shoulder. "Don't worry. He still wants you to join us. He told me himself just now."

"Is he angry I asked about her?"

Max shrugged then as though he could tell his answer worried Colin, and added, "If for some reason he is, I'm sure he'll get over it. Sean's a smart man. He isn't reckless. Tomorrow he won't even care. Let's get a drink. I'll warn you I can't return your gun until you leave. I'm afraid you might try to shoot McCarthy."

Colin saw he was joking and smiled. He followed Max out of the office.

Sean stood with Catherine at the bar as she drank a Shirley Temple garnished with a cherry. She seemed too innocent for her father's world. Sean glanced at Colin and Max but didn't appear to pay much attention to them as they sat at the other end of the long bar. Max asked the bartender to bring Colin a scotch. Colin tried not to look at Catherine in the presence of her father, but he felt her glancing at him in the shiny bar mirror. Max patted his back and they drank together.

13

"Why are you coming home so late? Where have you been?" Sheila sat at the small kitchen table in Colin's apartment drinking a cup of coffee.

"I had work."

"With who, Lana Turner?" Colin laughed at her joke. "With Tom?"

Colin didn't reply. "With who then?"

He stood behind Sheila and put his hands on her shoulders. "All you need to know, sweetheart, is that I'm finally working with my own kind and I'm going to be bringing in a whole lot more money soon." He kissed her graceful neck and then took his hands off her. "We won't be living here for much longer."

As a rule, bosses didn't want their men discussing business with their women, but Sheila pushed.

"That sounds really good, Colin. But, tell me, who are they?" He set his hands on her shoulders again and squeezed tightly.

"Don't be so curious." He backed away when she squirmed under his grasp.

"That fucking hurt, Colin."

He didn't say anything in return. Sheila continued to drink

her coffee and lit a cigarette. Colin could feel her watching him as he left the room.

~

Catherine McCarthy was beautiful, intelligent, and off limits to Colin. She was too young and too good for him, and her father would maim him if he touched her. And Colin wanted her.

He dreamed about her at night while he was in bed next to Sheila who was beautiful as well. Even as he was making love to Sheila, he'd imagine she was Catherine. When every day Sheila told him how much she loved him, he felt guilty but he still wanted Catherine.

He saw Catherine in person once, and if he was lucky twice, a week at her father's pub. He met with Max and Sean there in Sean's office to give a report on Tom and company. Sometimes Colin felt guilty visiting Sean and Max, but every time they embraced him as a Northerner and he got his hands on the cash Sean gave him, that guilt subsided a little more.

Colin was no longer living in his old childhood building fulltime. He had a secret place without Sheila on the Lower West Side, a large, more upscale apartment close to *McBurney's* that he'd bought after Sheila began to abuse morphine and he needed to distance himself from her when she'd refused help. But he still kept the apartment in the Bowery so Tom and Sheila wouldn't become suspicious. And he made sure to be there whenever he expected a phone call from Tom or a visit.

Sometimes though, he didn't make it there on time or Tom showed up without prior notice. And the next day Tom would ask Colin where he'd been. "What can I tell you?" Colin would reply and shrug his shoulders. "I've been having trouble with my lady. I went out for a stroll."

Catherine occasionally toyed with him, giving him flirtatious glances and little smiles. "Hello, Colin," she'd whisper in her low, beautiful voice. And then she'd turn around and be on her way. Sometimes, she'd wink. Other times she'd talk to him for a long while, and they'd tell each other about their day and their lives. Her interest in him seemed to strengthen because her father wanted her to have nothing to do with him. Colin never told her he had a girlfriend but somehow she found out.

"How's Sheila?" Catherine asked him one morning, after he had come into her father's pub for a meeting with Max.

She'd caught him by surprise. "Your girl, Sheila," she said.

"How did you hear about her?"

"Max told me."

"He did?"

Catherine nodded. "Don't be annoyed with him. He gets weak and will tell me anything if I pout." Her eyes softened. "How is she?"

"She's doing fine." He didn't want to trouble Catherine with Sheila's problems.

"Do you treat her well, Colin?"

"I believe I do."

"That's good."

"Why? Are you taking a survey?" Catherine laughed.

"No, just making sure."

"Making sure about what?"

"In case you and I are an item someday, I'm making sure you know what you're doing."

She had caught him by surprise once again. He stared at her for a moment. Then he smiled. "In a few years, maybe. Where's Theodore?"

"He's at home today."

With both McCarthy and Tom to deal with, Colin was busy. But some days he couldn't help but think about Johnny and the friendship they had long ago and had lost, and about Lucille and their fervent past. Other times he thought about his mother and siblings whom he hadn't seen in what felt like forever, or his father.

He was proud of his secret apartment. It was a beautiful place, tastefully furnished, with a large, airy bedroom. It had finished wood floors that shone, and long, windows that allowed light to pour inside. It was the opposite of his cramped, airless childhood Bowery home. But he had no one to show it off to.

Colin and Sheila had recently called it quits. It seemed the more money he made, the more morphine she bought off the street. Both Tom and Sean, although they had no problem distributing drugs to strangers, had certain appearances they wanted to maintain, and they expected their men, and their men's women and families, to stay clear of drugs. The men and their loved ones could drink, but Colin himself rarely drank anymore.

He hadn't known what to do with Sheila. He had told her countless times that she needed help and had tried to assist her, but she'd refused every time.

Another thing Colin liked about the apartment was that Sheila still didn't know where it was. He'd thought. Until one day she began loitering outside his building, hounding him into letting her inside.

He had been coming back from McBurney's, where he'd met with Max. He had another meeting in an hour with Sean and a few other associates. He had gone home to change into a fresh suit for the meeting.

"Why didn't you tell me you have a new place? I had to find out for myself by following you around all day. It's time you gave me some answers, baby. Does Tom know?"

"Sheila, you wouldn't dare." Colin used a firm tone.

"Maybe I would."

"Please go home."

"I don't have a home," she yelled at him.

He looked at her for a moment and wiped the tears from her eyes because he still cared what happened to her. She pressed her face into his hands and he kissed the top of her head. "Why didn't you let me help you?" he whispered into her soft hair.

"No one can help me," she said, looking up at him.

He shook his head and went up the stairs to his building and stepped inside. She followed before he could shut the door to the lobby.

"Come on, baby, I'll sleep with you if you want," Sheila said in the hallway.

She was still beautiful, but she was a mess. She started to cry and Colin again pleaded with her to go. It gutted him to abandon her, but Tom didn't like her and McCarthy didn't know about her problems yet, and that meant she was dangerous for him.

Sheila continued to follow him as he went upstairs to his apartment. He fiddled with his key in the lock. She made him nervous because despite everything he was still drawn to her. Colin struggled not to give in, and he pretended not to listen to her. He didn't even look at her.

"Colin, you know I love you, honey. Let me come in."

He felt brave enough to turn around and face her. "You won't let me help you so go home." He turned back to open his door.

"I don't love you anymore anyway. I was lying so you'd let me in."

Colin shut the door, leaving her standing there in the hallway. He lingered behind his closed door. He listened carefully to make sure she was gone, and when he was certain she was he opened the door again. He took a deep breath and picked up his newspaper from his doormat. Her strong perfume still circled in the air. He tried not to breathe in her familiar scent. He closed and locked the door.

He parted the curtains and looked out the kitchen window and watched Sheila crossing the street. She almost got hit by a car as she dashed through a green light and he winced. She made it to the other side and strolled to wherever she was going now that she was no longer Colin O'Brien's girl. He doubted she even knew where. Sheila had lost her job, and even her parents avoided her because of her drug problem. She could disappear and no one would miss her – Colin knew what that felt like.

He entered his new kitchen and started a pot of coffee. Then he made his way into the bedroom and sat on the edge of the bed. Wearing his clothes and shoes, he leaned back and collapsed into its clean softness. He wasn't going to give up this good life. He wasn't going to let anyone ruin it for him. Colin closed his eyes and he didn't open them until he heard the water boil.

"Look at him. The son of a bitch thinks he's king now," Tom said.

Tom sat with Colin in a pub on the Lower West Side and pointed at Sean McCarthy as he stepped out of an impressive car across the street. They had been on the West Side buying guns from a Chicago guy. Everyone used the guy, even McCarthy. After that they had left the guns in the trunk and then parked in front of the pub and gone in for a few drinks.

"Me and Sean used to be mates. Now he thinks he's the man because he has a penthouse with its own elevator and a summer mansion on Long Island. I also heard he collects art," Tom spoke with disdain.

Colin sat calmly in his chair. He shrugged and continued to

read the day's newspaper spread out in front of him on the table. His cup of black coffee grew cold at his right. Maybe he'd have a penthouse someday, or a large home on Long Island, or a brownstone house like Tom had. Maybe he'd have all three.

Rock 'n' Roll Singers Killed in Plane Crash!

Kennedy for President?

Tom slammed his chunky fist down on the table. "Colin, I'm talking to you."

"Sorry." Colin looked up and took a sip of the cold coffee.

Tom drank his Guinness. "Don't know how you can drink that shite, it's cold."

"It's still got the caffeine."

"I heard you're no longer with Sheila. Finally." Colin nodded.

"That was a good decision on your part." Tom took another drink. "Look at him now, that fecking McCarthy," he said as Sean walked back to his car with Max. "Look how proud he is of himself. I ought to go out there and teach him—"

Colin reached over and touched Tom's shoulder as he started to rise. Working for McCarthy had given him more confidence. "Don't get too upset, boss. You need to take it easy." He stared into Tom's pale blue eyes.

Tom was dying. Lung cancer.

Tom cleared his throat. Colin could see in Tom's eyes that although he was an old man who had lived a long life, the idea of death and the unknown still frightened him.

"Don't treat me like an ill old man. Show me some respect, won't you?"

Colin murmured an apology.

Tom took a gulp of Guinness and stared at the wall behind Colin. Colin knew Tom had assumed Errol would be the one to gain control of the Bowery after Tom's death. Now, Colin could see that the thought of Sean McCarthy possibly gaining control of the Bowery after Tom's death angered Tom.

"Sean's a greedy bastard, but I always thought that, out of respect for me, he would leave the Bowery to us," Tom said to Colin. "The Declans understood the code of respect. Sean? Not as much."

Colin waited for Tom to ask him for his thoughts on how Sean McCarthy had achieved such success within the Bowery in just a matter of months. He imagined the idea of McCarthy, who was Tom's former acquaintance, owning Tom's Bowery streets, didn't sit well with Tom.

Tom was determined to find the betrayer fast. He had had been discussing it with Colin in the car earlier as they'd parked by the pub. Tom had suspected that it was Little Bill. Colin didn't give his opinion then either. He watched the transition of power with indifference. Sure, Tom would buy Colin a cup of coffee, but because Colin was a Northerner, Tom would never show him genuine respect. He had finally come to realize that. Sean McCarthy was Northern like him and that meant something. He was also giving Colin more money, and since Tom had chosen Jack O'Clery to be his successor instead of Colin, Colin figured he had little to lose when Sean took control. He felt Sean would promote him soon.

Of all the things Colin had learned in the business, the one that mattered most was that betrayal was irrelevant so long as you were doing it to better yourself and could protect yourself from any consequences. That's how men survived in the streets.

14

A FEW YEARS LATER

A while back Catherine McCarthy had married Albert
Devine, the son of a wealthy and respectable business
associate of her father's from Boston, but now she was a widow.
Albert Devine was a young, budding politician. Who would
have thought he'd get stung by a bee and die two and a half
years after he and Catherine wed? He hadn't known he was
allergic. Catherine had lived in Boston with her husband, but
now she was back in New York. Colin hadn't seen her in all that
time. She now had a two-year-old daughter. Colin suspected
Catherine's marriage had been arranged by her father in order
to get her out of New York and away from Colin.

He ran into her at Sean's pub. "Colin O'Brien!"

Colin smiled and waved. Catherine had filled out, from the
pregnancy, probably, but her husband's death hadn't appeared
to have changed her much. She was even reading a book.

"Mrs. Devine."

Catherine blushed and set down her book on the bar.
"Please, call me Catherine." She smiled.

Colin nodded. "I heard about your husband. I'm sorry. I
truly am."

"Thank you." Her eyes reddened and he felt bad he'd brought up her husband's death. She seemed more mature than when he'd last seen her.

"How have you been doing?"

"All right. You?"

"Okay, thanks. I heard you have a daughter."

Catherine's eyes brightened. "Yes, I do. Her name's Violet. Do you want to see a picture of her?" She reached for her purse on the bar.

Colin sat next to her and she handed him the photograph.

It was a professional picture like the ones purchased from department stores. Colin gazed at the photo of the young child. She had her mother's dimples and shining blue eyes, and rosebud lips, but what must have been her father's red hair.

"She's beautiful." He handed Catherine back the photograph.

"Thanks. Are you still backstabbing for my father?"

Colin frowned. Then he grinned and he realized she'd made a joke.

"I was only kidding," she said as though she sensed his discomfort. "My father appreciates your help."

"Of course." Colin's face burned as he continued to sit with her.

His conscious was suddenly bothering him. "I have to go now."

"I'm sorry you're leaving so soon."

"I just finished meeting with Max, and I have to go to the bank before it closes." He didn't really have to go to the bank but it gave him an excuse to leave. He got up, and the bell which hung from the top of the door chimed as he left.

Tom wasn't a Northerner like Colin and Sean, but he'd given Colin his start in the business, and when Colin first joined the Woodlawn gang on the side, he knew it meant a betrayal of

Tom's trust. Yet those guilty feelings had diminished over time. Catherine had forced him to remember them.

Colin didn't make it to the meeting with Sean that evening. He didn't want to return to the pub. He had to think about things for a while and try to soothe his conscience. In the end he told McCarthy he was ill with a fever. He had to make it sound contagious because Sean detested germs and was paranoid about catching illnesses.

"Don't come," he told Colin over the telephone. "Don't come around again until you're well."

Four weeks later Tom's condition had deteriorated. Tom's doctor hadn't given him more than a few months to live.

From his bed Tom would give Colin the look a proud father might give his son and shame would overcome Colin in such a way that he could hardly look at the old man.

"Colin," Tom would say as Colin sat at his bedside. "Help my cousin. Don't let McCarthy take the Bowery from us."

Colin would sometimes nod after Tom spoke, but other times he'd say, "I will, Tom. I will."

Sometimes he didn't know what to say so he'd close his eyes and pretend to be nodding off. If Tom said his name over and over, trying to awake him then he would 'wake'. Tom would repeat what he'd said and Colin would agree.

"We'll take care of Jack O'Clery," Sean McCarthy said to Colin on a rainy afternoon one week later.

He did 'take care of' Jack. Two days later O'Clery was found strangled in his bed at his Bowery home. The week after Jack

O'Clery's death Sean McCarthy asked Colin to knock off Little Bill. McCarthy's goal was to quickly disperse the Salthill gang. Tom was nearly gone, and there were only a few members left to block McCarthy from taking control of the Lower East Side. Sean wanted Little Bill and a few other men cleared out so that when Tom died he'd be able to take over Tom's rackets and smoothly absorb them into his own without a battle. If Tom's high-ranking men were still around after his death, one of them might try to take over Tom's position and resist the assimilation.

Colin didn't know how he felt at first. After all, he considered Little Bill a friend and knew his family. But then he figured Bill's death would further establish his professional relationship with Sean. It would be a good way to show his devotion to the Northern guys.

"Are you sure you're all right with this?" Sean asked Colin in his office above the pub. "This guy is a friend of yours, isn't that correct?"

"He isn't a Northerner. And work is work," Colin said with confidence.

"You don't have to do it if you don't want to." But from the tone of Sean's voice Colin could tell he would be more than disappointed if he didn't.

"I want to."

"Good. That's what I assumed." Sean sounded pleased.

"How's Catherine?" Colin hadn't asked Sean about her since that first time.

Sean frowned. "Why?"

"I was just wondering how she and her daughter are doing now that they're back in New York."

"They're doing fine. I'm taking care of them."

"Are they living with you and your wife?" Colin had never met Mrs. McCarthy, but from what he'd heard she was an older version of Catherine.

"No. Cathy's staying somewhere else. She's seeing this fellow. She and Violet moved in with him. I don't care for him much but she seems to. I will say that he treats both of them with respect. She's a grown woman with a child, so I can't tell her what to do even though I give her money. The fellow is a poor bastard. He's a struggling actor. But I guess it's fine because he makes her happy. And I never thought I'd see her happy after her husband died."

"I'm glad to hear she's doing well," Colin said politely. Internally, he fumed at the fact that McCarthy would rather have his daughter be with a poor actor instead of him.

Sean cleared his throat, as if to stop his sentiment. Then he was back to business. "The Little Bill situation needs to be resolved two weeks from today." His eyes lit up as he looked Colin over. "I'm going to buy you a couple of new suits. I don't like the one you're always wearing."

The light-colored suit Colin had on was his favorite but he nodded and smiled.

"Is McPhalen dead yet?" McCarthy asked him on his way out the door. "I thought he only had a few months?"

Colin stopped in his tracks and didn't turn to look at Sean. "He was better for a while, but not anymore," he whispered.

Colin didn't stay long enough to find out whether the news delighted Sean. He didn't want to know, because seeing Sean's delight would have made him feel terrible.

Tom on his deathbed was like a dying king. People came to his brownstone house from all over the Bowery, and even beyond, to pay their respects to him. They'd make baked goods and hot food dishes for his family. They'd bring these along with flowers, Mass cards, and bottles of Jameson they couldn't really afford.

They felt that they owed him, for whatever help he might have been to them throughout the course of their challenging immigrant lives. For whatever rent or bail money he'd loaned to them or their loved ones, and overlooked when they never paid him back. For however he'd avenged them, their wives, husbands, children, or friends when they'd suffered an injustice. For whatever ways he made them feel safer, while at the same time subtly keeping them in their place.

It was no surprise to Colin that when he arrived to pay his respects, having received a phone call from Tom's wife saying her husband was nearing the end, he found a long line of visitors outside the ornate house.

Tom's wife noticed him standing in line outside and asked everyone else to step aside so he could enter.

"Colin." She embraced him.

"Mrs. McPhalen." He'd always addressed her formally.

He accepted the large, warm woman's embrace. He had avoided thinking about the upcoming killing of Little Bill and what it would mean for the future of Tom's empire, but now he couldn't help but feel a little ashamed. He liked Mrs. McPhalen. She was a good woman. She had shown him nothing but kindness, and now he was going to destroy her husband's legacy, betraying him in the worst way after she watched her husband, the love of her life, die.

"How are you?" Colin asked.

Her tired green eyes filled with tears. "I'm going to miss him so much."

Colin looked into her eyes and nodded. He did know something about loss. Then he wished he hadn't looked at her eyes, because she grabbed him for another embrace and sobbed on his shoulder. Colin rubbed her back to calm her.

"Bill's already here. Come inside." Mrs. McPhalen dried her eyes and gestured to the hallway. "Joseph will be visiting later."

Colin wondered if Joseph would be bringing the wife she disliked.

He followed the stout Mrs. McPhalen through the doorway into the living room where Little Bill slept on the couch. The shrine to Errol was still there. There were many empty glasses on the coffee table. He wouldn't be seeing Bill today though he would kill him soon.

Colin looked at the portraits and photographs on the walls of the McPhalens' living room. He had never really noticed them until now. For all of those occasions that he had been inside Tom's house over the years, he had never paid much attention to the photographs. He focused on them now because he needed to concentrate on something other than Tom's impending death and Little Bill's as well, a death he would cause.

There were a few old-fashioned images of Tom in his youth on the walls. It was strange to witness the old and dying Tom as a young man. There was no hint of the man Tom would become. Tom, with apple cheeks and a charismatic toothy smile as a boy, and a headful of hair and swaggering confidence as a young man, a cigarette hanging from his grinning lips. Then there was determination and an unapologetic smile in a photograph of Tom taken from behind inescapable prison walls.

Colin stopped in the doorway of Tom's room.

Mrs. McPhalen touched his arm and said, "He wants to see you." Colin entered the bedroom slowly. The room smelled of illness, as hospitals often do. The bitter smell of the fluids on the sheets mixed with astringent disinfectants that did little to hide the fetid odors, made him choke. Tom rested in his bed under blankets. To say he looked like a ghost wouldn't have been an exaggeration. His complexion blended into the white pillow.

Tom coughed up something foul and struggled to sit up when Colin approached his bedside.

"It's all right, Mr. McPhalen, you don't have to sit for me."

Colin found a handkerchief on the bedside table and tried to wipe the old man's mouth, but he grabbed the handkerchief from Colin.

Tom cleaned his mouth and smiled at Colin's formality. "How are you?" Colin asked.

"Me? I'm wonderful." Tom chuckled, his voice heavy with mucus. "And stop whispering. You don't have to speak to me like I'm an old woman. And don't call me Mr. McPhalen."

Colin smiled genuinely at Tom. He was surprised at his boss's cheerful disposition despite his fragile demeanor.

Tom put the handkerchief down. "Come closer, I want to have a good look at you."

Colin moved a little closer.

"What are you, afraid?" Tom laughed. Colin stepped next to the bed.

"You're all grown up, Colin O'Brien. And maybe this is the first time I've seen it clearly. You're almost an old man yourself."

Without hesitation, Colin knelt down at Tom's bedside. Despite the brutal acts Tom had sometimes directed Colin to commit, he had never feared Tom the way he feared Sean McCarthy because Tom had always seemed somewhat human. Colin trusted Max, but sometimes Sean reminded him a little too much of the loan shark who had pushed his father over the edge. Sometimes Colin reminded himself a little too much of the same man.

"You have come far, Colin. You've done a good job, a very good job. I'm as proud of you as I would be of a son. You are like a son to me, and I want you to know that even after I go, there will always be a place for you in my family."

Colin had a difficult time looking Tom in the eye, but he managed to thank him. He appreciated Tom's sentiment but wondered why he hadn't been chosen to lead. Colin contemplated what Max had told him about Colin's Northern heritage standing in the way.

Tom took Colin's hand with his cold one. "About Jack, I think Little Bill is betraying me. You must kill him for me."

Colin remained silent.

"You'll do this one last thing for me, won't you?" Tom said.

Colin didn't know whether to grin or cringe at the irony. He nodded.

"And always remember," Tom said, patting his hand, "who gave you your start in this business."

Colin wasn't sure why Tom had said that. He wasn't sure if Tom knew his loyalty was dissipating. And why, if he did think Colin was straying, had he asked him for that lethal favor?

Colin thought about Tom's words even after he'd left Tom's deathbed. He walked out of Tom's spotless house into the tainted streets of downtown Manhattan with the hope that maybe everything would turn out to be for the best.

A few days later Tom had died and Sheila was suddenly back at Colin's door. Soon he'd be expected to get rid of Little Bill.

Sheila showed up at his prized apartment on the Lower West Side early one dreary Wednesday morning. Colin wasn't out of bed when she came, and Sheila didn't seem to care that she might wake him up from a peaceful slumber when she knocked on his front door and shouted.

"Colin? Honey? Are you in there? I know you're in there. It's me. Let me inside."

He didn't have to ask who 'me' was. As soon as he heard the knocking and shouting he knew who it was. No one else knocked like that at this hour without any care about disturbing the neighbors, except for maybe Tom. But Tom had died the night before so it couldn't be him. In Colin's world it was rare for a man to not die at the hands of another.

Colin considered not answering the door and ignoring Sheila. But she wouldn't leave until he made an appearance and his neighbors would despise him if he didn't stop the noise soon. The building wasn't a tenement and the other residents tolerated very little. He groaned as he rose.

Colin put his pants on and walked out of the bedroom. He answered the door shirtless. "How did you get into the building?"

Sheila frowned. "One of your neighbors let me in as he was leaving." She smiled as she stared at his bare chest. "You're looking good."

He knew he'd lost weight, but he had no woman to admire that achievement. He looked her over. She seemed plumper and healthy. "You look good also. What happened to you?"

"I'm well now. I've been well for months. Oh, Colin, it's been a long time, too long."

He nodded. It had been months since he last saw her. She seemed better, but he was cautious. "What do you want, Sheila? Do you need something?"

"What do I want? I'm at your door so I must want money, right?" Her face flushed.

"Sheila," he pleaded.

"Do you know what your problem is? You don't know how to communicate with women when they expect more from you than furs and jewelry."

He was too tired to defend himself so he invited her inside.

Sheila frowned as if she was deciding whether she liked his response, but after a moment she entered, removed her raincoat, and made herself at home.

He stared at her suitcase. "You know you can't stay here."

"I'm not here to bother you," she said.

Sheila sat down on his new couch and draped her coat over the armrest. "Nice sofa. But you should really get your act together and get yourself a better place. This one isn't that great." She glanced around his apartment with her alluring dark eyes. "With the money you're making, you could do much better now. You need at least two bedrooms. And you should consider getting a television. My friend has one and it's fantastic."

"This apartment is perfect for a bachelor. I'll think about getting a television."

She turned to look at him, standing in the doorway of the kitchen and leaning against the doorframe. "You never will."

Colin chuckled and shook his head.

She glared at him. "I'd be more than happy to leave if you want me to, but then we can't, you know..." She dragged her tongue across her lips.

And then he felt her feminine presence. It felt good to have a woman in the apartment again. He hadn't brought a girl home for months. And she was a beautiful woman, with her radiant hair and intriguing eyes, her softness, and the sweet smell of her perfume. He wanted to take her into his arms and kiss her, and then bring her to his bed and make love to her. Then he remembered how much trouble she'd been in the past and it turned him off.

"We can't... Where have you been living?" he said.

"With a friend. A female friend. She's the one who has the television. Boy, am I going to miss that thing."

"Why? You'll see it when you go back."

Sheila didn't reply, and that worried Colin. How long did she plan to stay at his home? In prison, Colin had never been alone, and when he was released it had a strange effect on him. He enjoyed being alone. That made living with someone difficult.

"Do you have any soda to drink?" she asked.

Colin got the feeling she wasn't interested in leaving

regardless of what she'd said. She knew he never kept soda in his ice box and would have to go out and buy her a few bottles.

"Soda? At this hour? Sheila, are you planning something? I don't keep money in the house anymore."

A couple of months ago he'd found her in a poor condition outside his building again, and because it was cold outside he invited her inside his apartment against his better judgement so she could shower, eat, and rest for a while. They'd ended up making love. He'd fallen asleep and when he awoke, he discovered she was gone and that she'd stolen from him.

Sheila frowned. "No. I'm thirsty."

"I'll get you a glass of water."

"No, I want pop. Please?" She batted her long eyelashes. "You know where you can get my favorite."

"All right," Colin grumbled. "It's raining outside, but I'll go out and get you some. But don't steal anything."

Sheila held up her hands. "Don't worry. I don't do that anymore. Besides, you have nothing I can steal, right?" She winked. "It looks like it stopped raining." She peered out his window.

Colin put on a shirt and shoes. He looked around for his wallet and found it on the end-table by the door.

Sheila surprised him with a hug. "Thanks. You're the best," She put her long arms around his waist.

He protested a little but he liked having her arms around him, her warm body so close to his. So he allowed her to embrace him for a minute, and then he made his way out of her arms. She sighed, and he could tell she was disappointed and had expected something more in exchange.

"I'll be back soon."

He left his apartment feeling uncertain. What exactly had that embrace meant? Were they back together? Was he okay with that? He hadn't left anything valuable in the apartment that she could take, as she had done before on his 'soda runs' for her. She'd steal his belongings and pawn them to buy morphine. He'd buy them back a day later if he could. She had said she was well, and with her radiant appearance she looked healthy; but with Sheila he could never be quite sure. Sometimes she looked well even when she wasn't. When he'd left he had taken his gold watch and his gun with him as well, the only things that were of monetary value to him in his home. The bundles of hundred dollar bills Sean McCarthy had given to him as payments, or money he was holding for McCarthy, he kept in a safe deposit box in a posh foreign bank on Fifth Avenue that didn't question their customers' business ethics. Even his father's accordion he kept hidden under his bed.

The Lower West Side wasn't usually quiet in the morning, but today it was. Colin stepped out of his building and into the clean streets. That was one thing he liked about living on the West Side, the streets were cleaner. And people didn't recognize him there so they tended to leave him alone. He breathed in the sweet autumn air. Sometimes he felt like such a sucker because apparently there was nothing he wouldn't do for a woman.

In this case he took the bus to the Bowery to buy Sheila's soda because *Fleischer's* market sold the cola she favored. The closer the bus got to the Bowery, the more trash there was on the sidewalks; pieces of newspaper, old beer cans, broken glass, all blowing in the morning breeze. He wondered if the Bowery had become dirtier over the years and he hadn't noticed, or if he hadn't been there in so long it just looked that way to him now. Colin exited the bus and went across the street to *Fleischer's*. He waved to a traffic cop he knew from childhood.

Old man Fleischer had died years ago. Colin and Johnny had frequented his shop as boys. They used to buy bubblegum from Fleischer, and when they were older they bought cigarettes. Fleischer's son, Donnie, ran the shop now. After Colin joined

Tom's Salthill men, Donnie had asked him for a favor regarding a neighbor who didn't respond well to complaints about noise coming from large parties late at night. Colin had obliged. Donnie had no problems with noise from then on. All Colin had to do was have a conversation with Donnie's neighbor.

Donnie was a few years older than Colin. He was married to a spirited Irish girl Colin remembered from his childhood tenement, and they lived above their shop.

Donnie greeted Colin as soon as he entered the shop. "Mr. O'Brien! It's so good to see you. How are you?"

"Please, Donnie, call me Colin. I'm well. How are you and Fiona?"

"We're well. Thanks for asking." Donnie stood behind the shop counter.

Colin liked Donnie, he was always cheerful. He was never sarcastic or bitter like some of the other guys in the city. And Colin liked to think Donnie respected him, despite the fact that Tom had made Colin shake down Donnie for money. So maybe Donnie feared him a little, but he still respected him.

"What can I get for you today, Colin?"

"I need a few bottles of soda."

"How about a whole case? I can give you a case for free."

"You don't have to do that."

"I want to," Donnie insisted.

Colin grinned at him. "You sure know how to make a good deal."

"Anything for you, Mr. O'Brien. I mean, Colin."

Donnie stepped into the backroom. Colin began to browse the shop's shelves. He saw a bottle of perfume he knew Sheila would like. But he stopped himself before grabbing it and walking over to the counter where Donnie now waited with the case of soda. Things were going to be different now with Sheila. He wasn't going to spend too much money on expensive gifts for her. She'd have to show him a lot of commitment before he did anything like that again, and not the other way around, the way it had been before.

"Thanks, Donnie." Colin took the large crate of soda from the counter and tried to hand him a crisp twenty dollar bill.

At first, Donnie refused to accept the money. "It's not necessary. You're such a good, loyal customer, I want to give it to you."

Colin moved the bill between his fingers and the paper made a noise. "I insist, for all your troubles and hard work. Come on, buy Fiona something nice with it."

Donnie beamed as he accepted the cash. "Colin, you're so generous, the best fellow."

Colin nodded and then walked out of the market with Sheila's crate of soda. He took a cab home.

When he returned to the apartment he found that Sheila had made herself more than comfortable. The suitcase she had brought with her was open and empty on his bed. She had unpacked and arranged her dresses and shoes, and underwear and stockings in the closet and the dresser.

Colin realized he'd left the crate by the front door. He carried it into the living room and set it by her feet. It landed with a thud and she jumped a little on the couch. His back was still aching from bringing it upstairs. "Why did you put your things in my bedroom?"

"What does it look like, genius? I moved in."

"I can see that, but why?" He stared down at her.

She backed away from his commanding presence as if she thought he would strike her, but he never had. Then she stood up, and although she was tall and wore heels, she had to stand on her toes to face him. "Because I'm pregnant, Colin. That's why I got better. And before you say anything, I know it's yours because I haven't been with anyone since I was with you a couple of months ago—"

"Pregnant?" He tripped over the crate of soda and knocked it over. The bottles rolled out and scattered on the floor.

Sheila leaned over and picked a cola bottle up. "Don't hurt me. If you do, I'll smash this in your face!" She raised the glass bottle in the air.

"I've never hurt you, Sheila." He remained still as he watched her. Did he really believe she hadn't been with anyone else since him? He knew she'd be furious if he asked so he stayed quiet.

She gave him a cold stare and then she gradually softened. She lowered the bottle. "I know. But when you tell some fellas a thing like that, they sometimes get angry. I've heard about it happening to girls." She began to cry softly.

He stepped close to her and put his arms around her. "What am I going to do with you?" He touched her chin and when she looked up at him he smiled. He couldn't help it. He was tough in the streets but soft when it came to women. It'd all started with his sister whom he had adored as a child.

Sheila looked into his eyes. "You could marry me." Colin stepped back in panic.

"Us, get married?"

"Of course. What else am I supposed to do with the baby? Raise it by myself as a bastard?"

"No. There's adoption. Or I can pay for one of those doctors—"

"You want some strangers raising our baby?" She looked stunned. "And I'm a Catholic, Colin." She put the bottle down and sat on the floor and buried her face in her hands and started to cry again.

He knelt down next to her and attempted to soothe her. "It's going to be fine, Sheila." She was getting loud and he didn't want the entire building to hear their predicament. After all, this building wasn't a tenement. Weeping and screaming wouldn't be tolerated here like they had been in the Bowery. Sean McCarthy had found Colin's apartment for him, and some of the guys Sean had dealings with lived in the building or knew people who lived there. Colin didn't know how it'd look from the outside, and he didn't want it to look ugly.

"What the hell do you know?" she shouted. "I need to worry about myself, not you."

"Let's not get too loud."

Sheila jumped up, and when he followed she spat in his face. "You're only worried your fancy neighbors will hear us. I'm getting my things and getting out of here."

Colin wiped his face and grabbed her by the arm. "That was a nasty thing for you to do." His face burned with anger.

Sheila shook him off. "You've changed. You aren't the swell fella you used to be. You're a pig."

Colin watched her from a distance as she collected her belongings. He'd frozen because of what she'd said to him. *Had he changed for the worse?*

Sheila fumbled and dropped items as she collected them out of his closet and dresser and packed her suitcase. Yet she still walked out of his apartment with pride.

The way she left his apartment sparked something in Colin. He admired her.

A few days letter she sent blue flowers to his apartment. He read the note and smiled.

Colin—

I love you. Let's make it work.

Kisses,

Sheila

Colin called her to apologize, and they were married at city hall two days later. They didn't invite anyone. He didn't even tell Sean or Max he was getting married.

"Congratulations. I would've bought you two a gift if I'd known," McCarthy said to him a week later when he noticed Colin's ring.

Tom's widow sent over a bottle of fine non-alcoholic wine for Sheila and Bushmills for Colin. He wondered how she knew about the baby when they hadn't told anyone. The night before, Colin had removed the gold ring Tom's widow had given him and tucked it inside his dresser.

15

"You murdered my husband!"

Colin was with Little Bill having a few drinks at *Deegan's*. He turned from the bar to see who had shouted at him.

He saw a fatigued-looking woman standing behind him. Her eyes were red and swollen. She looked familiar. Those eyes, they were deep brown and pretty under the inflammation. Had she been crying because of him?

"Lila? How'd you get past the doorman?"

"Yeah, it's me. I waited until he took a break." She reeked of booze. "You had some nerve killing Johnny."

"I'm so sorry."

"That night we spent together—you knew and you didn't say anything. I always hoped I'd run into you one of these days so I could tell you to go to hell. You know, my brother wanted to kill you after what you did. It's not like the police would've helped us. They don't seem to care when gangsters kill each other. But I stopped my brother."

"Why did you?"

"Because what good would it have done? Killing you wouldn't bring back Johnny."

"Thank you," he whispered.

"Don't thank me. Sometimes I think I should've let him."

Colin tried to reason with her, but even he knew it was pathetic. "The order came from above after they killed Ronan. I'm very sorry for your loss."

"*Losses*. Or you don't remember my father's dead, too?"

"Again, I'm sorry."

"It's hard to come face-to-face with the loved one of the men you murdered, isn't it? Of course, I know there were others. Like your mother's lover." He'd told her private things the night they'd spent together and now she seemed to enjoy making him squirm. "Don't tell me Johnny and my father were orders. You had a choice. There's always a choice."

"There are times when I wish I'd died instead of Johnny. McPhalen—"

"You're trying to tell me that when that old man tells you to jump off of a bridge, you jump off of a bridge?"

"That's sort of how it went."

"Went?"

"Tom died."

"I didn't know that. I'm glad to hear it. How did he die? I hope he suffered."

"He had cancer. I truly am sorry, Lila. Johnny was the only friend I had when I came to this country. He was like a brother to me at one point in my life. How are you? I got married, and my wife's going to have a baby."

"I don't give a damn how you are. Some brother you were to my husband." She shook her head in disgust. "If you cared then you wouldn't have killed Johnny and my father. And just before Christmas. Is it you who's been sending me money every month?" Colin nodded."Do you send money to all the families of the people you kill?" she said. "You're going to be bankrupt. I want you to stop sending me money."

Colin shook his head and held Lila as she cried and smacked her fists against him.

"I hate you," she said, over and over again.

Little Bill had been sitting at the bar quietly watching the scene unfold. Now he opened his mouth.

"Colin, are you going to let this bitch talk to you that way? Aren't you going to ask her to leave?"

Lila stepped away from Colin, and he turned to look at Little Bill.

"It's the least I owe her. I broke her heart." He glanced at her and handed her his handkerchief. "Isn't that right, Lila?"

She glared at Little Bill. "That's right." She dried her eyes.

Little Bill shook his head. "Well, I'm not going to sit here and listen to it. Sorry, Colin, this witch is getting on my nerves. I'm going to walk." He rose and placed some money on the bar. Then he collected his hat and gave Colin a short wave.

"Your friend is rude. I don't like him," Lila said after Little Bill had left.

"He was. I'm sorry about that. Do you want to sit?" He sat at the bar and gestured to the stool Bill had vacated.

She hesitated and then sat. He turned to face her and she handed him the handkerchief.

"Did you really just run into me or did you come here to find me?" Colin asked.

"I guessed where you'd be." She held his gaze.

"You remembered I like coming here?" He didn't know what to say to her because he knew that nothing he could say would lessen her pain.

Lila nodded. "I know where you guys socialize." She glanced at the clock behind the bar.

Colin leaned on the bar and asked the bartender for another gin over ice. "Do you want a drink?" he asked Lila.

"Sure. I'll have a beer."

"Better make that a soda water," Colin called out to the bartender.

"I said I wanted a beer," Lila told him.

"You've had enough to drink."

Lila scoffed. "Are you paying?"

"I'm paying."

She stared at him with such anger he shivered. "I won't thank you."

"You don't have to. I know you miss him, miss them. I'm so sorry."

"I miss them very much."

"I'm sorry for ending their lives." That he could still show remorse amazed him.

"In a way you ended mine as well. I can't forgive you. Not ever."

"I understand."

"You're married now?"

"I got married five days ago."

"What's she like, your wife?"

"She's fun. She's pretty."

"Fun? Pretty? Aren't you supposed to say how much you love her?"

Colin shrugged.

"I used to be pretty," Lila said.

"You still are."

"After Johnny, I... I don't want to talk about it."

"Do you need more money? Because now I can send more."

"No. I work as a seamstress with my mother. We—my girl and I—get by fine. The men get killed. We women are left to pick up the pieces. I'm tired sometimes but I don't need more money. In fact, I don't want what you've been sending me. I don't use it. As soon as it arrives, I rip it up and throw it in the trash."

Colin nodded although he doubted that was the case. He

would continue to send her money. "You didn't move to Long Island."

"That dream died with Johnny."

He cleared his throat to remain focused. "How is your daughter?"

"I don't think you deserve an answer to that question."

"I don't." Her coldness wounded him, but what had he expected?

She hated him and he understood why.

"Did you knock up this girl you married?" she said.

"What makes you say that?"

"I did the math."

"I did." Lila's strong presence made him want to be honest with her.

A few minutes later she left to use the ladies room and he slipped a hundred dollar bill into her coat pocket and walked out of the pub.

Then a day after that, he put a bullet into Little Bill's head.

Colin told Bill, "It's a beautiful day. Let's drive to the shore and do that business we were going to do next week today instead."

Little Bill agreed and insisted on driving even though they made the trip in Colin's new car.

On the nighttime drive home from the casino, Colin asked Little Bill to pull over in the quiet wetlands so he could take a piss. Bill pulled over. Colin stepped outside to take his piss that never was, and then turned around with his gun concealed in his hand. He gestured for Bill to open the passenger window.

Little Bill leaned over and complied. "What's going on?"

Colin shot him, and Bill hadn't even seen it coming. He'd asked too many questions about Colin's new car anyway. Colin shoved the bloody body into the newspaper-lined trunk of his car, covered it with rags, and drove it into Queens like Sean wanted.

Later that night when Sean was done with viewing the corpse in an old garage he owned, Colin and Max put Little Bill on some plastic sheeting. They peeled off his fingerprints and used a small hammer to knock out his teeth. Then they wrapped the body with old bedding and rope, and put it into the back of Colin's car in the dead of the night. They drove the body to an isolated marshland on Long Island that Sean used as a dumping ground. After digging a deep grave and burying Little Bill, Colin and Max changed their clothes. They burned the dirty ones in a trash barrel fire on the beach and cleaned Colin's car back at the garage.

Over the next few days, Colin and Max abducted and shot Frank O'Neill and Michael M. at Sean's request. Mikey was only a soldier but Sean wanted him gone. He'd told Colin he couldn't take any chances. Colin liked Mikey but he needed to look out for himself. Afterwards, they again buried the bodies on Long Island.

Colin was now working fulltime for McCarthy, who had absorbed Tom's Bowery rackets and his mafia contacts.

Colin was in McCarthy's pub some months later. It was a few weeks after Sheila had given birth to their daughter, Camille, a healthy, beautiful baby with luminous skin, and blue eyes like her father's and permanently red lips like her mother's. Colin was in awe of his daughter, and he never doubted she was his. He hoped his mother's sadness wouldn't be passed on to her. When Camille was born and he held her tiny, delicate body in his large hands, he realized he could never leave Sheila because he could never leave Camille. He loved her that much, and he couldn't believe he had ever considered not having her in his life. She needed a father. He wanted to give Camille everything he never had as a child.

Yet sometimes Colin wondered, when did he become a man who could mutilate someone's body in a garage and then come home and kiss his daughter goodnight?

Catherine was sitting at the bar going over papers Colin assumed had to do with Sean's business. Catherine did the bookkeeping for her father's pub and restaurant now. Colin had heard she'd left her actor boyfriend and was living on her own with her daughter.

She had her back turned to him. "We're not open," she said as soon as he entered and the bell at the top of the door jangled. Then she looked up and over at him. "Colin, I didn't know it was you." She smiled.

"How have you been?" He found himself nervous around her.

"Good. You?"

"I've been well, thanks."

"We haven't talked in a while. I heard you got married."

"Yeah. Months ago."

Catherine laughed a little. "You sound unsure. Are you?"

Colin's face felt hot. "A lot has been going on. I don't know if you heard, but my wife and I just had a baby girl."

Catherine smiled. "Congratulations." She looked at him deeper, and he almost couldn't bear her beauty, her large eyes and dark hair.

"Thank you," Colin said.

"What's her name?"

"Camille."

"That's a pretty name. It's French like my mother."

"Thanks. My wife chose it."

"Your wife, what's her name?"

"Sheila."

"Right, she was your girlfriend. Sheila. What a lovely name. Is your wife lovely?"

At first Colin didn't know what to say. "She is. She's very lovely."

"I assumed she would be." Catherine didn't sound jealous, just curious.

"But you're beautiful." He'd spoken without thinking first.

Catherine gave him a subtle smile and he couldn't tell what she was thinking. Catherine was the kind of woman a man married and moved with into a large house in the country to create a big, loving family. The kind of woman a man settled down with for the rest of his life. What did that make Sheila? If Colin wanted the perfect life, had he started his with the wrong woman?

Sean walked down from his office upstairs, followed by Max.

Max approached him with open arms. He embraced Colin with passionate warmth. "How've you been?" He patted him on the back.

"Not bad," Colin said.

"Not bad? You have a gorgeous wife and a beautiful new baby. And Sean's going to promote you." Max patted him on the back again. "Cheer up."

Colin grinned at him. Sean promoting him meant he'd receive even more money and greater respect.

McCarthy glanced at Catherine and then guided Colin upstairs to his office.

Sean sat down behind his desk and smoked a cigarette. He poured a glass of whiskey and offered Colin, who was seated to the right of Sean's desk in a comfortable leather chair, a glass as well. Colin declined.

"You don't drink anymore?" Sean asked.

"No, I still drink sometimes. I just have a lot of things to do today. With the baby at home, you know. I need my head clear today."

"Being a father is the best thing in life. Better than fine whiskey, better than money." Sean smiled. "But you know what they say, you aren't Irish unless you can take your drink." He raised his glass high in the air as if to toast their fatherhood.

"I think I'm going to love being a father."

Sean put the glass down without taking a drink after his toast and looked at Colin. He leaned back into his desk chair. "You're a serious fellow, aren't you? A lot of you Bowery guys are serious. Some of you don't know how to take a joke, or make one. But I don't think you're like that, Colin. I think you can take a joke. But you are serious." He watched Colin while he talked about him.

Colin looked into Sean's cold, hollow eyes and realized how threatening Sean could be if he wanted to.

"I think your being serious is a good thing," Sean said after a while.

Colin breathed with ease.

"You heard what Max said downstairs about me giving you a higher place in our organization?" Sean asked.

"I did." Colin continued to stare at Sean's eyes. Very little frightened him anymore except for Sean's eyes.

"It's a good idea. In fact, it's Max's idea, and I like it. He likes you, and I like you. I appreciate the devotion you've already shown me. You've done a lot for us. But right now wouldn't be a good time for me to change things. Can you understand? I wish Max hadn't said anything. He came to me with the idea and I said I'd think about it. Well, I thought about it and I've decided against it."

It irked Colin but he didn't want to see Max punished.

"The reason I said no for now is because some of the older fellows, you know, the ones who've been working for me longer than you have, wouldn't like it. They'd be wondering why I moved you up instead of them. They'd think their commitment didn't matter. I just want to make sure all is right by you." Sean grinned in a fixed way that gave Colin the chills.

Colin nodded. What choice did he have if he wanted to make sure nothing came back to hurt Max in some way? "I understand."

"Great. When's the last time you went on vacation?"

"Excuse me?"

"Vacation. You know, like taking time off from work and getting out of town."

"Oh. No, I haven't done that."

"Never?" Sean eyes widened in disbelief. Colin nodded slowly.

"Would you like to?"

"I suppose I would, in the future."

Sean's somewhat blank stare turned into a large smile. "Catherine wants to go on vacation, and I'm not about to let her go off by herself. This world is a dangerous place. You're going with her."

"Me?"

"Of course."

"I appreciate the opportunity, but with Sheila and the new baby at home, I don't know if I can go away right now."

"It's your job, Colin. It's not really a vacation for you. For Cathy it is."

Colin smiled at the irony. "Where is she going?"

"Los Angeles. Cathy wants to try out for the movies. I think she's going to be great, don't you? With her looks, she's going to be famous."

"I didn't know she was interested in acting."

"Neither did I until a few weeks ago. Her former fellow got

her interested in it. They took some acting classes together. Will you go?"

Colin knew it was an order and he couldn't say no or maybe. He had to say yes. But in the past, Sean hadn't seemed to want him around Catherine. "Why me?"

Sean looked irritated that his motives had been questioned. "Because with your looks, you'll fit in in Los Angeles. My other fellows are too ugly to go." He chuckled.

"When do we leave?"

"Day after tomorrow. You'll be flying there with Cathy and my granddaughter. I bought the tickets already."

"What if I hadn't said yes?" Colin asked out of curiosity. Sean laughed like that never would have happened. "You knew of this in advance?"

"I did, Colin."

"I wish I'd known earlier. I'll go but it's kind of short notice."

"You know how things are. Business is business. Think of yourself as a soldier during wartime. You've been called into combat. Maybe you aren't so prepared, but you have to go. Do you know what I mean?" He leaned in toward Colin. "Besides, I didn't know if it was you who I would ask to go. I had another one of the fellows lined up at first, but then I thought you'd be better and more appreciative of the job. You want to work your way up a rank, Colin? Then this is a good place to start. It's a very important trip. If you do a terrific job with my girls out in Los Angeles, watch them closely, and make sure they don't break even a fucking fingernail, I'll make you what the Italians call a *capo*, a captain, when you return."

Colin sat there and pretended to be enlightened even though he was well-versed in how the organization's structure worked and how he was currently near the bottom.

"You'd make a lot more dough," Sean said. "Capo. Now that's

a promotion old Tom never would've given a Northern guy like you." He waited for Colin to agree with him.

"I appreciate that. How long will we be in Los Angeles for?"

"As long as Cathy wants, two weeks probably."

Colin nodded. Two weeks with another woman. Sheila would kill him, but she'd find out somehow if he didn't tell her before he left.

"I suppose you can sort of think of it as a vacation for yourself as well, a vacation from this whole goddamn city. And watch them, will you?" Sean spoke sincerely.

"I will."

"Here's your ticket." Sean handed him an American Airlines ticket. "The flight leaves at ten in the morning. Be there an hour before. Max will be at the airport waiting with Catherine and Violet out front. Max is going, too. He's ugly, but I've known him for a long time and he's never been to L.A. He'll give you a call at home the night before if the plans change, but I don't expect them to."

Colin left the office and the pub and headed out into the bright streets of New York, which he had mastered years ago. Now he was going to learn how to navigate Los Angeles a little. He figured he was on his way.

∾

Sheila didn't take the news well.

"If you're going to California for two whole weeks then we're going with you."

"It's for business, Sheila. McCarthy wouldn't like it if I took my family with me."

Colin packed his leather bag with shirts and trousers. He didn't pay much attention to what he packed. He stopped halfway through when he recalled he'd be spending the two weeks with Catherine. He better be more careful about what he packed. Colin put in a silk tie to go with his suit.

"What kind of business is he doing out in Los Angeles? Is it really just a business trip?" Sheila stood in the doorway of their bedroom as he packed. Sunlight trickled in through the windows. Camille slept on and off in the other room.

Colin glanced over at Sheila. Her tight white dress highlighted the baby weight she hadn't lost. Colin had told her he didn't mind that her once taut figure had vanished, even though he sort of did.

"Colin, I'm talking to you. Quit staring at my stomach."

"Sorry," he muttered.

"A silk tie. You're taking some nice clothes. What kind of trip is this?"

"McCarthy likes his guys to dress sharp."

She glared at him. "What are you doing there?"

Colin sighed. "I'm taking McCarthy's daughter there," he confessed.

"A woman? How old is she? Is she an infant? Why does she need an escort?"

"Because she's the boss's daughter. She's in her twenties. But before you start to panic, don't. She's a widow with a young daughter. She's traveling with her child. Don't be worried."

Sheila entered all the way and sat on the bed. "I shouldn't be worried that you haven't gone to bed with me in months?" Her face reddened with anger. "Are you fucking this woman?"

"No." Colin closed his bag and stared at her. "It's nothing like that. I never touched her. She's the boss's daughter, I couldn't touch her even if I wanted to."

"Do you want to?"

"No, of course not. It's a business arrangement. Sean needed someone to go to Los Angeles with his daughter and granddaughter. His daughter's going to try out for the movies there, and he chose me to go. I didn't choose to go. He chose me. L.A. is a big city. He wants someone to go with them to make sure they're safe. That's all it is. Do you want to get a big house in the country, like you talked about?" After Camille's baptismal, they had moved into a more expensive building with an elevator and a doorman. Now Sheila wanted to move to the country to raise their daughter. "Do we want a private school for Camille someday? We're going to be able to afford all those things and more after I make this trip."

"Are you getting a promotion?" When he didn't answer her, she beamed. "You are, aren't you?"

"Yeah, if I go on this trip."

"That's wonderful, Colin." Then Sheila frowned. "Is his daughter pretty?" she asked quietly. "If she's trying out for the movies she must be pretty."

"She is. But not as pretty as you are." Colin kissed her.

"Do you really have to go?"

"I do. I'll buy you a television for our bedroom when I return. So now you'll have two televisions. And I'll take you and Camille on a beautiful vacation soon. Okay?"

He watched her closely. She looked disappointed, and why shouldn't she be? Her husband was leaving to spend two weeks with another woman in beautiful, warm Los Angeles. He wrapped his arms around Sheila's waist, and she reached up and put her arms around his neck.

"Everything will be fine. I'll be back soon, and we'll have a great life," he whispered into her ear.

"Oh, Colin, just don't never come back. Or don't go, come back, and leave me."

"How can I leave you when I come back?" He smiled at her. "You're peculiar sometimes, Sheila, do you know that? That's one of the things I enjoy about you." He gently teased her as he leaned down and buried his face in her smooth neck, smelling of soft perfume. He breathed in her comforting scent.

"I have a bad feeling, baby."

"You sometimes have those feelings, sweetheart. They're just feelings, they don't mean anything." He kissed her lightly on the nose. Inside he felt as if he had consumed cold liquid too fast. His stomach ached. Maybe Sheila was right about something, but he didn't know what. "Sheila, you know I'd never leave you and Camille."

The pain persisted.

She looked up at him in silence for a moment, her pretty, brown eyes staring at his face. She rubbed his back and then gently broke free of their embrace. "Go on, finish packing."

Catherine always looked beautiful, but she looked stunning as she walked toward Colin at La Guardia Airport. Every male turned to stare as she sauntered by. Her long, dark hair framed her intelligent eyes and her soft, pink lips. She wore white gloves like an elegant woman.

He had arrived feeling down because he felt guilty leaving his family for two weeks, but seeing Catherine made him feel much better, especially the way she smiled at him. Her young daughter, Violet, was at her side. Violet was a quiet little girl and a real sweetheart.

"Colin, in that suit you look like a younger, taller version of my father."

Colin smiled but inside he wasn't pleased to have been compared to McCarthy. Sean had insisted he wear a certain kind of dark suit.

"Are you excited about the trip? I am," Catherine said.

"I'm glad to have the opportunity."

Catherine laughed.

"What's funny?" Colin grinned but he didn't get the joke.

"You. You're either too serious or nervous, I can't tell which one."

He laughed when he realized she was being humorous.

"I'm glad my father listened to me and sent you," she said. "It took a lot of coaxing on my part, as I'm sure you can imagine."

Colin took that to mean Catherine had requested him, which was news to him. Max said hello to Colin and helped Catherine with her luggage. Colin offered his assistance but Max told him he could handle it.

"Are you coming with us, Max, or are you helping with the luggage until we board the plane?" Catherine winked at Colin.

"Do you really think I'd leave you alone with him?" Max glanced at Colin as he cracked the joke. "I'm coming, sweetheart. I thought your father told you all this already."

Max stacked one of Catherine's small suitcases on top of a larger one. He let out an exhausted sigh. He'd never had much endurance, and his being overweight didn't help either.

"Yes, I guess he did." Catherine smiled down at Violet as the child tugged on the hem of her skirt.

"Let's go, mommy!"

Catherine held Violet's hand and started to walk ahead of Colin and Max.

She glanced at Colin over her shoulder. "Aren't you coming?"

Colin looked at Max struggling with the heavy luggage. He wondered if he should again offer his help and carry some of it over to the check-in area. He looked at Catherine, with her long legs appearing smooth in her form-fitting skirt, and he decided the luggage could wait.

Her high heels clacked as she began to walk faster, and he had to run to catch up to her.

Catherine stopped walking, turned around with Violet, and smiled at him. "You're a good servant," she joked.

Colin was so stunned at her impudence that he stopped in his tracks for a moment and couldn't form a reply. They went into the terminal building together. Colin walked closely at her side. He wanted to take her hand but didn't.

"Are you really excited, Colin, or do you just think of this trip as work?" she asked.

He almost stopped in his tracks again.

Catherine blushed and roared with laughter when she realized what he thought she'd meant. "Excited about the trip, that is."

"I'm excited."

They both laughed.

"What does your wife think about the trip?"

"She doesn't like it."

Catherine smiled at him.

When they were deeper inside of the terminal Catherine asked him to hold Violet's hand while she went to use the bathroom. The small girl's hand felt like a doll's in his. For a moment, he almost forgot he was holding Violet's hand, he was so preoccupied with watching Catherine walk away.

While he waited for Catherine to return, he made chitchat with the young girl.

"Are you happy you're going to California?"

Violet looked like a miniature version of her mother when she smiled. "Yes. So happy."

She reminded Colin of his daughter back in the city with Sheila and, again, he felt guilty that he was leaving for such a long time without them. He considered calling Sheila now from the airport to see how things were at home. But that call could wait a few more hours.

Max went up to Colin and Violet and stood in front of them

out of breath. "Hey, big guy, you could've given me a hand," he said with sarcasm but not anger. "I had to check all that luggage in by myself."

Colin grinned at Max and shrugged. "You said you didn't want help."

"Maybe I'm too proud sometimes." Max chuckled. "Where's Cathy?"

"She went to use the ladies room."

Then Catherine strode toward them, and Colin couldn't focus on anything else.

Max noticed Colin's admiration. "Ah, I see. She's beautiful, isn't she?"

"My mommy's going to be an actress," Violet said. Colin smiled at her.

"Be careful," Max told Colin. "She's like fire, pretty to look at, but cruel if you touch it. There are repercussions."

Colin frowned, and before he could ask Max what he meant by the remark, Catherine stood in front of them.

"Hello, you fellows," Catherine said in her sensuous, clear voice. A voice that was noticed and admired as much as the beauty of its speaker. Colin felt proud to be standing with her.

"Hi, sweetheart," Max said.

Catherine smiled at him and took Violet's hand. "Thanks for watching her, Colin."

"Was she in there a long time?" Max whispered to Colin. His voice had a serious tone, and his eyes darkened.

"No. Not for too long." Colin wondered if he had done something wrong and what. It seemed from the look on Max's face he had.

"You didn't check on her?"

"No. She went to the ladies room. She asked me to stay here and watch Violet."

Catherine attempted to intervene but Max cut her short.

"Didn't Sean tell you to keep an eye on her at all times?" Max said to Colin.

"I assumed there are exceptions. I mean, she was in the ladies bathroom."

"You didn't keep an eye on her at all times?"

"Not at that time, no. I wasn't going to follow her into the ladies room."

Max waved him off. "Not inside. You should've waited outside for her with Violet."

Colin still thought Max was joking, so he said, "I don't think it would've been appropriate for me to loiter outside the ladies room."

Max eyed him closely. His face looked like stone. "I might have to report back to Sean on this one. I might have to give him a call right now, before we leave. He might have to send another guy over here who's going to do his job right." His face flushed and then he began to walk over to the phone booths behind them.

"What the—" Colin raced after him. He grabbed Max's arm from outside the booth and prevented him from picking up the phone.

"Don't," Colin said. "I need this opportunity so much, more than you can imagine. My wife just had a baby. Please."

Max backed out of the phone booth and stared at Colin in a welcoming way. He put his arm halfway around Colin and patted his shoulder. "Relax, Colin." Max led him to where Catherine stood with Violet. "I was only fooling you." He winked. "But don't get too interested in Catherine. You're married, after all, and she is the boss's daughter."

Colin looked at him stunned. "What the fuck, Max?"

"Consider it your initiation. Now that I scared the shit out of you, you really are one of us."

Colin shook his head.

Max removed his arm and shrugged. "We've all gone through one."

"Right, an initiation." Colin spoke like he understood but he couldn't disguise how much he sweated, and his heart beat faster than it ever had before. He had been scared, and now he was outraged. He didn't like anyone frightening him even if it was a joke. Sean McCarthy had weird moods. If Max had called him to complain that Colin had done something wrong, Colin knew Sean was capable of killing him in a heartbeat.

They arrived where Catherine and Violet stood. Colin took his handkerchief out of his pocket and wiped his forehead.

Catherine, seeing that everything now appeared fine between the two men, smiled at Colin and gestured at Max. "Was he joking around again?"

"Yeah," Colin said. "A joke, that's all it was."

Catherine laughed and looked so beautiful that he pretended not to have noticed her cold sense of humor. Her deep blue eyes glistened and her teeth shone, and Colin forgot all about before for a moment.

Violet hummed, sweetly and off-key; it was a Connie Francis song Colin recognized.

"Come on, let's get on the plane," Catherine broke in.

They boarded the commercial airplane and Catherine sat next to Colin, and Max sat with Violet.

"I made sure you'd sit with me," Catherine said to Colin.

"You didn't want to sit next to Max?"

"I don't mind Max, but you're much more pleasant to look at. I wonder what they're going to serve for lunch."

"Whatever it is, it probably won't taste very good."

"Yes, airplane food is notoriously unpleasant. Have you ever been on a plane?"

Colin shook his head.

Catherine smiled at him like that amused her. She squeezed

his hand. "How exciting for you. The last time I was on an airplane was when I toured Europe a few years ago with my mother."

"Did you enjoy it?"

"Yes, very much, especially Rome."

"You're well-spoken," he said. "Did you go to college?"

"I completed a year of college when I was married. We had a nanny. I took classes at night."

"How did you like it?" Colin figured he could learn from Catherine.

"I loved it. It helped me stay sane. I loved my husband, and I love my daughter, but it can get boring being just a wife."

He wondered whether Sheila would get bored now that she no longer worked and what that would mean for their daughter and him. "I didn't make it that far. I didn't even make it to high school. It's good you did."

"Most of the fellows who work for my father didn't. My father is the exception. He graduated from college. My husband, he went even farther, college and then graduate school."

There was a sadness in her voice, but Colin didn't think it was only for the loss of her husband. For her youth maybe, that she had ended it so soon by marrying young. Catherine lowered her gaze and he put his hand over hers in a tender way. He wasn't trying to put the moves on her and he sensed she knew that.

A stewardess caught them off guard. "Would you like a drink?" She had short, blonde hair and brown eyes.

"I'd love a martini," Colin said. "Gin. Two olives."

The smooth fabric of her uniform brushed his hand. "Great choice." She smiled and seemed to notice Catherine only then. "What would you like, ma'am?"

"I'll have the same." If Catherine was the least bit jealous of the stewardess's flirting with Colin, it wasn't obvious. Colin was a little disappointed. But then again, maybe Catherine was one of those women who didn't get sore over that.

"Is that your favorite drink?" Colin asked her when the stewardess stepped away.

"It is."

"Same here, currently. Most of the fellows I know, all they drink is whiskey or Guinness. Now that I'm getting on in my years, I have to be careful about my health."

"You aren't that old." Catherine laughed a little. "I can't stand whiskey myself. Too much bite, not enough smooth flavor."

He smiled at her. He didn't think whiskey tasted like that, but the way she said 'smooth' had turned him on.

The stewardess arrived with their martinis. She handed Catherine hers first. She took more time with Colin's drink and gave him a wink. Then she passed to each of them a cocktail napkin with the airline's logo. Colin half expected to find the girl's phone number written on his napkin. He thanked her for his drink but focused on Catherine.

"So, you're going to be in the movies?"

Catherine sipped her martini. "Hopefully. A friend of my father's friend says I have the talent."

"And the looks." Colin smiled. "Your old man knows someone in the movie business?"

"Yes, a producer. My father's friend sent them a reel of me."

"You're going to shine up on the big screen."

Catherine blushed. "Do you really think so?"

"I know so."

"Then when the heck do we get to Los Angeles? I can't wait."

"Relax. Let's have another drink."

"All right, but you're paying."

"A gentleman always pays." He smiled.

16

LOS ANGELES

"It's me." Colin was surprised to find Lucille still had the same phone number and that she hadn't moved.

"Who?" she said.

"Lucille, it's me."

"Colin, I asked you not to—"

"I know, but it's been a while, so I thought I'd try again."

"I heard about Johnny. Why, Colin?"

"It became McPhalen and us against Bernal and his men. They'd take us out if we didn't take them out first. We took them out before they could get us."

"What happened to you? You sound just like a gangster."

"You know what happened to me."

"How can you be so selfish? Johnny had a family."

"I'm giving his family money every month."

"Every month?" Lucille laughed bitterly. "That makes what you did all right?"

"It doesn't, but that's what I'm doing."

Lucille sighed.

"How is your family doing?" he asked.

"Please don't... I'm going to hang up now."

"I know we can't be together, but I still care about you."

"Christ, why are you still trying to be in my life? It can never be the same as it once was. I haven't changed my mind about that."

"I care about you. That's the only answer I have. I've been doing a lot of thinking since I got out here."

"Where are you?"

"Los Angeles."

"What are you doing all the way out there?"

"I'm on business."

"My brother told me you're working for those other guys now."

"Yeah."

"I hope you believe you made the right decision. McCarthy went to church with McPhalen and look how he treated him. What makes you think he's not going to treat you the same someday?"

"He won't."

"You're sure?"

"He won't. Why, did you hear something?"

"No. I just care about you."

"I'm glad to hear that." Colin smiled. "I have to tell you something."

"I know, you care about me," Lucille said.

"Yeah, I care about you, but I need to tell you something else."

"If it's one of your gangster stories, I don't want to hear it."

"Of course not. I realize now that I shouldn't have done it, and I'm sorry I got you involved."

"What do you mean?" Lucille sounded exasperated.

"I shouldn't have killed Carmine. I could've stopped him but not killed him. I should've just scared him and kicked him out so that he'd be too afraid to return. Carmine—he didn't just beat

Maureen. He forced himself on her. I never told anyone the whole story. It was kept a family secret for her sake. You know how people can talk. My family went along with my plan."

"My God. That's why you... You went to jail to protect her. You gave up your life."

"But I should've had more self-control. If I had just hurt him enough to scare him, then I could've been with you, and maybe *I'd* be married to you and we'd be living where the weather was warm and beautiful. Then I could've been the father of your children. I loved you."

"Please... you don't know how difficult it was for me." Lucille got quieter. "Every day I'd think about you in prison. But I didn't plan for your return. I moved on, and so should you. My brother told me you got married and have a child. You *are* a father. Congratulations."

Lucille had been his secret from Sheila—he'd kept the rosary beads hidden from her—and he'd clung to Lucille because she'd reminded him of the old times, but now it was time for him to let her go.

"Thank you, Lucille. I'm not going to bother you any more so you don't have to worry. I just wanted to hear your voice one last time and let you know I'm sorry for everything."

The sunlight hurt his eyes as he stood outside on the balcony of his extravagant hotel room in Beverly Hills. In a few days he'd have a deep tan. Catherine had hurried into her red two-piece bathing suit with white polka dots and jumped into the blue pool with Violet immediately when they arrived.

Colin liked Los Angeles. The days were warm and filled with sun, and there were vibrant people and film stars everywhere he turned. He dined next to Marlon Brando his first night there, and he could have sworn he saw Ava Gardner a day later. He thought he could get used to living in a place like that. In Los Angeles, everyone was treated like a star, it didn't matter if you were once a poor boy from Kilrea. As long as you wore an expensive suit and had a beautiful woman on your arm, you were accepted as one of them.

He started sleeping with Catherine the first night they arrived. She didn't take things slowly. She simply asked him, "Do you want to go to bed with me? I've never slept with someone who worked for my father."

Colin loved his daughter, but he didn't love Sheila, although he was fond of her. He'd married her for Camille's sake. He felt guilty about Sheila and their daughter back at home, but he still went to bed with Catherine. They were careful to keep it a secret from Max.

"How are things going with my daughter?" Sean asked him on the telephone four days after they arrived.

"Things are going very well."

"You two aren't getting comfortable, are you?"

Colin could tell Sean wasn't kidding. "Of course not, Mr. McCarthy. I'm just here doing my job with Catherine and Violet. I'm keeping them safe."

"Good." Sean cleared his throat on the other end of the line. "Put Max on the phone. I want to speak to him."

"Max is out at the moment."

"It's you two alone, eh? You and Cathy in the hotel? Is she in her own room? Is she in your room? Where is she?"

Max, Colin, and Catherine and Violet had adjoining rooms.

Colin nodded, except Sean couldn't hear him. "Colin, are you there?" Sean sound irritated.

"Yeah, sorry."

"Where is she?"

"She's in her room with Violet."

"Tell Max to give me a call as soon as he returns." Had Sean believed him?

"Sure thing, boss." Colin hung up.

"Who was that?" Catherine had just stepped in from the outdoor pool and into Colin's room wearing only her bathing suit and a towel. Her long, dark hair dripped water on the plush cream carpet. Her firm skin was also kissed with water, like dewdrops on the grass at dawn. Max had taken Violet for a drive to see the ocean.

"It was your father."

"What did he want?"

"He wanted to know how things were, and why I was alone with you."

"You told him I was alone with you?"

"Not exactly, but I told him Max was out. He wanted to speak with Max. What was I supposed to do, imitate Max's voice?"

"You could've told him Max was in the bathroom. You could've lied. You didn't have to say he left the hotel." She dried her hair with a thick, white towel.

"Come on, Cathy, you know your father. He would've made me drag Max right off the toilet or out of the shower." Colin felt comfortable enough to use her nickname.

Catherine couldn't stop laughing. "Yeah, you're right."

Colin smiled. "Come here."

"You want some loving?" She stopped drying her hair. He nodded.

Catherine stepped close, and he sighed as she pressed her lips to his.

"I think I'm in love with you," Colin said.

She smiled but didn't say anything. He draped her over his shoulder and set her on the bed.

"I'm nervous," Catherine said outside of the studio door.

They had been in Los Angeles for a week relaxing and shopping, and today they headed out to the movie studio where Catherine said she had been promised a screen test and maybe even a small part in a film. She'd hired a sitter to watch Violet at the hotel.

"You're going to do terrific," Colin said.

"Are you sure you like this dress?" Catherine stroked the red fabric.

"You look like a star!" Colin nudged Max's shoulder. "Doesn't she?"

"She sure does. She looks like a success."

Catherine hugged both men, and Colin noticed Max blushing. "When are you supposed to go inside?" Colin asked.

"In two minutes."

"That's soon," Max said.

"You're making me more nervous."

"All right, Cathy, you better go in now. You don't want to be late." Colin put his hand to Catherine's back and gently pushed her toward the door. He started to follow her but Max held him back.

"Sean said she could go in by herself. He trusts them."

"Really?"

Max nodded.

Catherine knocked on the studio door and gave her name, and was let inside by an older woman with blonde hair and cat-eye glasses.

"Do you want to get a drink?" Max asked Colin after the red door had shut.

"Shouldn't we wait here for her?"

"She'll be fine. Her father knows them."

"Maybe we should check on Violet."

"Her mother paid that babysitter a good amount of money to watch her. Let's go to a bar and relax."

Colin nodded but he quietly wondered why Max was now being less protective of Catherine and Violet.

"Did Sean really say Cathy could go in on her own?" he asked.

"Of course he did," Max replied. "Why would I lie?"

True, Max had no reason to lie.

"I heard of this place down the street," Max said. "It's supposed to be a real pub. You look like you could use a pick-me-up."

The sidewalks in Los Angeles were quiet and clean compared to New York. Everyone drove in L.A.

"Colin, did I ever show you my new gun?"

"I don't believe you did."

"Sean got it for me. He told me that when we return he's going to buy you one, too. It's a very decent piece. Let me show you."

"You want to show me right here in the street?"

"Why not?"

"We're in the middle of the street, that's why."

"No one's around. No one's going to notice." Max removed the gun from his coat pocket. "Isn't she a beauty?"

Colin stroked the cool, black gun. "She's very nice."

Bang. Bang.

The gunshots echoed in the streets and bounced off the buildings. Max had dropped the black gun to the ground and shot at Colin's chest with a small gold pistol. He must have had a secret pocket on the inside of his suit jacket. Colin took out his gun and managed to hit Max once in the shoulder, but he fell to the ground when a third shot pierced his heart.

Colin wanted to ask "Why?" as his back met the sidewalk. He had hit his head when he fell and he could feel it bleeding onto the street. He moved his lips but his voice didn't seem to work. The more he bled, the more his mind seemed to fade. Soon he became drowsy. But he wasn't going to lie to himself. It hurt. It hurt a lot. Getting shot hurt like hell. Right then he would have traded places with an ordinary man and given up the years he had lived in glory as a gangster in New York City. It hurt so bad he would have traded places with a Bowery vagrant.

Max glanced at him. He didn't talk but the glance said everything. Now that McCarthy had gotten what he wanted, and Tom and the rest of his men were gone, he didn't need Colin anymore. Was Max sympathetic? Colin couldn't tell.

A blue car pulled up alongside the sidewalk and Max hurried inside with his hand pressed to his bleeding shoulder. A young woman with long, dark hair drove off. Catherine. There was no audition.

Colin lay sprawled on the warm Los Angeles sidewalk, blood pooling around his body. Looking up at the clear blue sky he thought about his life as he embraced death. How his father had cut his own life short because he couldn't handle the grim existence that had been handed down to him. Of his childhood friend whom he had once loved like a brother yet hadn't saved, a friend who had tried to warn Colin about his own fate. How Sean McCarthy had ended everything for him, and his beautiful daughter had helped. Of Sheila, who'd told him every day that she loved him, and Camille—who would take care of them now? He wondered what Sheila would think when she found Lucille's rosary beads in his dresser.

He didn't want to stop seeing that clear blue sky, and so he forced his eyes open every so often as he bled. A crowd gathered.

"Someone call an ambulance." The man in a tan coat and black hat bent down and looked over Colin's face and wounds. "He's dying!"

"There's a phone in the diner up the street," said a plump woman wearing a green dress with white pearls.

Colin smiled. Things had turned out for him the way they had to. Some don't have choices, and he knew this firsthand. Some are born into the life they will lead forever. Colin's eyes felt warm and wet, and when he touched them he saw blood on his fingertips. He left this earth with sirens approaching and a newsman with a camera snapping his picture. He closed his eyes for the final time. Even Colin knew what a terrific headline his death would make.

A NOTE FROM THE PUBLISHER

Thank you for reading this book. If you enjoyed it please do consider leaving a review on Amazon to help others find it too.

We hate typos. All of our books have been rigorously edited and proofread, but sometimes mistakes do slip through. If you have spotted a typo, please do let us know and we can get it amended within hours.

info@bloodhoundbooks.com

ABOUT THE AUTHOR

The Trouble Trilogy
Book 1: The Trouble Boys
Book 2: The Trouble Girls
Book 3: The Trouble Legacy

Best-selling author E.R. Fallon knows well the gritty city streets of which she writes and has understanding of the localized crime world.

Printed in Great Britain
by Amazon